Evely

C000271251

Evelyn James has alway
the work of writers such as Agatha Christie. She began
writing the Clara Fitzgerald series one hot summer, when
a friend challenged her to write her own historical
murder mystery. Clara Fitzgerald has gone on to feature
in over thirteen novels, with many more in the pipeline.
Evelyn enjoys conjuring up new plots, dastardly villains
and horrible crimes to keep her readers entertained and
plans on doing so for as long as possible.

Other Books in
The Clara Fitzgerald Series

Murder on the Mary Jane

by
Evelyn James

A Clara Fitzgerald Mystery
Book 12

Red Raven Publications
2018

© Evelyn James 2018

First published as ebook 2018
Paperback edition 2018
Red Raven Publications

The right of Evelyn James to be identified as the Author of this
work has been asserted in accordance with the Copyrights,
Designs and Patents Act 1988.

All rights reserved. No part of this book may be reprinted or
reproduced or utilised in any form or by any electronic,
mechanical or other means, now known or hereafter invented,
including photocopying and recording, or in any information
storage or retrieval system without the permission in writing
from the author

Chapter One

New Year's Eve 1921. The clouds were thick over the moon and there was a hint of rain in the air, but aboard the Mary Jane the atmosphere was electric. The old passenger liner had been tarted-up for the last day of the old year. She bore lights all along her rigging, illuminating her presence like some giant star on the ocean. The light fell on the waves and gilded them with an orange tint.

The music was loud. A full band was strumming out number after number, fuelled by a steady stream of champagne provided by uniformed waiters. People danced and laughed and drank. Saying goodbye to the last year, with all its good and ill, and preparing to welcome in a brand-new year, full of promise and excitement. Everyone was a little tight and a little high.

In the background the Mary Jane's crew kept the vessel on a steady course. She would sail in a large circle all night to keep the old engines ticking over. She was a relic from another age, a number of her crew had not been born when she was built. As majestic as she was, (the wise old lady of the sea, as her captain referred to her) she was well past her time as a sailing vessel. There was an anticipation among those who knew her well that this would be her last voyage, the next trip would be to the scrapyard. Her engines were largely held together by the willpower of her engineers and there were so many leaks and cracks throughout her hull that everyone had stopped keeping track. She was a grand old girl on the outside, but on the inside she was dying.

Some said the thought that this was the last time Mary Jane would sail had made the captain maudlin. He was still circulating with the party guests in his dress uniform, as he was supposed to, yet there was a hint of melancholy in his stride and his smile was forced. It was also whispered he had drank rather a lot of champagne, more than he normally would, anyway.

Mary Jane heaved through the sea, gently creaking, cutting her path as she had always done. The sea was where she was meant to be; twenty years serving the shipping lanes between England and Belgium, taking passengers back and forth in comfort and style, before the war had interrupted her career and passenger trips had been mothballed. For those four terrible years she had turned into a military transport, carrying soldiers to war rather than civilians to their holidays. All the time she had been captained by the same man, Frederick Pevsner, and when war had ceased, with Mary Jane not incurring so much as a scratch, a new future stretched out before them. Mary Jane was no longer fit for the daily journey between home and the Continent, but she could do coastal cruises and special events, such as the New Year's Eve celebrations. She was also popular for weddings at sea. Captain Pevsner had found a new lease of life for them both.

Imagining that all to soon be at an end was slowly killing him.

Captain Pevsner glanced seawards, a slight sway to his feet. He saw something he didn't like. Walking to the rail of his vessel he picked up a strand of lights that had gone out – one of the bulbs must be faulty. He grumbled to himself as he twisted each dead bulb in its socket in turn, trying to find the culprit. A sound caught his attention, a tentative scrape at the hull. He glanced down, almost idly, his mind on the bulbs. What he saw gently bobbing against the hull of his old ship made the colour drain from his face.

Dropping the dead bulbs he hastened to find his first mate, who was somewhere among the party-goers. Alfred Cinch was almost as old as his captain, but he had foregone skippering his own ship to remain on the Mary Jane. He was feeling as morose as his captain that night.

"Cinch!" Captain Pevsner hissed at him, catching Cinch by the arm and moving him away from the crowd of passengers. "We have to evacuate the ship!"

"Captain?" Cinch looked at him in bafflement.

"There is a mine, Cinch! A mine tapping at our hull! We abandon ship or we get blown up to Heaven!"

~~~*~~~

Clara Fitzgerald pressed a wet cloth to her forehead and took an uncertain breath. She was lying on the bunk in her cabin. Every one of the guests had been assigned a cabin where they could place their belongings and change from day clothes to evening clothes. Clara had retreated to hers unexpectedly early when she had discovered that the combination of a gently bobbing ship and cheap champagne did diabolical things to her stomach.

Sitting beside her was Captain John O'Harris, ex-air force, rather than sea captain. O'Harris and Clara were working on becoming something more than just friends, but it was proving a tentative process, each reserved for their own reasons. Fortunately, neither was in a hurry.

Captain O'Harris was smirking slightly as he watched Clara.

"This is not amusing," Clara growled, opening an eye and peering from beneath the cloth. "I can tell you are smirking with my eyes closed."

"Sorry," O'Harris said, "but it was very amusing the

way you suddenly went green and ran to the ship rail."

"I fail to appreciate the humour," Clara huffed.

"Do you want any more of the bicarb and water?" O'Harris proffered a glass containing a cloudy liquid full of bubbles, the product of mixing bicarbonate of soda with water. The mixture was soothing for the stomach and, on a night such as this when everyone expected to drink and eat too much, the ship's doctor had stocked up. When Clara had first become ill O'Harris had hastened to fetch her some.

"I don't think I can bear any more of that stuff," Clara cringed as she eyed the glass. "My stomach feels better."

"Want to try swallowing the seasickness pill the doctor gave me?" O'Harris offered as an alternative.

"I've never been seasick before," Clara grumped, embarrassed now the worst had passed.

"He said it would help," O'Harris cajoled.

Clara sighed and slowly sat up. She dropped the damp cloth from her forehead and took the pill with a fresh glass of water. It tasted chalky on her tongue and felt the size of a cricket ball as she endeavoured to swallow it, but it went down alright.

"Not quite how I expected our evening to go," O'Harris was smirking again.

"I fully intend to be back on deck for the chiming of midnight," Clara told him firmly. "I shall not let you down."

"I never doubted you," O'Harris said playfully. "I guess we won't be toasting the New Year in with champagne, however."

The look Clara gave him had him laughing.

"Sorry, old girl, couldn't resist. I am very glad you are feeling better though."

Clara softened.

"I'll stick to lemonade in the future," she replied, before pausing. "What's that?"

Over their heads, on the deck above, there was the noise of feet stampeding; as if someone else was in a desperate rush for their cabin.

"Maybe another guest found the champagne disagreeable?" O'Harris suggested. "Though, how anyone can call what they were serving us tonight champagne beggars belief. If I was French I would be ashamed."

The first set of running footsteps were now followed by several more. Clara frowned.

"I can't believe everyone found the champagne that disagreeable," she said.

There were shouts now, and a scraping sound of something heavy being moved. Captain O'Harris stood up, his eyes focused on the ceiling as if he could look through it and see what was going on. Clara was looking up too, baffled. They both jumped when someone knocked on their cabin door.

"Ship's steward!" A voice called out.

Captain O'Harris opened the door and they both saw a red-faced man in the corridor outside.

"The captain apologises, but we must ask you to evacuate the ship. If you can make your way calmly, but swiftly, to the upper deck you will be placed in a lifeboat," the man said in a rush, before moving off to the next cabin.

"Evacuate the ship?" Clara had jumped up from her bunk, but the man was already gone.

She and Captain O'Harris stepped out into the corridor and noted that a number of crewmen were hammering on the doors of each cabin to see if they were occupied and, if they were, informing the occupants to abandon ship. Clara looked at O'Harris in astonishment. The ship was cruising just off the coast of Brighton. The weather was calm and there should be no other ships out here to potentially cause a collision. What could possibly have gone wrong.

"Do you want to take your bags?" O'Harris asked Clara, ducking back into the cabin.

"Just my handbag," Clara said. He picked it up and tossed it to her. "We best get into a lifeboat!"

They made their way up on deck where the only signs of a problem were the hysterics of various passengers who had taken the news of the evacuation badly. Some were panicking for no better reason than that they could. Since there was no obvious sign of fire, or of the ship sinking, it seemed ridiculous to lose your head. Not that that would help if there was a fire or the ship was sinking, anyway. Most of the passengers were milling about, waiting to be assigned to a lifeboat. Looking gloomy at having their celebrations cancelled, rather than scared.

Clara and O'Harris joined the others and were rapidly handed lifejackets by a passing crewman.

"What has happened?" Clara tried to ask him, but he scuttled past without speaking.

No one seemed to know what was going on. After about fifteen minutes of waiting around for the first lifeboat to be loaded and launched, the initial fright at the word 'evacuate' was diminishing and people were growing restless. Some wanted to go back to the sun deck where the band was still playing on, by the order of the captain. Others were proving belligerent, especially with several glasses of champagne under their belt. The crew was having a hard time keeping order.

Just as matters seemed to be getting out of hand, Captain Pevsner appeared on the balcony of his bridge and looked down on the assembled passengers. Calmly and clearly he addressed them all.

"I apologise for this inconvenience ladies and gentlemen," he began. "I hope to resolve the matter very swiftly, but for your own safety we must temporarily evacuate you from the ship."

"What is going on!" A man from among the passengers yelled.

"As you all know, the sea lanes around the British coast were a prime hunting ground for the German U-boats during the war. To counter the threat, the sea was salted with thousands of mines. Despite the best efforts of the sweepers after the war, some of these mines remain and the Mary Jane has had the misfortune of encountering one," there was a collective gasp from the crowd which Captain Pevsner ignored. "The mine, thankfully, has not exploded and, as I have a number of men aboard who once served on minesweepers, I have every hope we can remove the threat and prevent any damage to the ship. However, as a precaution, I am asking you all to go in the lifeboats and wait at a safe distance. My priority is the wellbeing of my guests. I dearly hope to have you all back aboard before midnight."

More questions were thrown at the captain from the crowd, but he refused to answer them.

"Please cooperate with my crew to the best of your ability. This will speed the evacuation and ensure you can all return before midnight. This is but a temporary interruption to our evening, ladies and gentlemen. Thank you for your patience."

Captain Pevsner walked away and into the bridge cabin, the questions of the passengers still pursuing him to no avail.

"What a nightmare," Captain O'Harris reflected. "I didn't realise there were still mines out here!"

"Not many," Clara reassured him. "But the odd one or two. How I understand it, they might have originally sunk too deep and then something occurs to cut their mooring and they resurface. I've read stories about fishermen dragging them up in their nets."

"What a catch!" O'Harris shook his head.

The man stood just ahead of them was growing impatient. He was drunk and already in a temper. When a crewman came to ask him to step into a lifeboat he pushed the man away.

"I ain't getting in no lifeboat!" He barked.

He stumbled backwards and spun around to face the other guests.

"What bloody nonsense! I ain't getting in no lifeboat!"

With that he started to stalk off in the direction of the sun deck and the music.

"Sir!" The crewman went to chase him.

Another crewman stepped over to the gathered passengers.

"Would you care to get in the lifeboat?" He asked O'Harris and Clara.

"Not really," Clara groaned, looking at the swaying white lifeboat. "I have been watching how you launch the things."

The crewman started to look worried, thinking they had another stubborn passenger on their hands. Captain O'Harris patted his shoulder.

"She doesn't mean it," he promised.

Clara raised an eyebrow.

"Ask an honest question, get an honest answer," she replied, stepping forward towards the nearest lifeboat. "I don't care to get in, but I will."

Clara lifted her skirt and managed to get one foot into the lifeboat before it started to rock. She grimaced and screwed up her eyes for a second, the seasickness pill still only just taking effect. Then she swung in her other foot and wobbled for a moment, before rapidly finding a space on one of the benches in the boat. Captain O'Harris joined her, along with several others, then the boat was lowered towards the sea, the process slightly jerky as the winches were turned by hand. The sea seemed to slap the boat as it came down onto the surface. To Clara's delicate stomach it felt like a blow. The ropes were released and the lifeboat was rowed by a crewman away from the ship to where several others were already sitting.

As the Mary Jane fell behind them Clara felt a chill come over her, almost like a premonition something bad was going to happen. She tried to ignore it, but she doubted she was the only one sitting in a lifeboat and waiting in tense anticipation for the sudden explosion of a mine.

Chapter Two

"How will they go about removing the mine?" Clara asked the others in her lifeboat.

Glances were exchanged between the passengers and the crewman who had rowed them out. They had been sitting in the lifeboat for almost half an hour and everyone was becoming cold and agitated. Clara had asked the question as much to distract everybody from their predicament, as out of curiosity. People mumbled among themselves, then an older man sat towards the prow gave a polite cough. Eyes fell on him.

"I might be able to answer the question," the man declared modestly. He was dressed in a dinner jacket and purple bowtie. He had the side whiskers of a man from another generation and the twist to his mouth suggested he was used to talking with a pipe clenched in his teeth. "I was with the Royal Naval Reserve during the war. I served on a yacht that did some minesweeping."

"They used a yacht for minesweeping!" A woman near Clara remarked with a gasp.

"They used yachts for a lot of things," the RNR man explained. "But this one was used for minesweeping. I served aboard her for about six months. When you sweep for mines you use nets, which is why a lot of fishing boats were converted for the purpose. When you snagged a mine in the nets, you would carefully bring it to the surface and then, in general, you shot at it with a rifle to make it explode a safe distance from the vessel."

"But this mine is already near the Mary Jane," Captain O'Harris pointed out.

"And it hasn't exploded," the RNR man raised a finger. "That tells me it is faulty. These mines were designed to go off at the slightest bump. The horns on them were like triggers. Knocking one caused the whole thing to explode. Others were magnetic and would be attracted to a metal hull. You might get away with skimming one if you were a very light craft, but not a passenger liner. I've known a fishing boat gently nudge one and be blown sky high."

The phrase 'blown sky high' caused several people to shudder and cast anxious glances across to Mary Jane. She looked quite peaceful in the water.

"You think the firing mechanism is faulty on this mine?" O'Harris said.

"That would be my surmise," the RNR man nodded. "If they can move it away from the hull and then steer the Mary Jane to a safe distance, they should be able to explode it with rifle fire."

"If they have a rifle," O'Harris pointed out.

"Old seadog like Captain Pevsner knows what can lurk in these waters. He'll have a rifle or two onboard."

"Are you saying these waters are full of mines still?" A young man in the party startled at the revelation and he, along with several others, started to glare at the water around them suspiciously.

"Thousands of mines were laid," the RNR man explained patiently. "By both the Germans and the British. We have swept this channel over and over, but we are all aware that we missed mines. The ones that sank to the bottom for some reason or slipped their mooring. Every now and then a fishing boat finds one. Could be generations before we discover them all."

Now everyone was feeling less comfortable in the lifeboat.

"Look, the Mary Jane's moving!" Someone shouted from behind Clara.

They all looked over at the hulk of the passenger liner as she started to move. She was going very slowly, making the smallest ripple possible in the water.

"Now we will discover if the mine was magnetic," the RNR man observed nonchalantly.

The Mary Jane continued on her course for several minutes, then she turned her prow and seemed to be coming around on herself. The next moment her engines went into reverse and she came to a tentative halt. Everyone held their breath.

From the rail of the ship movement could be seen beneath the lightbulbs. Suddenly there was a series of bangs and flashes. Rifles! Bullets flew into a seemingly empty patch of water. No one in the lifeboat could see the ominous globe that was the mine bobbing on the water's surface. The first volley brought no results. There was a pause as the crew lined up for the second attempt. More bangs rang out and more flashes of light. The water was peppered again but, this time, a faint metallic 'ting' suggested that the mine had been struck.

"Really is a dud…" the RNR man puttered just as there was a massive explosion.

A huge plume of water whooshed into the air and fell back down like heavy rain. The ocean heaved and, even at a safe distance, the lifeboats felt the surge and were rocked back and forth.

Almost as fast as the explosion had occurred the waters returned to normal and the waves caused by the mine died down. Everything became calm again.

Clara let out a sigh of relief. She had not realised she had been holding her breath until that moment. Aboard the Mary Jane signals were now being shown to inform the lifeboats they could return. The oarsmen went back to their work and the small boats were rapidly drawn back to the liner. Rope ladders were thrown down and guests worked their way back onto the deck; most of the ladies complaining how difficult it was to climb in dress shoes.

When it was Clara's turn she slipped her shoes off and jammed them in the belt of her dress.

"Forever practical," O'Harris grinned at her.

"I am not a fool," Clara replied with a smile, then she clambered up the rope ladder in her stockinged feet. She was over the rail and safely on deck faster than most of the other ladies.

"There is only one downside," Clara remarked to O'Harris as he appeared on deck. "My feet are now wet. Never mind."

Clara slipped on her shoes and grabbed O'Harris' arm.

"Nearly being blown up by a mine does wonders for a girl. I want to dance!"

"Clara Fitzgerald, whatever has come over you!" O'Harris teased.

"Well, I am cold, and I don't know anything better for getting you warm again like a little bit of fast movement," Clara replied in mock seriousness.

"Want some champagne too?"

Clara scowled at him.

"Alright," he laughed. "I won't push my luck! I want that dance!"

The band had been instructed to play throughout the ordeal of the mine. Unlike the guests, they had not been permitted to leave the liner during the drama. Captain Pevsner had reminded them of the noble efforts of the band on the Titanic who played until it went down. When this seemed not to convince the musicians, he bluntly informed them that all the lifeboats were gone and they would be best to distract themselves from possibly impending doom by playing. Reluctantly, they had obeyed.

With the drama over they were recovering themselves, their nerves more than a little shot to pieces and the odd wrong note being played as they endeavoured to get themselves back into the party spirit. For the guests the ordeal seemed to have been little more than a temporary interlude and they were all laughing and dancing nearly as soon as they were back aboard. There were still several hours before midnight and there was plenty of champagne to drink and food to consume. Why dwell on the mine? No harm had come of it, after all.

The band was playing a waltz, they weren't quite up to anything faster just at that moment. O'Harris escorted Clara to the dance floor on the sun deck and slipped his arm around her waist. They took a moment to get into the rhythm of the waltz and then they were moving in time with the other dancers. Clara felt herself relax properly. She had asked to dance, even though she was not a keen dancer, because she had needed to do something to burn off the agitation she had felt in the lifeboat. Awaiting the fate of the Mary Jane had been torturous and had left her fizzing. She needed to do something to take away those nerves.

It also felt good to be close to O'Harris. Clara was beginning to like dancing after all.

"Watch out," O'Harris whispered in her ear as they swayed to the music.

"Watch out?" Clara asked.

"Captain Pevsner, if I am not much mistaken, is heading straight for us with a look on his face like a sour haddock."

"You have no idea what a haddock looks like, do you?" Clara replied.

"I was trying to go with the nautical theme of the evening," O'Harris countered. "Most fish look sour, don't they?"

"Miss Fitzgerald."

Captain Pevsner had arrived at their side and O'Harris had been right, even if his analogy was slightly flawed. The man looked worried and upset.

"Might I have a moment of your time?" Captain Pevsner asked Clara.

"It is urgent?" Clara asked, though she had no doubt it was.

"Yes. Might you come up to my bridge? Captain O'Harris, you are welcome too," Pevsner had added the last as an afterthought.

"Something has happened," Clara said with a sigh. "Right then, I guess it is time to be a detective again."

Captain Pevsner led them up to his bridge. At another time Clara would have been distracted by the marvellous view from the large glass windows. You could see for miles. But now was not the time for admiring the outlook.

"I apologise for disrupting your evening further," Captain Pevsner said as soon as they were on the bridge. They were alone, even Alfred Cinch was not present. "A situation has arisen that I could use your help resolving."

Captain Pevsner gave a long sigh and walked over to the table in the middle of the room that held charts. They were a token gesture, since the Mary Jane no longer traversed routes her captain did not know like the back of his hand. They were memories, however, and they stayed in a place to remind everyone that once the liner had sailed real oceans.

"I am right in understanding, Miss Fitzgerald, that you are a private detective?"

"Yes," Clara confirmed.

"And you have worked on cases alongside the Brighton police?"

"I have a very good working relationship with the police. I aim not to tread on their toes, however."

Captain Pevsner seemed satisfied.

"There is a situation aboard my ship that I would like to see resolved speedily and discreetly. If possible before we dock tomorrow. I would very much prefer not to have the night's festivities disrupted further, or my guests unsettled by a police presence."

"What has happened?" Clara took a pace towards the captain, all seriousness now.

"My cook was evacuated from the ship with the

guests," Captain Pevsner explained. "When he returned to the ship's kitchen a short while ago, he was distressed to find a gentleman lying on the kitchen floor. Sadly, the gentleman was dead. Worse, he was one of the guests."

Clara's shoulders sagged.

"An accident?" She asked, knowing if that was the case she would not have been summoned.

"It would appear he was murdered," Captain Pevsner explained miserably. "And that places me in a tricky predicament. I could radio to the police, but I imagine they will ask me to dock at once and thus my guests will not get their expected New Year's at sea. Equally, once I have docked there is a greater chance of the killer leaving the ship. Right now, he, or I suppose she, are trapped. I had hoped you might investigate the matter discreetly. If you could locate the murderer while we are still at sea, I could detain them and hand them over to the police tomorrow with a minimum of fuss."

"Clara is here for the festivities too, you know," Captain O'Harris pointed out, his tone stern.

"I am aware of that," Captain Pevsner responded, his own tone was dull, as if he was struggling to comprehend what was happening. "Another time I would not have asked but this year…"

Captain Pevsner looked wistfully out the window of the bridge, down to the sun deck where his passengers danced. He smiled faintly.

"The Mary Jane has seen many years of fine service. She has helped her country in time of war and she has brought pleasure to a great many people. I have been her captain for almost twenty years. Before that, I was first mate aboard her. She is a friend as much as my vessel," Captain Pevsner turned his eyes to Clara. "Old seadogs tend to become sentimental about their ships. Perhaps it is because you spend so much of your time together. This old girl is in my blood and that makes this last voyage all the harder."

"Last voyage?" Clara asked.

"Mary Jane has had her day," Pevsner creased his mouth into that faint smile again. "She is worn out. The sea has taken its toll. I have been denying it for a long time, but in my heart I know this will be our last venture. When I sail back to Brighton in 1922, so I will be saying goodbye to an old friend. The next stop for Mary Jane is a scrapyard and, perhaps, it will be time for me to hang up my sea-boots. I wanted this last voyage to be special, to be something to remember her by. I don't want it spoiled by a police investigation. I don't want my passengers leaving angry and upset. Not on this occasion. Not when I can't redeem myself and Mary Jane.

"I want my old girl to have a grand last voyage, not tarnished by spilt blood. If you can find this killer without alerting the passengers, all the better. I want people to go away with happy memories of the last time Mary Jane sailed, not memories of a murder."

"What if one of the passengers is the killer?" Clara said.

Captain Pevsner shook his head.

"They were all on the lifeboats."

"At least one was not," Clara reminded him.

Pevsner paused.

"Your point is taken. But, still, if you can find who did this without a fuss, then this evening would not be ruined."

"The evening is already ruined for our dead man," Clara said. "But I do understand, and there is wisdom in trying to solve this before the Mary Jane goes back to harbour. I'll need full access to the ship and the cooperation of the crew."

"You will have it," Pevsner promised.

"Then I shall take the case."

"Clara!" O'Harris protested. "We are supposed to be celebrating New Year's."

Clara glanced back at Captain O'Harris.

"As I said before, I fully intend to be stood on the sun deck when the clock chimes midnight," Clara assured him.

"I won't let you down."

O'Harris sighed, but then he smiled.

"Do I get to tag along?"

"I'm supposed to be spending the evening with you, so I hope so!"

Captain Pevsner looked relieved.

"Thank you, I really appreciate this."

Clara shrugged.

"You best show me this body of yours."

Chapter Three

Captain Pevsner led them below decks. The Mary Jane seemed quieter down here with the guests all up on deck. The music from the band just penetrated the closed confines; a faint echo in the corridors. However, the steady thrum of the engines as they descended further into the bowels of the ship, overrode the soft melody of the waltz from upstairs.

The kitchen or, in nautical terms, the galley, was a long room set in the centre of the ship. Thus it had no windows and operated day and night by electric light generated via the engines. Even on a cold December night the kitchen was humid and brought Clara out in a sweat barely moments after she entered. Great ovens blazed out heat, no one had turned them off when the ship was evacuated. There was a smell of charred food as whatever was inside was burned to a crisp. The room would usually be steamy from all the pans of water bubbling away, but they had been removed from the heat when the kitchen was abandoned and now stood upon counters, their contents cold.

The kitchen crew were nowhere to be seen. Clara glanced at Captain Pevsner for an explanation.

"They are waiting in the chart room," he explained.

"When they came back in and discovered the body, they summoned me at once. I told them to wait in the chart room while I considered what to do."

"How many kitchen crew are there?" Clara asked as Captain Pevsner lead them down the length of the room.

"Five. The cook, two assistants and two boys who deal with the cleaning and lifting."

The room was divided by long metal island units. They were rivetted to the floor with great bolts. Each served as storage space as well as a table to work on. Captain Pevsner led them down the right-hand side of these islands, finally turning at the end and stopping. The body was lying in the gap between the islands and the left-hand wall of the kitchen. From the waist down, the island masked the body from view, but the shoulders and head were sticking beyond the counter and easily visible.

"It's the drunk we met on deck!" O'Harris exclaimed. "The one who refused to get in a lifeboat."

Captain Pevsner seemed startled.

"What is this?"

"This gentleman," Clara pointed to the corpse, "refused to get in a lifeboat when he was asked to and stormed off. It appears he never got in one."

"It was not your crew's fault," O'Harris hastened to add. "The man was belligerent. Only way to have put him in a lifeboat would have been with his lights knocked out."

Captain Pevsner was not appeased.

"Do you know who this man is?" Clara asked, stepping closer to the body and crouching down.

There was a large kitchen knife sticking out of the man's right side, it had not been possible to see it from the angle she had been standing, but now she was closer she could make it out clearly. There was also a lot of blood pooled on the right side of the body. He had not died quickly.

"I know a lot of my guests," Captain Pevsner said. "But this man's face I don't recognise. Obviously, anyone with the money could buy a ticket to this event."

Clara took a better look at the victim; he was probably in his thirties with dark hair and a blotchy complexion that even in death was noticeable. Clara guessed he was a habitual heavy drinker. He had a strongly defined face – strong chin, strong nose, high cheekbones. The combination made his features handsome in a sturdy fashion. Age and drink, however, would likely strip that rugged charm and replace it with a sagged, swollen ugliness. But he was still young enough to carry his excesses lightly. When not drunk, Clara could imagine the man was very attractive to women.

He wore a smart dress suit. She opened the jacket and found a label for a tailor's shop in Brighton.

"Parker's," she read out the label.

"A very high-end tailor," Captain O'Harris said. "Nothing 'off-the-rack'. My uncle used to buy his suits from there, had a new one every few years. I remember the fittings could go on for weeks."

"This suit looks new," Clara turned back the cuffs of the jacket and ran her finger over the satin lining. "There are no signs of wear and tear. Ah!"

She retrieved something from the inside of the cuff, it was a tiny piece of cardboard.

"He had failed to remove the tag," she showed the slip to Pevsner and O'Harris. The cardboard was a name tag, indicating that the jacket belonged to a particular suit, and thus for a specific customer. Unfortunately, the tag did not indicate a full name, only the initials. H. K.

"I could compare that to my passenger list," Captain Pevsner said.

"That would be helpful," Clara nodded. She continued to look over H.K's body, searching pockets from which she produced his ticket for the night's event and a tin of breath mints. There was nothing else.

"Why was he down here?" Pevsner puttered, glaring at the body as if it offended him, which it probably did. It was upsetting his well-ordered ship and disrupting the night's proceedings.

"The man, from the little I saw, was dreadfully drunk," O'Harris said. "It was early in the evening as well. I would guess he was looking for another drink."

H.K. had a champagne glass by his hand. It had rolled into the pool of blood. Clara carefully picked it up and placed it on the island counter to her right.

"That would confirm your theory," Clara said. "The waiters scrambled into the boats with everyone else."

"The logical place to find more alcohol would be the kitchen," O'Harris nodded. "Or a room near it, at least. I doubt, in his state, he fully appreciated the situation that was occurring all around him."

"And that leaves a very big question," Clara stood up and rearranged the skirt of her dress. "Who killed him, and why?"

"A crewman?" Captain Pevsner asked anxiously.

"We can't rule out that another passenger avoided the lifeboats," Clara responded. "In which case, it would seem someone followed this man and killed him. Whether that was a spur of the moment thing, or whether someone was planning this, we can't say for the moment."

"It's interesting that no one appears to have missed him," Captain O'Harris mused. "Most people do not come to these things alone."

"No one has come to me and said their husband or friend is missing," Captain Pevsner confirmed.

"So it would seem no one aboard cares much about the fellow," Clara sighed, feeling sorry for the man on the floor.

H.K. was clearly a wretch and a drunk, but most people came to such a predicament through ill-circumstances. Who knew what was in the man's past that spurred him on to drink? And, had it contributed to his murder?

"Might we ask the ship's doctor to take a look at him?" Clara asked.

Captain Pevsner looked perplexed.

"Why? He can't be helped?"

"The doctor may offer some insight into how he died," Clara explained patiently.

Captain Pevsner seemed somewhat unconvinced, but he agreed to go and fetch the doctor.

"Nasty business," O'Harris frowned once they were alone.

Clara was looking at the champagne flute which was smeared with blood down one side.

"If only he had climbed aboard the lifeboat," she said. "He would be still alive."

"No wedding ring," O'Harris noted. "We can exclude the possibility of a wife."

Clara glanced down at the man's hands and saw they were bare.

"Who comes to a New Year's Eve party like this alone? It is hardly the sort of place you would expect to meet someone. Everyone would have come as couples."

"Maybe he came with a girlfriend," O'Harris answered. "And maybe the girl got fed up with him when he started to hit the booze."

"That is possible," Clara agreed. "He doesn't look like the sort of fellow who would have trouble finding a girl to accompany him."

"How do you mean?" O'Harris asked curiously.

Clara smiled.

"He is good looking and well-off. He dressed smartly for the evening, took time over his appearance. He is not so chronic a drunk that he neglects himself. A girl who met him and did not know about his drinking would be attracted."

"You think he was a chronic drunk?" O'Harris tilted his head to look at H.K.'s face from another angle.

"His face is covered in broken veins, the sort you see on someone who has either worked out in the cold a lot or drinks heavily. From his appearance I guess the latter. He has that look to him," Clara felt sadness creeping over her again as she looked at H.K. "I think he was a regular heavy drinker. I could be wrong."

"What about the knife?" O'Harris moved around to study the blade that protruded from H.K.'s side.

"Kitchen knife," Clara shrugged. "Hardly hard to find one in here."

"An impulsive act, then?" O'Harris offered.

"Maybe," Clara still had that frown on her face. She didn't like what she was looking at, and not just because it was a dead body. She felt there was something sinister behind this, something that went beyond an argument turned bad.

Captain Pevsner returned with the ship's doctor. The man was knocking on the door of retirement. Ex-Navy, as the medals on his jacket demonstrated, he had a naval pension to live off, but couldn't quite let go of the sea. He had a thick mane of white hair and even thicker eyebrows. He seemed competent enough, at least he had been polite and friendly when Clara had visited him earlier. Now he nodded to her.

"You look better."

"I feel better. That pill worked wonders," Clara replied.

Captain Pevsner led the doctor around the far side of the islands, so he had a view of the dead man from the feet up.

"Oh dear," he said as the corpse came into view, though his tone sounded more puzzled than alarmed. "A stabbing."

"I wondered if you could tell me anything about how he might have died, beyond the obvious," Clara said.

The doctor carefully dropped to his knees. The process involved a lot of creaking from his protesting joints. He crouched like a gargoyle over the body, his crown of hair making him seem all the more otherworldly. He touched the handle of the knife gingerly.

"I would say the knife went into a lung," he scrunched up his eyes as he assessed the angle of the blade. "The thrust would have been an upwards jab, which means the knife would have missed the ribcage and gone up beneath it. But it is too low to strike the heart, may I?"

The doctor pointed at the knife and glanced at Clara, indicating he wanted to remove it.

"Go ahead," Clara said. If she was going to resolve this matter before the police came, she would need all the clues she could get. No doubt Dr Deàth, Brighton's coroner, would not be happy with the tampering, but she was in a tricky position. Besides, she doubted Pevsner was going to allow the body to remain here. He wanted his kitchen back up and running.

The ship's doctor removed the knife. It was a kitchen knife, as Clara had predicted. The blade was about seven or eight inches long and had a bend at the tip.

"Scraped a rib after all," the ship's doctor noted of the bent blade. "It wouldn't have reached the heart, not from this angle and thrust so low into the body. But it would have gone into the right lung, puncturing it. That alone would not have been fatal, at least not swiftly. Do you know what happens when the lung is punctured?"

Clara had worked as a nurse during the war and had seen her fair share of accidents and emergencies.

"The punctured lung would leak air into the chest cavity with every breath the man took," she said. "Eventually, the air in the chest would cause so much pressure that the healthy lung would collapse and the man would suffocate."

"Ah, you have some medical knowledge," the doctor smiled at Clara warmly.

She was beginning to like the man.

"I was a nurse in the war."

"And you are quite right, but the process takes time and I don't think our friend here had reached that stage. No, I think he bled to death," the doctor took a good look at the blood pooled around the body. "I wonder…"

He rose with difficulty, having to lever himself up using the counter top of one of the islands. His knees protested heartily. Once upright, he stepped over the blood pool and arrived at the dead man's head. The process of crouching down, with the protest of his joints, was repeated until he was able to bend forward and lift H.K.'s head.

"There!" The doctor pointed out to Clara a bloody patch on the floor and a wet looking wound on the back of H.K.'s head. "He must have fallen backwards with the shock of being stabbed, or someone pushed him, and he hit his head so hard he passed out."

The doctor sniffed.

"The man reeks of alcohol. That would have helped to send him unconscious for a while, long enough at least for him to bleed out without rousing."

"And that's how he died," Clara said.

The doctor was rising up again like some old pneumatic machine that needed oiling.

"At least he didn't know about it," he observed. "Not after he fell and hit his head, anyway."

"Can I move him now?" Captain Pevsner glanced at Clara. "I need my kitchen back."

"I don't think we can learn anymore from him," Clara agreed. "I will need to talk to your kitchen staff, though."

Captain Pevsner was a little disgruntled, but understood.

"The chart room is back along the corridor. They should be all there. I'll get the body removed while you talk to them. I could do with a hand," Pevsner looked up purposefully at Captain O'Harris.

"I'll remain here," O'Harris said, with a barely perceptible groan.

Clara patted his arm.

"Come join me when you are done."

Then she headed off to locate the chart room and her first set of witnesses.

Chapter Four

"Which of you would be the cook?" Clara asked as she entered the chart room.

Several unhappy faces turned towards her. The kitchen crew were all men and they all looked as though they had just burned the captain's dinner.

"I'm the cook," a rugged man with the girth of an elephant levered himself up from a wooden chair. "Theobald Schilling."

"German?" Clara asked.

"My father was," Theobald shrugged. "Who are you?"

"Clara Fitzgerald," Clara introduced herself. "I am a private detective and Captain Pevsner has asked me to discreetly unravel the mystery of the dead man in your kitchen."

The men looked uncertain.

"You?" Theobald asked. "Alone?"

Clara made a play of looking over her shoulder to see if anyone was behind her.

"It looks to be that way," she remarked to Theobald. "Would you like me to inform Captain Pevsner you do not wish to cooperate with me?"

Theobald jerked in surprise at the statement.

"No," he said quickly. "I was only a little taken aback."

Clara mellowed. She knew that, for many men, finding themselves confronted by a female private detective took some getting used to.

"Mr Schilling, were you the first to discover the man in your kitchen?" She asked.

Schilling shook his head.

"That was Robbie," he pointed to a man of about forty who had been sitting next to him. "Robbie is my assistant, but like the captain's first mate."

Charlotte turned to Robbie. He was a complete contrast to his boss; skinny where Schilling was fat, calm when Schilling seemed anxious. He seemed rather bored with the whole situation, as if it was an inconvenience, like an oven stopping working.

"Robbie," Clara addressed the man. "What might be your surname?"

"Bunting," Robbie huffed, he looked unimpressed at talking to a woman detective too.

"You went into the kitchen first?" Clara persisted.

Robbie shrugged, indicating he thought that obvious.

"Did you touch or move the body?" she asked.

Robbie snorted, clearly thinking that a stupid question.

"I stopped in my tracks and turned around to cook," he answered. "Why would I touch him?"

"Maybe if you thought he wasn't dead," Clara suggested.

"He had a kitchen knife sticking out his side!" Robbie laughed nastily at her.

Clara was becoming annoyed.

"Then you recognised the knife?" She asked him sharply.

Robbie seemed wrong-footed for a moment.

"What?"

"You recognised the knife as belonging to the kitchen?" Clara said.

Robbie glanced at Schilling, a sudden uneasiness creeping over him.

"It was a knife," Robbie grumbled. "The handle looked like the ones we have in the kitchen."

"Did you notice anything else?" Clara resumed.

Robbie regained his earlier arrogance and sneered at her.

"The fellow was dead and bleedin' all over the floor. I noticed that."

Clara narrowed her eyes at him, but said no more. He was not worth the aggravation. Instead she turned to Schilling.

"When the evacuation was declared, what happened in the kitchen?"

"We turned off the hobs," Schilling hefted his shoulders. "Left the ovens on though, because Pevsner hoped we would not be long. The ovens are old and temperamental. They take a while to heat up to the right temperature. I prefer not to turn them off and let them get cold if I can help it."

"You fully expected to come back," Clara observed. "You were confident Captain Pevsner could deal with the mine."

"Pevsner is an old hand at this," Schilling replied. "He has dealt with mines before, admittedly that was during the war, but I didn't doubt him."

Schilling seemed the honest, loyal sort. The sort who does not think too hard about possibly bad consequences. One of those souls who was forever hopeful that everything would be alright. It seemed he had absolute faith in Pevsner.

"Did you all head to the lifeboats together?" Clara asked.

"We did," Schilling confirmed. "I made sure everyone was aboard a lifeboat before they launched."

"The band did not get the same consideration," Clara pointed out. "Why was Pevsner happy to let you off and not the musicians?"

"Isn't it obvious?" Robbie snapped. "The musicians could keep playing and hold up peoples' spirits. We were of no use aboard. No point cooking for people when they are all out at sea!"

"You might have helped dispose of the mine," Clara retorted, fed up with the snide man.

"None of us know how to shoot a rifle," Robbie told her promptly, which provided Clara with an opening to respond.

"Really? Surely you served in the war?"

Schilling gave a strange cough. His second assistant, who had yet to be introduced, seemed to try and lean away from Robbie, distancing himself. The kitchen lads made no comment, keeping to themselves. Robbie's sullen look had become ingrained, but now he seemed to be scowling at the universe at large. No one answered Clara.

Clara folded her arms across her chest.

"I seem to have touched a sore spot," she reflected. "You did not serve in the war, then?"

Robbie made no answer. Schilling cleared his throat once again and then spoke.

"Robbie was a conscientious objector," he explained. "He spent most of the war in a prison for his views."

Clara now saw why the topic had caused such concern, and why the second assistant, who was probably a fraction too young to have served in the conflict himself, seemed to have an issue looking at Robbie. Schilling tried to deflect attention.

"I never passed the medical," he slapped his belly. "The recruiting sergeant took one look at me and said it would be too much work and effort to get me into shape. I offered to cook for the army. They said they couldn't find a uniform to fit me. So, I ended up back with Captain Pevsner, cooking for his crew and the men he was transporting."

"I can see why Pevsner let you board the lifeboats," Clara replied. "No point keeping you aboard and risking your lives for no reason."

She wondered if the band would see things that way.

"Before you left the ship, did you happen to glimpse

the man in the kitchen? Maybe on deck, or heading down a corridor?"

"I didn't see him," Schilling shook his head, then he glanced at his kitchen crew. "Did any of you see him?"

The others shook their heads.

"Why was he in the kitchen anyway? Why didn't he get in a lifeboat?" Robbie grumbled.

"He was pretty drunk," Clara explained. "I don't think he realised the gravity of the situation. He appears to have gone to the kitchen looking for more champagne."

"He wouldn't have found it there," Schilling said. "Too hot. There is a cold room further along the corridor. The champagne is in there."

"Who would kill a random drunk looking for champagne?" Robbie blurted out. "Surely everyone was either tackling the mine or leaving on a lifeboat?"

Clara could not answer him, it was a question she had pondered herself. Had someone spotted an opportunity for revenge? Or had there been an argument that had turned nasty?

"Do you know who the man is?" Schilling asked.

"Not as yet. No one seems to recognise him," Clara replied. "Captain Pesvner is having the body removed from the kitchen. You should be able to get back to work soon."

"Good," Schilling said with relief. "The guests will be getting through my last batch of canapes. I need to get cooking again."

Clara was not entirely surprised that Schilling's primary thought was his work. She had investigated a few murders and people reacted to the discovery of a corpse in many ways. Some were overcome, while others merely annoyed by the inconvenience the body caused them in their work. Schilling was clearly one of the latter.

Clara thanked them for their time and then went back to the kitchen to see how things were progressing. H.K. had been removed to the cold room for the time being. Captain Pevsner was personally mopping up the blood from the floor, while O'Harris was talking to the doctor. He glanced up when Clara returned.

"Anything?"

"They were all on a lifeboat when the murder occurred," Clara replied, frowning.

"It would have been a bit too obvious to be one of them," O'Harris agreed. "What do you want to do next?"

"I can't do a lot until we have a name for the man," Clara said. "Hopefully Captain Pevsner can supply that."

"I shall aim to do so," Captain Pevsner looked up from his mopping. "As soon as this is done and my kitchen can return to normal."

"In the meantime, let's see if we can track down the crewman who was trying to get H.K. into a lifeboat. He may well be the last person to have seen him alive, besides the killer," Clara said.

Captain O'Harris joined her as she left the kitchen and headed up to the deck. The music was still playing loudly and none of the other passengers appeared to have caught wind of the murder. They all seemed to be enjoying themselves.

"I only glimpsed that fellow who was trying to wrangle H.K. into a lifeboat," Clara said. "I hope we can spot him again."

"I have a vague idea of what he looked like," Captain O'Harris assured her. "Between us we should locate him."

They walked the length of the ship looking for the crewman. There now suddenly seemed to be a lot of staff aboard the ship and they had a nasty habit of looking all alike. Clara was beginning to feel a tad frustrated when Captain O'Harris nudged her hand and pointed to his right.

"Is that him?"

Clara stopped and watched a crewman who was making sure the lifeboats were securely fastened back aboard. He had his head down, but Clara could see him in profile and there definitely seemed to be something familiar about him.

"Yes," she decided. "That could be him!"

They hurried over to the crewman and introduced themselves.

"Might you be the gentleman who was trying to get that drunk guest into a lifeboat?" Clara asked.

The crewman stood up from his work and looked at them with a puzzled expression.

"I had to get a few drunk passengers into lifeboats," he explained.

"But this one stormed off," Captain O'Harris interjected. "I believe his exact words were 'I ain't getting in no lifeboat'."

"Oh, him!" Understanding dawned on the crewman's face. "I remember him. He stalked off to the sun deck."

"Did you pursue him?" Clara asked.

"I tried to," the crewman nodded. "After I had everyone else in the lifeboats I went to find him. He was sitting in a chair on the sun deck listening to the band. He looked depressed. I approached him and politely explained the situation and that he should get aboard a lifeboat. He used some very foul language and told me to go away."

"Did you?" Clara felt sorry for the crewman having to try and coral the irate drunk into a lifeboat. Probably those already in the lifeboat would be glad he had not succeeded, had they known about it.

"Not at once," the crewman said. "I knew the captain would not be happy to have a guest left aboard. I tried to think of another way to get him in the lifeboat. I even suggested there would be more champagne if he got in. I'm afraid he just swore at me again."

"Not a nice fellow," O'Harris sympathised.

"I think he was upset over something," the crewman said, unexpectedly defending H.K.'s belligerence. "He seemed hurt. I felt he was lashing out at me not out of spite, but because he could not lash out at the person who had really upset him."

"Had he come to the party alone?" Clara asked.

"Maybe you saw him with someone earlier?"

The crewman shook his head.

"Sorry. Until I was trying to get him into the lifeboat, I had not noticed him."

"Did any other passengers refuse to board a lifeboat?"

The crewman gave this some thought.

"No one else argued with me, but I suppose someone might have opted to remain. People can be odd like that, some of them are terrified of the lifeboats because they seem small compared to the liner," the crewman scratched at his chin. "You can never guarantee that everyone has left the ship, you just do your best. I made the effort with that man, I really did. But, other than trussing him up and dragging him to a lifeboat, I could do very little. He wouldn't leave the sun deck voluntarily."

"When did you last see him?" Clara asked.

"I suppose I was trying to persuade him for about fifteen minutes. The band must have seen, they were playing the whole time. Eventually I gave up and went to see what was happening with the lifeboats. That was when I realised they had all been launched and I couldn't have got the man aboard one even if he had agreed to it. I went to help the captain after that."

"You never saw the man again?"

"No."

The crewman drew his brows into a deep crease across his forehead. He was holding a piece of rope in his hands and he slowly twisted it around his palm.

"Why are you asking all this?"

Captain Pevsner was keeping the incident in the kitchen very quiet and Clara had hoped to do the same, but avoiding a direct question could lead to greater suspicion. The last thing anyone needed was wild rumours flitting about the liner.

"The gentleman who remained aboard had an accident and was injured," Clara said carefully. "Captain Pevsner has asked me to investigate the circumstances.

"Am I in trouble?" The crewman started to panic. "I

honestly tried my hardest to get him into a lifeboat."

"You are not in trouble," Clara promised. "No one is being blamed. It is just we are trying to understand the circumstances. As it was, you endeavoured to get him into a lifeboat right until the point there was no lifeboat to place him in."

The crewman nodded quickly.

"Yes, I did try. I hope the captain understands."

"No one is blaming you," Captain O'Harris offered his own assurances. "The man chose to stay behind."

"He did," the crewman started to relax. "I hope the accident was nothing serious."

Clara had no response to that. Death was probably the most serious outcome of any situation.

"Thank you for speaking with us," she gave the crewman a cheery smile and let him go back to coiling rope.

She walked along the ship and found herself at the corner of the bridge, with a view across the sun deck. Captain O'Harris joined her.

"Now what?" He asked.

Clara narrowed her eyes at the assembled guests, talking and dancing.

"Now we see if we can find someone who appears to have lost their dance partner."

Chapter Five

Captain O'Harris and Clara drifted to the edge of the sun deck, near where the tables for food had been placed and covered with large white tablecloths. The band was back in the swing of things and was playing an upbeat number that had the younger party guests full of enthusiasm. Clara glanced at her delicate wristwatch, the one she always wore when on an evening out. It was only just seven o'clock, there were several hours before the finale of the evening. All the more remarkable at how fast H.K. had managed to get himself drunk.

"And who is this fellow?" O'Harris spoke.

Clara glanced in his direction. He was looking along the line of buffet tables. A boy was wandering along the edge of the tables looking worried. He was in evening attire and so was presumably one of the guests, but that did not explain why he was all alone.

"Are you all right?" Captain O'Harris called out to the boy.

The child walked up to him. He had blond hair left long and just touching the starched collar of his shirt. He looked up at O'Harris with big blue eyes that had the wet appearance of someone close to tears.

"I'm lost," he said, jutting out his lower lip.

"Oh dear, old chap," O'Harris crouched down before the boy. "Who are you missing?"

"My mum," the boy explained. "She made me get in a boat without her. She said she would be waiting for me, but I can't find her."

His lower lip trembled and the tears fell.

"We will soon enough find her," Clara appeared next to the lad and bent over so she could look in his face without looming over him. "Now, what is your name?"

"Bert," the boy answered.

"Short for Robert?" Clara asked.

The boy gave her a puzzled look, then glanced back at O'Harris for reassurance.

"She's a detective, old chap," O'Harris informed him. "Very good at solving mysteries and finding missing people."

Bert's expression lifted a little, a ray of hope drying the tears. He took a better look at Clara.

"Can you find my mum?"

"It is the sort of thing I do all the time," Clara replied.

"How will you find her?" Bert asked with the persistence of the very young.

"By asking questions," Clara informed him. "Such as, what is your mother's name?"

Bert frowned, he gave O'Harris that uncertain look again, as if Clara was some strange creature he could not quite get his head around. Then he answered Clara.

"Mum."

"Yes, but she has a name also?" Clara pressed.

The frown deepened.

"Her name's 'mum'."

"Ok," Clara gave up on that one, trying to pretend she could not hear O'Harris chuckling under his breath beside her. "What about your surname? You are Bert, who?"

Bert scratched his head, clearly finding these questions alarmingly hard. Then inspiration dawned.

"Nightingale," he said.

"You are Bert Nightingale?" Clara asked.

Bert nodded.

"Ah, then we have a start!" Clara smiled. "Now, Bert Nightingale, let us proceed to the captain's bridge and see if he can help us."

Bert gave a little sniff to hold back his tears, then he reached out and grabbed Clara's hand. She was surprised and stared at this little person who had suddenly latched onto her. Clara did not spend much time with children.

"How old are you, Bert?" Captain O'Harris stood up.

Bert gave this a good deal of thinking time.

"Six?" He said uneasily.

"Not sure about that?" O'Harris asked.

"No," Bert shook his head.

They started to walk back to the bridge.

"Can you describe your mum?" Clara asked Bert.

Bert became more animated.

"She is taller than me and wears a dress!"

"Describes every woman on this ship," O'Harris said to Clara with a grin.

"What colour was her dress?" Clara continued.

"Black."

"That narrows it," O'Harris said with amusement.

"Let's try this again Bert. Your mother is Mrs Nightingale, so what would you call her as a first name?"

Bert gave a groan, he was getting frustrated too.

"Mum!" He informed her crossly.

"Fair comment," O'Harris shrugged his shoulders.

Clara gave him a look.

"What does your father call your mother?" Clara asked Bert.

"He is dead," Bert answered, though it was a statement and didn't seem to affect him much. "He died when I was just a baby, fighting in the war."

"Right," Clara sighed.

They had reached the stairs up to the captain's bridge. Clara hoped Pevsner was inside and could supply information on Bert's mother. The sooner she could deposit the boy with someone else and carry on her investigation the better. They were halfway up the stairs when Bert piped up again.

"Actually, I think I am five."

"Sure about that, old man?" Captain O'Harris asked him.

After a pause, Bert nodded.

"Well, at least we have that resolved." Clara smiled at him gently.

Bert's hand was soft and hot in hers and he had a tenacious grip, as if he feared she might suddenly disappear on him.

"Why did your mum put you in a lifeboat alone?"

"There wasn't space for her," Bert thrust out his bottom lip and the tears threatened again.

"I'm sure she is fine," Clara promised him, giving his hand a squeeze. "No one was hurt during the evacuation."

She corrected herself mentally; one person was hurt, but it was not Bert's mother and there was no need for the boy to know about H.K.

They reached the bridge and found Captain Pevsner sitting at the chart table, going through a large ledger.

"Ah, Miss Fitzgerald, I was going through the passenger list," Pevsner rose as she entered.

"We have a lost boy," Clara indicated Bert with her free hand. "He says his mother put him aboard a lifeboat that did not have space for her and said she would be waiting for him. He can't find her."

"Oh dear," Captain Pevsner said sympathetically, turning to Bert with a gentle smile.

"His surname is Nightingale," Clara continued. "We thought you might be able to get your crew to find his mother."

"Nightingale?" Pevsner looked puzzled, then he shook his head. "I have just been through this whole book of passenger names and there is no one called Nightingale in it."

Clara was disappointed. Bert looked first at her, then at O'Harris with a very worried expression.

"Can't you find my mum?" He asked.

"Old boy, are you sure your last name is Nightingale?" O'Harris crouched beside Bert again.

Bert's worried eyes refilled with tears.

"I thought it was," he said hopelessly. "Is it not?"

"Don't worry," Clara told him brightly. "I am sure your mother is looking for you, all we need do is settle you in the bridge and put the word out you are here."

"Ah, I don't think that will be possible," Captain Pevsner quickly butted in. "I have a lot to attend to and I can't have a child left alone on the bridge. You best keep him with you."

Clara was irritated, she had the distinct impression Captain Pevsner's statement was based on the fact she was a woman and therefore a more obvious choice to look after a lost child than the captain.

"Might I remind you I have my own duties to attend to?" Clara said. "You were the one who asked for my help."

"I appreciate that, but I cannot play nanny while acting as captain," Pevsner informed her coolly. "And my crew is currently extremely busy."

Bert was following the conversation with the look of a damned man – or rather boy – as if he feared he was to be abandoned again. O' Harris interrupted the argument.

"I'll keep an eye on Bert," he volunteered. "He can tail along with us. I'll make sure he doesn't bother you while you are working, Clara."

He gave Clara a wink and then nodded at the child. Bert was looking utterly downcast, clever enough to understand what the adults around him were arguing about. Clara felt guilty.

"Never mind, Bert," she turned to the boy. "You are stuck with us until we find your mother."

Bert gazed up at her with unhappy eyes.

"She can't have gone far," Clara reassured him. "And she will be looking for you. Now, you have nothing to worry about. Stick with Captain O'Harris and we shall make sure you are fine."

Bert turned to O'Harris, his sorrow briefly eclipsed by a burst of excitement at O'Harris' title.

"You are the captain of a ship too?" He asked, for the first time showing a glimmer of enthusiasm.

"No, I flew aeroplanes in the war," O'Harris explained with a smile.

"You were in the war?" Bert's eyes widened. "Did you know my dad?"

"It was a big war," O'Harris apologised, Bert's expression fell again and he quickly corrected himself. "But maybe I did."

"Now that is resolved...," Captain Pevsner remarked, "I can tell you what I have found out."

"Which is?" Clara asked keenly.

"Our man in the kitchen," Pevsner said, careful not to use words that might upset Bert, "goes by the name of Henry Kemp. It appears from the register that he was part of a group from Noble and Sons, it's a firm of wine importers in Hove. They are very well respected."

"I always get my wines from them," O'Harris agreed. "They have been established nearly a hundred years and they only sell the very best."

"Fine job for an alcoholic," Clara pointed out.

Captain Pevsner merely smiled.

"I'm afraid my register does not tell me anymore. But I can give you a list of the five other guests aboard from the same company."

"Yes, do," Clara let go of Bert's hand and picked up a piece of paper from the chart table. Pevsner handed her a pencil.

"The guests are Arthur Noble, Simon Noble, Elias Noble, Jane Dodd and Charles Walsh," Pevsner recited.

"Alfred Noble inherited the business from his father," Captain O'Harris elaborated. "Simon and Elias are his sons, I believe. I couldn't say who the others are, but I imagine they are part of the senior management team."

Clara jotted this all down.

"I would very much appreciate it, Captain Pevsner, if you could have these people rounded up and brought to somewhere private where I might speak with them. They must be informed of the death of their colleague."

Captain Pevsner nodded his understanding.

"Did the kitchen crew offer any insight?"

"Only that the knife was from the kitchen," Clara replied. "And that they were all aboard the lifeboats. I take it you have never heard of Henry Kemp?"

Captain Pevsner gave a crooked smile.

"No. You may have noticed from the quality of the champagne I have served tonight that I did not use Noble and Sons as my supplier. They are out of my price range, unfortunately."

"Then we might imagine your crew are similarly ignorant of Henry Kemp?" Clara postulated. "They are unlikely to move in the same social circles."

"Are you implying this was a crime committed by one of the guests?" Pevsner looked bleak. Suspecting his crew of murder was one thing, suspecting his guests was quite another.

"I am not ruling anyone out," Clara hastened to add. "I merely mean to imply that it is difficult to see how your crew might have a connection to Henry Kemp. At least, at this juncture. Was a list taken of those who got aboard the lifeboats?"

Pevsner shook his head.

"There would hardly have been time," he tapped his fingers on the chart table. "In a situation such as that, you rely on people wanting to get off the ship."

"So, someone other than Mr Kemp could have stayed aboard?"

Pevsner nodded, the bleak look had not left his face.

"This was not how I wanted Mary Jane's last voyage to be," he gave a faint moan and then sat down in the chair behind the table. "I wanted to finish in a dignified fashion. I wanted people to have happy memories."

"Most still will have," Clara promised him. "I intend to

resolve this discreetly and swiftly. The majority of the people aboard are not involved, so why should they not continue to enjoy tonight?"

"Thank you, Miss Fitzgerald, I appreciate your keen understanding of the situation."

"If you could round up the guests from Noble and Sons, I can continue with my investigation," Clara hinted.

Captain Pevsner walked to a speaking tube in the corner of the bridge and called down to those crew who could hear it that he wanted to see the first mate, at once. Alfred Cinch appeared within a few minutes.

"Captain!"

"Cinch, I need you to find the following people," Captain Pevsner handed him a list of names, similar to the one Clara had written out. "I wish you to bring them to my private cabin. Express upon them the matter is urgent, but be discreet."

Captain?" Cinch had not been informed of the body in the kitchen, though Clara was surprised it had not so far been gossiped about. A ship was a closed community and rumours flew around quickly.

"I'll explain later, Cinch," Pevsner nodded at him.

The first mate briefly looked at Clara and O'Harris as he left, clearly curious but wise enough to obey his captain without quarrel.

"I'll show you to my private cabin," Pevsner rose from the chair. "Oh, and I will spread the word about the lost lad."

Clara glanced at Bert.

"That would be appreciated, his mother must be going spare."

"I'll have my crew attend to it at once," Captain Pevsner placed his captain's cap on his head and straightened it until he was satisfied with the fit. "In the meantime, I have a New Year's Eve party to host."

Chapter Six

Pevsner's private cabin was larger than Clara had imagined it would be. She had expected it to be a poky space with just enough room for a bunk bed and perhaps a desk. Instead she discovered the captain had quite spacious quarters with the sleeping area divided from a study or dining room, and a separate bathroom. Pevsner's 'parlour' consisted of a cosy, if well-worn sofa, a round table firmly bolted to the floor and several cabinets or chests of drawers. A porthole gave a view outside, though a curtain was currently drawn across it. There was an instant feeling that this was personal space, a place few rarely entered without invite.

Pevsner motioned for them all to sit at the table. Papers and a couple of books were spread across it and the captain collected them up roughly and deposited them in a drawer.

"Can I provide you with a drink?" he asked, going to another cabinet and revealing a series of decanters and bottles. "I don't suppose you are wanting alcohol, but I do have a bottle of mineral water?"

"That will do," Clara agreed.

Bert was wandering around the room, looking up at the many nautical pictures on the wall. Captain Pevsner watched him, his expression softening.

"Here you go, young man," he picked up a glass bottle from out of a cabinet. It contained loops of white rope and a nail. "This is an old seaman's puzzle. You have to work out how to extract the nail from the bottle without either breaking it or undoing any of the knots in the rope."

Bert was handed the puzzle and ushered to a large wooden chair with arms near the porthole.

"You see if you can work that out."

Clara smiled at Pevsner's kindness. Bert had relaxed in their company and seemed less disturbed at being lost. Now he was a typical curious child who would need distracting while Clara interviewed those who knew Henry Kemp. The puzzle should keep him occupied for a while, at least.

"If he gets tired, he can rest in my bed," Captain Pevsner told Clara.

"Thank you."

"I'll put the word out for his mother, hopefully it won't take long to find her."

There was a gentle rap at the door of the cabin and Alfred Cinch popped his head inside the room.

"I have the guests here you asked for, Captain."

He had hardly finished speaking when a large, burly man shoved him out of the way and stalked into the room.

"What is this all about?" He demanded angrily.

He was an extremely fat man and his tailor had clearly had some difficultly accommodating his belly within his suit jacket. Discreet tucks and darts could not mask that here was a man whose gut poured over his belt and who had no intention of doing anything about it. He was flushed in the face, and a fine sweat hovered on his forehead, despite the weather being considerably cold. He wiped at his face with a handkerchief from time-to-time.

"I was enjoying the party," the fat man continued. "Now I am told I have to come down here and talk to…"

He turned his gaze on Captain O'Harris.

"So, you are the detective who has requested to speak

with me and interrupt my evening!"

"Actually," Clara rose from her seat, "that would be me. I imagine you would be Arthur Noble?"

The fat man scowled at her, an incredulous look on his face. Then he snorted in derision.

"Now I have seen everything!"

"Have you seen Henry Kemp recently," Clara quickly asked, wanting to catch Mr Noble on the wrong-foot and not intending to get into a debate about female detectives.

Arthur Noble opened his big mouth and then paused. He had probably been about to say something about being interviewed by a woman, he was that sort of man, but Clara's question had registered in his mind and suddenly had him thinking. He looked out the door to where Alfred Cinch was doing a better job of keeping the others of his party from entering the cabin. It was obvious that it was just dawning on him that Henry Kemp was not with them.

"Mr Noble, I did not ask you to come here to ruin your evening. I asked you because Henry Kemp has been found deceased in the ship's kitchen," Clara said patiently.

In the corridor outside the cabin the only woman in the Noble and Sons party gasped at the statement. Clara surmised she was Jane Dodd. Arthur Noble had become briefly uncertain, an obvious rarity for him. He shook it off.

"Henry?" He seemed to be processing the idea that his employee was dead. "But that is preposterous."

"Hardly," Clara waved at the chairs about the table. "Would you and your party like to sit? Then we can discuss this properly."

"With you?" Arthur Noble returned to his previous train of thought.

Clara was concluding the man was rather stupid, though clearly he had a finesse for business – or very good managers.

"Our other option is to sail back into harbour this very instant and summon the police," Clara explained, hearing

Captain Pevsner make a strangled noise behind her. She ignored him. "If you want to get back to the party with reasonable speed, you would be best advised to have a chat with me."

Arthur Noble blanched, unused to being ordered about by anyone, let alone a young woman. Clara waited, standing with one hand on her hip and not dropping her gaze from the fat man's eyes. She had her own evening arrangements and was not about to waste time. The sooner this matter was resolved, the sooner she and Captain O'Harris could return to celebrating the last few hours of 1921.

"I have never been spoken to in such a fashion!" Arthur Noble blurted out.

"You perhaps mean you have never been spoken to so honestly before?" Clara challenged him. "Really Mr Noble, you are not the only one who has had their evening interrupted. Personally, I would rather like to be on the sun deck dancing right now. I imagine Henry Kemp would much rather be up there too."

Arthur Noble was fighting with himself – a part of him wanted to continue arguing and protesting at being confronted by a woman claiming to be a detective, but the other part of him – the small, sensible part – realised that doing so would only waste his own time further. He huffed and puffed but, in the end, they all knew he was going to sit down at the table and talk.

"This best not take long," he grumbled, finally taking a seat.

The chair groaned under his weight and Captain O'Harris raised his eyebrows at Clara. She knew he was debating the possibility of the chair collapsing into fragments beneath Noble's mass. Clara returned his look with a roll of her eyes and O'Harris nearly laughed, having to put his hand to his mouth and cough to disguise it.

Alfred Cinch allowed the other guests into the room. Simon and Elias resembled their father in their round, flushed faces. A family trait, it would seem. They were both overweight, but nowhere near the size of Arthur. They had his sour expression, however, and sat down with looks of sufferance on their faces. Clara was wondering if they behaved in such a way to their customers, or maybe the senior Nobles never dealt with those who bought their goods. They were belligerently arrogant and she was making a mental note never to provide them with her trade.

The other two members of the group looked more as would be expected of two people who had just heard a work colleague had died. Jane Dodd was older than Clara had initially anticipated; somewhere in her forties. She seemed upset at the news and pulled out her chair with her hands trembling. In a complete opposite to her employers, she was rail thin and had a tendency to stoop her shoulders. This masked the fact that she was actually taller than Arthur Noble. She was dressed smartly, but not extravagantly, and pulled her embroidered wrap tighter about her shoulders once she was sitting, as if she was feeling the cold suddenly.

Charles Walsh was the youngest of the group; Clara guessed he was in his mid to late twenties. He wore a good suit and was smartly turned out, his blond hair carefully oiled back and his moustache trimmed. He sat down between Arthur Noble and his two sons, avoiding making eye contact with anyone.

"Now," Clara began with everyone seated, "I understand who you are, Mr Noble, and that these are your two sons, but might I ask how Miss Dodd and Mr Walsh fit into your company?"

If anyone was surprised that Clara knew all their names, they did not show it. They probably guessed Pevsner had acquainted her with the details. Despite the captain's indication that he had a myriad of duties to attend to and could not supervise Bert, he was now hovering at the back of the room and clearly too intrigued to leave. Alfred Cinch, however, had quietly departed.

Arthur Noble finally decided it was best to get on with things and cooperate with Clara. He made the introductions of his staff.

"Miss Dodd has been my secretary for almost twenty years, she is a part of the family," he said gruffly, though there was a tenderness to his words that Clara had not expected. "Charles is our youngest senior manager. A rising star in the company."

Charles Walsh reddened at the compliment.

"What about Henry Kemp?" Clara asked.

"Henry was also a senior manager," Arthur Noble explained. "He was extremely good at his job and will be sorely missed."

"I take it you arranged this evening, Mr Noble?" Clara was trying to get him talking before she probed further into Henry Kemp's character.

"Every year we do something for New Year's," Arthur Noble shrugged dismissively. "Miss Dodd makes the arrangements."

Naturally, Clara thought to herself. Arthur Noble would not lower himself to such petty labours. Clara turned to Miss Dodd.

"You booked the tickets for this evening?"

"With Mr Noble's approval," Jane Dodd answered hastily. "I thought it would be a rather different way to spend the evening."

"And you always invite the senior managers?" Clara turned back to Arthur Noble.

"They are like family too," he displayed his boredom for the questioning with a yawn.

"What about guests? You all attended singly? I assume you have a wife Mr Noble, does she not come?"

Noble gave his nasty snort again.

"This is a male only event, excluding Miss Dodd, naturally," he nodded to Miss Dodd with that remarkable hint of sensitivity once more. "The arrangement is we attend alone, no wives or girlfriends. I insist. Women are such a nuisance."

He directed this last statement firmly at Clara and she felt inclined to retort but held her tongue. She felt that Mrs Noble was probably hugely relieved she did not have to spend New Year's with her boorish husband.

"Was Henry married?" Clara asked instead, thinking there might be someone on shore who would be heartbroken to hear the news, certainly more heartbroken than Arthur Noble.

"Henry never married," Noble answered. "Tragic, actually, his father was badly hurt in an accident and Henry devoted his time to caring for him and his mother, outside of work. It was a trying existence."

Clara thought of Henry's drinking.

"I have to ask, was it usual for Henry Kemp to drink so much?"

"It's a party," Arthur Noble shrugged gruffly.

"Yes, but it is also very early in the evening, and I note that none of you are drunk, whereas, when Henry was last seen alive, he had clearly had too much to drink."

"What are you implying about my managers?" Arthur Noble growled, his tone sharp.

Captain O'Harris, who was taking a backseat in events, now bristled and narrowed his eyes at the man. Clara was unfazed.

"I am not implying," she said. "I am stating. Henry Kemp was extremely drunk when last seen alive, I witnessed this for myself. He refused to get into a lifeboat and it would seem he came down to the kitchen looking for more champagne. All I wish to know is whether this was a common occurrence for him."

"I don't employ drunkards!" Arthur Noble slammed his fist on the top of the table.

Bert, who until then had been fully absorbed in his puzzled, startled and looked up. Captain Pevsner spoke quietly to him and turned his chair so he faced out the porthole.

"Mr Noble," Clara said coldly. "Your obstructive attitude is not assisting any of us. I am not questioning your business practices, I am asking about tonight. Was Henry Kemp in the habit of drinking to excess in his leisure time?"

"And I am telling you that I only employ people of the strictest of character!" Arthur Noble pointed a fat finger at Clara, jerking it at her as he made his point.

Captain O'Harris had endured enough.

"Put your finger down before I break it, old boy," he said, his tone level but sinister.

Arthur Noble's eyes switched to him. His face reddened to a dark shade of crimson.

"You are threatening me?"

"Old boy, if you don't start behaving like a gentleman and answer the questions you are being asked, then I shall do more than just threaten you," O'Harris leaned back in his chair and spread his hands on the table. "My family has had an account with your company since 1862, you know. I have always been a deeply loyal and, might I add, prolific customer."

"You have an account with us?" Charles Walsh asked suddenly.

Clara saw something in his eyes, a look almost of panic. As she had suspected, while Arthur and his sons were the figureheads of the company, it was the senior managers who made sure it ran smoothly and the last thing they needed was for one of the Nobles to upset a good customer.

"The O'Harris account," O'Harris said with pleasure. "I admit there was a bit of a dip last year due to my absence, but on the whole I believe you will agree I provide you with a lot of trade."

"The O'Harris account is one of our oldest and most profitable," Charles Walsh now turned to Arthur Noble and Clara noted he was no longer the abashed employee. He was telling Noble, in a subtle but firm fashion, to shut up and cooperate. "The O'Harris account brings in a lot of outside trade too."

"Yes, I am generous donator to a number of societies

in Brighton and I have always encouraged them to source their supplies through Noble and Sons," Captain O'Harris said lightly. "When I donate wines to these societies for their dinners, I always use your company. It would be a shame if, because of a silly row, that was to come to an end."

Arthur Noble had lost some of his puff. He blinked rapidly.

"What are you saying?" He asked, looking first to O'Harris then to Charles.

"I am merely saying that I don't care for your attitude towards my good friend, Clara Fitzgerald," O'Harris purred. "And that might influence my buying habits in the future."

Clara was amused. She knew the battles she could win alone and the ones where she would need help. As much as she liked to consider herself an independent woman, she was aware that some men would simply not talk to her without leverage. Arthur Noble was one of those men and no threat she could propose to him would change his attitude. However, O'Harris could kick him where it hurt, figuratively speaking, right in his bank account. If that made him keener to talk, Clara was not going to protest.

"Mr O'Harris is one of our best customers," Charles Walsh hissed at Arthur Noble.

He was angry and impatient with his boss. Arthur Noble no longer looked so confident.

"I would like to remain one of your best customers," O'Harris smiled pleasantly. "All it takes is a little cooperation."

Arthur Noble, now completely cowed, glanced to Charles then turned his face to Clara. He took a deep breath and, in his most polite and obsequious manner, stated;

"Miss Fitzgerald, might we begin again?"

Chapter Seven

"Henry Kemp joined the company five years ago," Arthur Noble told Clara when she asked him about Henry. "He came highly recommended from another importing company, one that specialised in exotic goods such as spices and tea from India and China. He had doubled their profits."

"And then he left?" Clara asked.

"Henry was a native of Hove. The firm he was working for was based in London and he wished to move back to the coast to be nearer his parents. As I said earlier, his father is infirm and he wished to be nearby to help his mother. It never interfered with his work," Arthur Noble seemed to consider this a rather irrelevant aspect of his employee's life. It did not relate to him or the business, therefore it was out of his scope of interest. "Henry was a very good senior manager. He helped the business to prosper, I had no reason to fault his abilities. He was responsible for hiring Charles, a decision that has also been beneficial to the company."

Arthur Noble was really laying it on thick now. Like a lot of puffed up bullies, the moment the tide turned against him he was left desperately treading water to save himself. He seemed to feel the need to appease Charles

Walsh, who had been the one to point out the significance of Captain O'Harris' account.

Clara was starting to see the man in a new light. It seemed he was somewhat at the mercy of his senior employees and felt the need to mollify them. Here was a man who knew he could not run his company himself. For that matter, considering the stony silence of Simon and Elias, she guessed they would not be running it any time soon. The result was that he was dependent on men like Henry and Charles and that gave his senior managers a power over him that was simply remarkable.

Clara squirrelled this information away in her memory for future reference.

"Did Henry Kemp seem happy in Hove?" Clara asked.

Arthur Noble seemed a little fazed by the question. His employees' happiness was not a great concern of his unless it damaged the business.

"I only really saw him twice a week for the company meeting. Monday morning and Thursday afternoon. He was always very proper and efficient at those."

"You had not noticed his drinking?" Clara pressed.

Charles Walsh seemed to flinch a little at the question, Arthur Noble, however, did not hesitate this time.

"I had no cause for concern in that department. Henry might have liked an odd tipple here and there, we are wine importers. We go to tastings and regularly must sample our own produce," Arthur Noble's tone had taken on a superior edge once again. He seemed to have lifted his head and be staring down his nose at the others round the table. "I noted at once, for instance, that the champagne served tonight was not from Noble and Sons, nor was it of a quality to compare with what we would supply."

Captain Pevsner was more amused than insulted by the remark and did not take it to heart.

"I imagine you like to reward your employees' hard work, Mr Noble," Clara was playing to the man now, as a means to get him to speak more freely. He was arrogant, but insecure, and liked having his arrogance fed. "Which is why you arrange evenings like this?"

"It is traditional. My father began the practice," Arthur nodded, he glanced at his silent sons. "When I leave, my boys will continue what I have started."

Simon and Elias made no comment on that.

"Did you spend the night together once you were onboard?" Clara asked him.

"It was a bachelor evening, aside from Miss Dodd, who is always very welcome," Arthur Noble cast a sideways look at the secretary. "Miss Dodd worked for my father before he retired. She is part of the family."

Clara was somewhat amused at how Arthur Noble kept repeating that phrase. She wondered what Miss Dodd felt about being an honorary part of this 'family'? Perhaps she and Charles Walsh could have thought up a lot better way to spend their New Year's Eve. Or, rather, they could think up other people they would much prefer to spend it with.

"So, you stayed together as a party during the evening?" Clara wanted to pin down that information.

"Well, there was not really much else we could do," Arthur Noble babbled, seeming confused by the question. "We ate, we listened to the music. Miss Dodd was gracious enough to partner me in a slow waltz."

Charles Walsh had been growing more and more restless as his boss talked. Clara had her eye on him. He seemed to want to say something, but was not quite prepared to speak up. His fingers fidgeted on the table, and he was chewing on his lower lip, as if trying to keep from speaking.

"Can you tell me what you all did when the evacuation was announced?" Clara asked Arthur Noble.

Noble suddenly grew animated, he pulled himself up and thrust out his chest.

"Quite the moment!" He declared, looking at Captain Pevsner with a smile. "I was in the Royal Naval Volunteer Reserve in the war. I used my father's yacht. We came across the odd mine in our time, I tell you. When I heard what was happening I offered my services to Captain Pevsner. I was a good shot in the war and my eyesight remains near perfect, according to my personal optician. Captain Pevsner, however, felt I was too important to risk my life in such a fashion and insisted I must preserve myself by heading for a lifeboat."

Clara couldn't help but glance at Pevsner, who was resisting the urge to smirk. His amusement was palpable. Pevsner would know how to play to his guest's inflated ego to get him out of his way.

"Instead, you took charge of ensuring your party was safely evacuated?" Clara suggested to Noble, pampering his sense of self-worth.

Arthur Noble had puffed himself up like a peacock and it was fascinating to watch.

"I did indeed. Nothing could be more important than the lives of my employees. Unfortunately, by going to offer my assistance to Captain Pevsner, I had had to separate from the others. I told Charles to get everyone in a lifeboat."

Clara's eyes turned to Charles, she didn't have to ask a question to get him talking, he was already desperate to speak.

"That's true," he said. "Mr Noble said he was going to go see Captain Pevsner and inform him he was formerly in the RNVR and could be of assistance. He instructed me to ensure that everyone else went aboard the lifeboats."

"Where was Henry Kemp at this time?"

"Henry had been standing at the edge of the sun deck," Charles explained. "He had drunk a little too much champagne, or maybe it wasn't the quality he was used to and it went to his head faster than he expected."

Charles was protective of his work colleague, even in death. Clara would have liked to get him on his own to discover what his true relationship with Henry was like.

"Henry wasn't in a great mood tonight. I thought something had upset him," Charles continued. "When the evacuation was ordered and Mr Noble told me to see everyone on the lifeboats, I went up to Henry and said we were leaving and he ought to come. He protested, said he hated small boats and wanted to stay on the liner. I managed to persuade him that it would be best if he joined us, but, when we reached the lifeboats he became even more agitated. Every time I suggested he climb in, he pressed one of us to go ahead."

Charles sighed, slowly it was dawning on him that those last few minutes with Henry had sealed his fate. How different would it have been if he had just boarded a lifeboat?

"Eventually we were all on the lifeboat and there was no one for Henry to tell to go ahead of him. A crewman tried to help him onto the boat, but I think he panicked. He went as white as a sheet and froze. Then he became angry and point-blank refused. He stormed off in a temper," Charles looked miserable. "Henry was a proud man. He would not be seen to be scared. He would get angry rather than have people think less of him."

"Was that the last you saw of him?" Clara asked.

"I started to get out of the lifeboat to follow him," Charles explained. "But a crewman told me I mustn't and that he would find Henry. I never saw him again. I assumed he had been put aboard another lifeboat."

"And when you returned to the liner, did you wonder where he might be?"

Charles shrugged.

"I did look for him, but I thought he might have gone off by himself. He might have felt embarrassed by what happened. Henry did sometimes go off to be on his own."

"All of you were on lifeboats while the mine was being dealt with?" Clara looked between them for confirmation. "You as well Mr Noble?"

"What a foolish question, of course!" Noble snorted. "I went on a lifeboat after Captain Pevsner insisted."

"What happened to Mr Kemp?" Jane Dodd suddenly spoke.

Her voice broke the tension of the room so abruptly that Arthur Noble seemed to startle. Jane Dodd had turned her attention to Clara. Previously she had concentrated on the table before her. She had a sharp and incisive gaze. Clara sensed that she had a strength to her that had enabled her to survive at Noble and Sons for the last two decades. She was certainly not a stupid woman, but she played things close to her chest.

"Mr Kemp was stabbed down in the kitchens," Clara explained, seeing no reason to honey-coat anything.

She was interested in the reactions of the party.

Miss Dodd did not flinch, her stare remained firm and serious. Arthur Noble looked slightly sickened, though whether that was because his employee had been murdered, or because of the manner in which it had happened, Clara could not say. Charles Walsh looked miserable and hung his head, perhaps feeling responsible. Simon and Elias did no more than blink. Clara was starting to wonder if they actually had brains in their head, they seemed almost like puppets, brought along to perform by their father. If they thought for themselves, they certainly didn't show it.

"He was murdered?" Arthur Noble whispered the word.

"Yes, and that is why I must discover what happened."

"It could not have been an accident?" Miss Dodd asked pointedly.

Clara shook her head.

"That seems extremely unlikely. Someone stabbed Henry Kemp, someone who did not leave the ship on a lifeboat," Clara glanced around the table. "Did you know of anyone who might have felt animosity towards Mr Kemp?"

"Enough to want to kill him?" Arthur Noble was astonished. "Henry was a tough negotiator when it came to wine contracts, but no one would kill him for that, surely?"

"What of his private life? Do any of you know about

his life outside of work?"

Charles Walsh looked up with sad eyes.

"Henry was a closed book. His private life was just that. Our association began at eight o'clock in the morning at the offices of Noble and Sons and ended at five o'clock. Apart from events such as this, arranged by Mr Noble, I never saw Henry outside of those hours."

"He did not talk about his family? Or what he was planning to do in his free time?" Clara asked in some surprise, even the most private of people usually gave some glimmer of what they did in their non-work-hours.

"He never mentioned anything to me," Charles confessed. "When we talked, it was always about work. I sometimes used to ask about what his plans might be for the weekend, but he always had a habit of deflecting questions rather than answering them. He was clever like that."

"He had a bicycle," Arthur Noble volunteered. The news that Henry had been stabbed had obviously shaken him and he was now trying to be helpful. "I believe he was a member of a cycling club. I only know because I was once driving my car through Hove's countryside and I spotted him. He had a flat tyre and I offered him a lift. He would only go as far as the bus stop, however."

"He wouldn't let you take him home?" Clara asked, wondering if that was significant.

"Henry said he did not want to inconvenience me and that the bus would get him near enough to his home for him to walk the rest of the way."

"What about his parents?" Clara enquired. "Do you know their names? They will have to be informed."

Arthur Noble cast looks at his employees, but no one said anything. A grimace came onto his face.

"I don't know their names, perhaps Miss Dodd has them in Henry's employee records, but that is back ashore."

"Henry never mentioned his parents to me," Charles added. "If I had not learned from Mr Noble that he had moved here to be near them, I would have assumed they were dead."

"And none of you can say if he had an enemy? Or if he was arguing with someone at the party tonight?"

Everyone at the table shook their heads. Clara had learned all she could. She thanked them all for taking time out of their evening to speak to her and then said they could return to the party. They were all deflated as they walked out of the cabin. Arthur Noble, in particular, had lost his bluster. As he made his way back on deck, he had to squeeze past a woman in the corridor. Or rather, she flattened herself against a wall and Noble walked past without acknowledging her.

The woman glanced at the open door to the cabin and quickly darted in.

"I am looking for…" her eyes darted around the room and alighted on Bert who was still working over Pevsner's puzzle. "Herbert!"

Bert glance up sharply.

"Mum!"

He flew from the chair and to his mother, who grabbed him up in her arms. Bert's mum began to weep softly.

"I have been looking for you everywhere!"

Clara looked to O'Harris and smiled. At least that was one problem resolved.

Chapter Eight

Bert Nightingale proved to actually be Herbert Nightly.

"But I always call him my little nightingale," his mother explained. "Bert Nightingale, I call him."

Hence the small boy's confusion. Mrs Doris Nightly had bought the tickets for the New Year's Eve party as a special treat and to change what was usually a sad day for her and Bert into something special.

"My husband was killed on New Year's Eve," she said forlornly. "I always think of him on New Year's and it was making the whole thing so sad for Bert. I wanted to change that. It is just me and him now, and we need to make the most of it."

With her profuse thanks for taking care of her son, Mrs Nightly departed with Bert. He grinned and waved at them over his shoulder, before they disappeared around a corner.

"At least that is sorted," O'Harris smiled.

"Just our Henry Kemp mystery to deal with," Clara nodded. "And a mystery it truly is. We have no idea who might have wanted to kill him."

"I ought to get back to my guests," Captain Pevsner excused himself. "Feel free to use this room as your headquarters for the evening."

Alone together in the cabin, Clara and O'Harris mused over the case.

"He must have encountered someone on the ship he knew," O'Harris said out loud. "We can exclude anyone from Noble and Sons as they were all together."

"There are over two hundred passengers on this liner," Clara said thoughtfully. "Not to mention the crew. That is a lot of potential suspects. Assuming, of course, this was something that had been brewing a while and was not due to a sudden argument."

Captain O'Harris shrugged.

"We can't exclude that, either."

He strode back and forth across the room for a few minutes, then he turned to Clara with a boyish grin on his face.

"I like being your assistant, Detective," he chuckled. "I can see why you do this, it is both frustrating and intriguing at the same time."

"There is that element to it," Clara agreed with her own soft smile. "Helping people find justice plays its part as well but, at the root of it all, is a deep desire to solve the puzzle. I won't deny that. This one, however, is proving a real teaser. There seems to be nothing to get your teeth into, no real lead to chase down."

"I thought Charles Walsh wanted to say more than he felt he could with his employer present," O'Harris suggested.

"Yes, I had that impression too," Clara pulled a face. "Jane Dodd, for that matter, seemed to have something on her mind. Getting them alone will be the tricky part."

Clara paused and then smirked.

"On the other hand, I rather doubt Simon and Elias Noble had minds, let alone anything on them!"

"I can see why the company needs good managers," O'Harris agreed with a roll of his eyes. "Arthur Noble is just a figurehead, oh, and the one who gets all the money from others' hard work!"

"Still, it would be interesting to get the sons alone and

see if they have any views on Henry Kemp. One day they will inherit the business and you would imagine their father is preparing them for the role by involving them in the day-to-day running."

"You mean his twice weekly meetings?"

"Yes, those," Clara gave a sarcastic snort. "What a way to live! I wonder how he spends the rest of his time?"

"Eating?" O'Harris postulated.

Clara was going to reply when there was a polite knock on the cabin door, which remained open. They both turned, Clara feeling a little embarrassed about her idle talk and wondering if it might be one of the Noble and Sons party behind them. It was not. It was a crewman.

"Captain Pevsner has instructed that anyone who saw Henry Kemp on the liner during the evacuation ought to speak to you," the crewman said. He was no more than a lad, probably sixteen or seventeen. He still had that slightly high pitch to his voice that signalled he was only just progressing out of childhood and into adulthood. "I saw him and thought I should tell you."

Clara welcomed the young man into the cabin. He wandered in a little uncertainly and it was plain that, on any other day, the captain's private cabin would be considered strictly off-limits. He looked around him with something akin to awe, before taking a chair at the table that Clara offered him.

"Let's begin with your name," Clara suggested.

"Ronald Long," the crewman answered promptly. "Though everyone calls me Ronnie."

"And what is your role on the ship?" Clara asked.

Ronnie shrugged his shoulders.

"I am technically the cabin boy, I suppose. I get all the odd jobs. I do a lot of mopping, but I am also learning the ropes ready for promotion. I want to make a life out on the sea, maybe have my own liner one day."

Clara liked his ambition. He was a bright boy and clearly keen. She hoped his future panned out as he wished.

"You saw Henry Kemp after the evacuation of the Mary Jane was announced?" Clara asked.

"I did. He was at the food tables on the sun deck, muttering to himself."

"Was this after he had refused to get into a lifeboat?"

Ronnie scratched at his head.

"Maybe. No one else was on the sun deck, except the band. Captain Pevsner instructed them to keep playing no matter what," Ronnie shrugged his shoulders, as if to say he had not understood the point of that.

"What were you doing during the evacuation?" Clara changed tack.

"Captain Pevsner wanted me to make sure everyone had left the ship. I went with the steward below to knock on all the cabin doors and check they were empty, then I came back on deck to see if anyone was still about."

"Which was when you saw Henry Kemp?"

Ronnie pulled a face.

"I did try to get him to leave the ship. I went up to him and asked him if he was aware of the evacuation order," Ronnie sighed. "He told me to clear off, and then he asked me for champagne. The waiters had all boarded lifeboats by that point, so there was no one around to offer him a drink. I explained again that the ship was being evacuated and he replied that that was no excuse for a man to risk becoming sober."

"He seemed upset?"

"Belligerent," Ronnie shrugged again. "Might have been the drink. He absolutely refused to accompany me to a lifeboat, said he wasn't going to set a foot in one of those things. I explained the situation once more, but he refused to budge. I had the impression he was more scared of the idea of getting in a lifeboat, than of being blown up by a mine."

"How long did you talk with him?" Clara asked, intrigued that Ronnie might have been the last person, barring Henry's killer, to see him alive.

"I don't know, a few minutes. I wanted to get him on a

lifeboat, but I couldn't convince him. I went to find someone to help me, which is when I realised all the lifeboats had been launched anyway."

"So, you couldn't evacuate Henry Kemp, even if he had agreed," O'Harris noted.

"I thought I better keep an eye on him, nonetheless," Ronnie continued. "If things went badly, we would need to get everyone left on the liner off, including Mr Kemp. I went back to the sun deck and he turned on me and demanded to know where the champagne was kept."

"What did you say?" Clara asked.

"He startled me. I just blurted out that it was all downstairs, in the kitchens and told him he would have to wait until the emergency was over. I was getting rather cross now," Ronnie looked abashed, it was the role of the crew to be eternally polite to the passengers, even when they were being unreasonable. Ronnie was ashamed that he had lost his temper, if only by a fraction. "I wanted him to stay where I could see him. The best place for him would be on the sun deck with the musicians. At least then I would know where he was, but there was no reasoning with him. When I asked him to stay put, he started shouting and telling me I could not order him about, he was a free agent, a guest on the ship and could go where he pleased. That was when he marched off, heading below-decks. I really didn't want him going down, that would be really bad if the mine exploded."

"You followed him," Clara guessed.

"I had to. I kept calling to him and asking that he come back on deck, but he wouldn't listen. He was muttering to himself all the time and wandering about seemingly randomly."

"How did you lose sight of him?" Captain O'Harris asked, knowing that Ronnie must have, at some point, stopped following Henry Kemp; otherwise he would have also witnessed his murder.

Ronnie flushed bright red.

"Please don't tell Captain Pevsner this," he begged,

sucking in and chewing on his lower lip. "I neglected my duty, I know, but I was tired with Mr Kemp and I didn't think I could persuade him to come back up top until he had a drink and…"

Ronnie came to a halt in his dialogue. He pursed his lips like he had just taken some foul medicine.

"And?" Clara pressed him gently.

"As I was passing one of the cupboards on the third deck, I noticed Jack."

"Jack? Another crewman?"

"The ship's cat," Ronnie admitted, hardly able to look up at Clara. "We had all been looking for him from the moment the order to evacuate was given. He has the run of the ship, you see. Well, someone had left the door to the cupboard ajar and Jack must have slipped in. He was nestled up in a pile of old towels. Only reason I spotted him was because I heard him meow. Jack knows when something is up, I think he was curious as to what was going on. He's a clever cat."

"Jack distracted you," Clara elaborated. "What did you do?"

"I wasn't going to lose track of the cat now I had found him," Ronnie explained. "I picked him up and I carried him all the way to the captain's bridge, where I put him in his basket and locked the door. If the worst happened, I would know where to find him at least."

Ronnie hung his head.

"I lost sight of Henry Kemp because of that. And I didn't bother to go back and look for him. I should have done, but I… I was so fed up with him…"

"Ronnie, I understand," Clara promised him. "You had your hands full and a belligerent guest who did not want to cooperate was the last thing you needed. Besides, what harm could he come to?"

"Exactly, that's what I thought to myself. What harm? By then they had managed to push the mine away from the ship anyway and were planning on sailing round so they could shoot it."

"Where precisely did you last see Henry Kemp?" Clara asked him.

"Ah, that's easy. I was on the fourth deck, the kitchens are at that level. I last saw Mr Kemp passing the chart room. I thought he might be doubling back to return to the top deck after all."

"Did you see anyone else while you were down there? Really think about this Ronnie."

Ronnie obeyed Clara and gave the question some thought, going over in his mind what he had seen while he was down below. He tapped his fingers on the table as he mentally progressed down into the bowels of the ship.

"I thought we were alone," he said at last.

Clara frowned.

"You thought? What does that mean?"

"At the time I thought we were alone," Ronnie clarified. "Now, however…"

He frowned deeply again.

"I might be making it up, I can't be certain."

"Tell me what is bothering you," Clara was leaning forward, keen to hear what Ronnie was about to say.

Ronnie took a deep breath and for a moment it looked as if he was going to change his mind and say he was mistaken, that the corridors were empty and that anything else had been added by his imagination later on.

"You know when you go into a room and someone comes in behind you, and even if they are as silent as a lamb, you sense they are there?"

"Yes," Clara nodded.

"It was rather like that. When I was retrieving Jack there was this moment when I could have sworn someone was just behind me. I remember thinking to myself that perhaps Mr Kemp had walked back towards me. But he hadn't," Ronnie contemplated the question further. "And there was something else, something I barely paid attention to at the time. I might be mistaken, but I think I saw a shadow, as if someone was passing down the bottom corridor at the prow-end of the ship. That couldn't have been Mr Kemp, he could not have made it there that fast. But if it was someone else, I can't tell you who they were. As far as I knew, everyone except myself and Mr Kemp were either on deck or in a lifeboat."

"You are certain all the crew were up on the top deck?" Clara asked him now, trying to jog his memory. People made sweeping statements, such as, 'everyone was on deck', when they did not actually know them to be true, it was just something they had assumed. Say the same thing often enough and it tended to become a reality in your mind, but just pause a moment to analyse that assumption and suddenly everything was turned on its head.

This was what Clara was hoping. Ronnie was frowning and trying to put together what he believed had been the case, against what he knew to be true. The two different concepts were failing to align.

"I thought everyone was on top deck," he said at last. "But I didn't actually see everyone on the top deck."

"Then a crewman might have been below, like you?"

"Yes," Ronnie said reluctantly.

"What about other passengers, are you certain Henry Kemp was the only one to remain behind?"

Ronnie was about to say he was, but the words died on his tongue. He looked miserably at Clara.

"I don't know. I don't think anyone knew who was left aboard and who was not," Ronnie's face fell. "If only I had kept my eye on Mr Kemp he would have been all right."

"This wasn't your fault," Clara reassured him.

Ronald Long did not look convinced.

Chapter Nine

After Ronald's confession that he had seen someone else below decks with Henry Kemp, Clara knew she needed to go back to the members of Noble and Sons and learn more about the dead man. So far, she had no motive for his murder and certainly no suspect. Henry Kemp might have been a drunk, but he did not seem to be the sort of person to purposefully upset people, at least from what little she had learned.

Before going up on deck to pursue her only leads in the matter, she stopped briefly by the cold store – a large refrigerated room which could be used to house huge amounts of meat and produce that benefited from being kept chilled. Once the store would have been filled to capacity to feed the many passengers on the liner. These days it looked largely empty, though an impressive stack of champagne bottles at the rear of the room did at least supply it with a function.

Captain O'Harris walked over to the crates and inspected their label.

"Never heard of the producer," he declared with some satisfaction.

"You are rather a wine snob," Clara teased him.

O'Harris put on a hurt look.

"I prefer to call myself a connoisseur."

Clara didn't argue with him, merely gave him a wry smile to indicate she was only being silly. Then she crouched down beside what might look, to innocent eyes, to be a pile of blankets tucked under the lower shelf of one of the many metal racks that lined the walls. It was, in fact, a stretcher containing the body of Henry Kemp and covered with thick woollen blankets to disguise its presence. Not that any of the kitchen staff coming into the cold store would have been fooled. Clara pulled out the stretcher and lowered the blanket from Henry Kemp's face.

He was already looking less 'alive'. The colour had vanished from his skin and he now had a grey hue, fine blue veins visible in some places, as if his flesh had become translucent. He had stiffened in the first stages of rigour mortis and his jaw had slackened and fallen open, revealing neat upper teeth, but rather twisted and stained lower ones. The doctor had closed Henry's eyes and he no longer stared out at the world with a slightly incredulous expression.

"What are you looking for?" O'Harris asked as Clara pulled the sheets back further.

She had not said anything when they had left the captain's cabin, except that she had to visit the cold store again.

"I want to rule out a possible motive," Clara explained as she rummaged through the pockets of Henry's dinner jacket.

She pulled out a few shillings, which she laid on the floor beside her. Then she examined his wrists and neck.

"Gold cufflinks, gold watch, silver tie pin, and this ring appears to be quite expensive too," she pointed out a ring on Henry's left hand little finger. It looked to also be gold with a large red stone.

"A ruby?" O'Harris postulated.

"I would guess so, considering the quality of the other items he is wearing," she tried his trouser pockets and produced a wad of pound notes. She counted them quickly. "Twenty quid."

"Tips for the serving staff!" O'Harris said, mildly astonished. Even he did not carry that sort of money to an evening party.

"I wanted to be sure this was not a simple crime of opportunity. That he had been robbed by someone who happened upon him and saw a drunk, rich man unable to fight back," Clara returned the money to Henry's pocket. "If he had just been wearing the cufflinks and watch, I might have still wondered, but the fact he has all this money in his pocket untouched convinces me he was not robbed for his valuables. Someone could have easily taken this money and no one would ever know."

"Hard to imagine someone on this ship mugging the man," O'Harris frowned.

"But not impossible. Someone might have slipped aboard with the intention of robbing the guests. It would be easy to do and I imagine many of the cabins have been left unlocked. I had to rule it out, because that also means ruling out that the killer was someone Henry did not know," Clara stood up and carefully adjusted her skirt which had rumpled when she crouched. "We are back to the idea that someone had a grudge against him and deliberately sought him out."

"And that brings us all the way around to the same question again – who?"

Clara pushed Henry's body back under the shelves. Covered with the blankets it was almost possible to forget there was a dead man resting there.

"I want to talk with Charles Walsh. It seems to me he knew a lot more about Henry than he was letting on. He couldn't say much in front of his employer."

"Arthur Noble is a certified oaf," a touch of anger entered O'Harris' voice. "The sort of man who has earned none of the luxuries he enjoys and yet thinks he is better than anyone else."

"I meet a lot of those," Clara said mildly. "They are not

worth getting cross about. Mostly they are fools who eventually get their comeuppance."

"Did he not offend you?" Captain O'Harris had been offended on Clara's behalf.

"If I spent my time getting offended by all the oafs I confront in this job, I would be perpetually offended," Clara told him lightly. "He annoyed me, that is certain. But I won't take it to heart, I have too much to do."

O'Harris followed Clara out of the cold store.

"I didn't realise this is the sort of thing you face regularly. Are a lot of men so disrespectful to you when they learn you are a detective?"

Clara smiled at him.

"Oh yes, which makes it all the more satisfying when I solve a case, especially if the man who was rude to me is the culprit," Clara's smile shaped into a wicked grin. "Come on, let's find Mr Walsh."

Charles Walsh was stood near the band, drinking a flute of champagne in slow, small sips and seemingly thinking of things other than celebrating New Year's. He was alone. Arthur Noble had asked someone to bring him a chair and was now stationed permanently by the buffet several feet away. His sons were loitering nearby. Miss Dodd had found a dance partner and was now executing a gentle waltz with surprising aplomb. No one appeared to notice Clara approach Charles.

"Mr Walsh? Might we talk a while in private," she asked as she arrived at the man's elbow.

He seemed startled by her appearance, he had clearly been deep in thought. He glanced at Clara, then at O'Harris.

"I could do with talking to you," he said after a moment. "I was debating seeking you out."

"Why is that?" Clara asked.

Charles Walsh took a deep breath and braced himself, as if he was about to face some unspeakable danger.

"I want to be honest with you about Henry Kemp. Maybe it will help to find his killer. I won't lie and say I much liked the man, but I wouldn't see him hurt," Charles hesitated. "I was always told you don't speak ill of the dead and Henry was my superior."

"Let's make one thing plain," Clara told him firmly. "In a case of murder, honesty is paramount, even when what you say might be unpalatable. Killers have escaped justice because people were not prepared to speak plainly about the deceased. Now is not the time to be polite. I would like to know all I can about Henry Kemp, as that might point me in the direction of his killer."

Charles Walsh took this all in with a nod of his head.

"All right then, let's talk."

They headed back to Captain Pevsner's cabin and Clara offered Charles a glass of water before they began. Charles accepted and placed his champagne flute to one side. He hunched forward in his chair, elbows on the table and both hands wrapped around the glass before him.

"Where should I start?" He asked.

"Tell me about your relationship with Henry Kemp," Clara suggested, it was an easy way to kick off the conversation. Hopefully it would put Charles more at ease. He looked unhappy, despite saying he wished to talk.

"Henry hired me to work for Noble and Sons," Charles explained. "Mr Noble I see maybe twice a week at the company board meetings. I barely know him. But I worked all week with Henry and I often saw him at weekend functions too. This job eats away at your life, you end up with very little free time. Not that I am complaining, I just want you to understand how much time I spent with Henry."

"I understand," Clara assured him. "You must have known Henry well?"

"Maybe," Charles frowned, the question worrying him. "I knew an aspect of Henry, I think that is the better way of stating things. I am sure there was a lot I didn't know about him, and probably there was a lot he didn't know about me. You share only a part of yourself at work, the part that is relevant to what you are doing."

"That is logical," Clara agreed. "Tell me what you knew about Henry through your work. Did you get on, for instance?"

The frown was still creasing Charles' forehead.

"I would say we did. He never complained about my work, at least. Henry was quiet, insular. If he gave you praise or criticism it was always in the same solemn tone, as if he begrudged giving anything at all," Charles ran one finger up and down the side of the glass of water. "I can't say I liked him, but I didn't mind him. He was not bad to work with. He set me tasks and let me get on with them. I appreciated that."

"Did he speak about his personal life?"

Charles shook his head.

"He was very private. You know how it is, you come into work on a Monday after the weekend and you talk about things, like the roast dinner you ate with the family, or your plans for Christmas. Well, Henry never did that," Charles was watching the water in his glass, he seemed unable to look away from it. "Sometimes you would forget yourself and ask him outright a question about his home arrangements. For example, the first year I was at Noble and Sons I received my invitation, which is really more of an order, to attend the New Year's celebrations and I was unhappy. I am seeing this young lady, well, actually we are engaged."

"Congratulations," Clara said warmly.

Charles blushed and ducked his head a little further, though the smile on his face seemed to indicate he was delighted with the praise.

"I wanted to spend New Year's with my fiancé, when I learned that I was expected to go to the Noble and Sons party and I could not bring her, I was upset. I moaned about it to Henry and I ended up asking him what his family did on New Year's. He just shrugged at me, 'pretty much the same as any other night,' he replied. He would not say anymore."

"You don't know if he had girlfriend then?" Clara

asked.

"No. I had a vague idea his parents were alive and he had moved back to Hove to be near them, but I think I learned that from Mr Noble rather than Henry himself. I really don't know anything about him outside of work. Sorry, that isn't very helpful," Charles looked up and caught Clara's eye. "But there is other stuff I do know. Henry's drinking, for instance, it was becoming a problem."

"So, tonight was not unusual?" Clara had suspected as much.

"I can't be sure when it began," Charles explained. "I didn't notice anything when I was first working with him, but as the months passed I detected little changes. He was always on time for work, but some mornings he looked so ill I wanted to suggest he go home. I thought he was catching a cold at first, but then the episodes became more frequent and I realised his symptoms indicated chronic, late-night drinking. I never saw him touch a drop at work, he was always the professional, but I think the second he was home he began to drink and did not stop."

Charles paused and his eyes drifted to his champagne flute, perhaps imagining his own potential fate if he continued to work at Noble and Sons. The strain of the job, the long hours and the demands of the Noble family might all conspire to produce a detrimental result in him too. He took a long sip of water.

"I noticed that a few weeks ago he had taken to having several drinks at lunchtime. We get forty-five minutes for lunch. Some days I take food in, but a couple of times a week I will go to the pub down the road and order something there. I learned about the place from Henry. He used to do the same, then he started spending more and more lunchtimes at the pub, until that was all he ever did. I used to go in for my lunch order and I would see him drinking. It might be whisky, or it might be gin, it was not normally beer. In any case, I realised he was consuming a lot of alcohol when he slipped out at lunch. I also think he had stopped caring if anyone saw him. He didn't seem to worry that I had noticed him."

"It didn't affect his work, though?" Clara asked.

"Not yet," Charles replied. "If he carried on the way he was going, it would have impacted eventually. I don't like to think about it, but if he hadn't of been killed, I think he would have started to drink at work and would have lost his place at Noble and Sons. Arthur Noble would not have stood for it."

"Did he seem unhappy?" Clara asked, knowing that most people drank excessively to escape the world.

"It was hard to tell when he was anything," Charles answered. "He hid himself away."

"And was there anyone at Noble and Sons who might have disliked him enough to wish him harm?"

Charles gave the question a lot of thought and it was apparent he was reluctant to answer. Finally, he coughed and said.

"Simon Noble. He and Henry had a falling out, but I don't know what over."

Charles fixed his eyes on Clara, for the first time losing his nervousness.

"Simon Noble might not look it, but he has a nasty streak. If anyone had a grudge against Henry, it was him," then Charles abruptly grimaced. "Yet, he was in the lifeboat with the rest of us, so it couldn't have been him, could it?"

Chapter Ten

Clara went back on deck with Charles and they found Miss Dodd. She had recently finished her second waltz and she was out of breath and looked a little flushed, but there was a smile on her face. The smile faded when she saw Clara.

"Miss Dodd, would you spare a moment to talk to Miss Fitzgerald about Mr Kemp?" Charles asked her politely.

Jane Dodd fanned herself with a hand, despite the cold night air she had become quite heated dancing.

"I suppose I could do with a little sit-down," she reflected. "I don't know how much help I will be, however, Miss Fitzgerald."

"We won't know until we talk," Clara replied politely.

Still fanning herself, Miss Dodd followed Clara down below. The music faded as they went down the gangway.

"I haven't danced in a while, I forgot how much it takes out of you," Miss Dodd remarked, excusing her breathlessness.

"It can be exhausting, especially in new shoes," Clara pointed out her own feet. "I can feel blisters forming. I should have broken them in a little better."

"Mine are not so new," Miss Dodd smiled shyly. "I

have had this dress pair at least five years. I only wear them perhaps three times a year, so no reason to buy new."

"Mr Kemp did not seem so sensible with his resources," Clara noted. "He was wearing some very expensive accessories tonight."

"Mr Kemp did not stint on his appearance," Miss Dodd agreed. "I doubt the man wore the same shirt in a month. Not that I am belittling his desire to look smart. He could afford it, after all."

"Senior managers earn a good income at Noble and Sons?"

"Very much so," Miss Dodd nodded. "It is a very prestigious role."

"Who will replace Mr Kemp? Charles Walsh?"

They had reached the threshold of the captain's cabin and Clara stepped back to allow Miss Dodd to enter first. She automatically said thank you and entered, smiling an acknowledgement at Captain O'Harris who still sat at the table. They were seated and the cabin door was shut before she answered.

"Mr Walsh would seem the logical candidate. He has worked under Mr Kemp since he joined the company and has a strong working knowledge of the business. I doubt Mr Noble would consider hiring someone else, someone who had not worked within the company."

"Will that mean a pay increase for Mr Walsh?" Clara asked.

Miss Dodd considered for a moment.

"I believe it would mean a sizeable increase. I am not privy to the details of company salaries, but I would have thought it would be a healthy amount," Miss Dodd dropped her voice almost to a whisper as she realised the implications of all this. "Not that I think Mr Walsh would kill for the job, not at all! He was certainly not poor and he got along with Mr Kemp."

"I wasn't implying anything," Clara promised. "I was just curious. Can you tell me a little about Mr Kemp? You must have known him for a number of years."

The colour slipped from Miss Dodd's face.

"I still can't think of him being dead," she spoke softly. "I remember Mr Noble hiring him. I was present when he signed his employment contract. He seemed a very bright, but reserved young man. I thought to myself…"

Miss Dodd hesitated, seemingly uncertain about what she had been about to say.

"Please Miss Dodd, honesty is vital now," Clara said gently.

Miss Dodd winced, and a slight flush returned to her cheeks.

"It's a little embarrassing, but I recall thinking when he was hired that such a handsome man as Mr Kemp could not be long without a wife. I was younger then. I still thought about my own prospects of matrimony," Miss Dodd sighed sadly. A thin smile, more a grimace than a pleasing look, distorted her lips. "I have gone past that now. Seemingly, so did Mr Kemp. He never spoke of a lady friend and, as far as I could tell, he never considered marriage. He seemed dedicated to his work."

"What about his drinking?" Clara asked.

Miss Dodd paused once more, she was clearly having issues, much like Charles, about talking ill of the dead. She sucked in her lower lip and seemed to be contemplating how much to say. Finally, she looked up directly at Clara.

"Mr Kemp, like all of us at Noble and Sons, knew his wine and liked it. It would be rather impractical to have a teetotaller as a senior manager. Drinking is part of the job, and most of the company employers are certainly not shy about it. However, the last couple of years I grew concerned that Mr Kemp was drinking more than was healthy. It was subtle things at first; looking unwell when he came to work, always asking for aspirin as if he had a perpetual headache and his skin always had this clammy look to it," Miss Dodd rumpled her forehead as she remembered what had caused her so much worry. "I thought at first he was a consumptive. I had a sister who went that way. Her symptoms were alarmingly similar. I desperately wanted to take him aside and offer him some assistance, there are places that offer treatments these days for tuberculosis, but I never quite found the right moment. And then I realised it was not consumption."

"What changed your mind?" Clara asked.

"Mr Kemp was working late, that was not unusual. What was, was that I had been asked to stay behind with him, to type up some urgent paperwork relating to one of our accounts. That meant I was in Mr Kemp's office and I noticed he was becoming more and more agitated the longer I sat there working," Miss Dodd shook her head. "I couldn't understand it at first. I felt as if my presence was resented. At last, Mr Kemp said something along the lines of 'I can't stand it anymore' and opened the bottom drawer of his desk and took out a bottle of whisky. I pretended not to notice, but I watched him pour out and drink four glasses of whisky before the next hour had passed. I was trying to work as fast as I could, you see, I felt so uncomfortable in that room.

"I managed to get finished and I placed the report on Mr Kemp's desk and said I would be off home. He glanced up at me and his eyes looked so miserable and watery, like an old man's. 'You won't tell anyone, will you Miss Dodd?' he asked me. I really couldn't say no to him, not when he looked at me that way. I promised I would say nothing, and then I bid him goodnight."

"When was this?" Clara enquired.

"About eight months ago," Miss Dodd said. "I had no idea what to do, so I kept his secret. In any case, it was not harming his work and therefore it was not anybody's business, was it?"

Miss Dodd said the last much more firmly, and with a challenge in her tone, as if defying Clara to tell her she had been in error.

"Do you think Mr Kemp was becoming a chronic alcoholic?" Clara asked without responding to Miss

Dodd's question.

"I imagine that is what a doctor would call him," Miss Dodd shrugged her shoulders. "These last couple of months he really declined. I could smell alcohol on him some days. His complexion became very blotchy and I found errors in his work, nothing serious, just spelling mistakes or poor grammar. He was always very fastidious about that."

"There was nothing to indicate why Mr Kemp had started drinking so much?" Clara raised a few possibilities. "Perhaps he was finding himself under a lot of pressure at work? Or there were stresses at home that were troubling him? Most alcoholics start heavily drinking due to an emotional stress they are trying to relieve."

"I don't know," Miss Dodd smiled wistfully. "He always seemed such a capable man, and rather good at his job. I never thought of him as particularly stressed or anxious. However, Mr Kemp was extremely private and he spoke very little about what he was thinking or feeling. I never really knew him well, if you see what I mean."

"Then you cannot tell me anything about his parents? Mr Noble said Kemp had moved down to Hove to be closer to them?"

"Ah, on that I can assist you!" Miss Dodd said with some relief. "I did know some of Mr Kemp's family arrangements as they were noted in his employment records, which I typed up. Also, he asked for occasional leave to help with his invalid father, and his request had to be written and I typed that up too."

"What can you tell me about his parents?"

"He is an only child, I know that. His mother and father live in Hove and they are his nearest blood relations. As far as I am aware there are no aunts or uncles, and no grandparents. His father was in an accident before the war and the poor man lost both legs."

Captain O'Harris winced. Miss Dodd glanced at him, her look understanding.

"Yes, it was a terrible thing," Miss Dodd continued. "Mr Kemp had a job at a prestigious importation firm in London. He had been there some years and he was spoken of highly. Unfortunately, his mother was struggling to cope with her now crippled husband and Mr Kemp felt he needed to move closer to home to be of assistance to them both. He applied for the opening at Noble and Sons in early 1909. Mr Kemp has been with us ever since, apart from the time he spent serving his country in the war. That was a tough time for the company. Mr Noble was not really able to run it all by himself. A retired senior manager had to be called in to help, just for the duration."

"Mr Kemp was fortunate, then?" Clara said. "Just at the time he needed to move back to Hove, so Noble and Sons needed someone to assist them."

"I suppose so," Miss Dodd agreed. "I only met his mother once. There was a company picnic arranged last year for the families of employees. Mr Kemp brought his mother. She was a very overbearing woman and she clung to him the whole day, demanding he fetch her this and that. I didn't really like her."

"Do you know of anyone who did not get on with Mr Kemp? Maybe someone in the company he had had cause to complain about?"

Miss Dodd thought hard, racking her mind for possibilities. Clara sensed that the woman genuinely wanted to help, that, despite Mr Kemp's reserve, she had been fond of the man. She pulled her lips in tightly, as if she was holding her breath to think. Then her mouth relaxed and she looked up at Clara.

"I'm sorry, but I don't know of anyone with a grievance against him," Miss Dodd was most upset to have been unable to offer more. "He never spoke of someone being angry with him or complained. Then again, Mr Kemp being so private, I doubt he would have said anything. Did you ask Mr Walsh? He might know more."

"I asked him, but he did not," Clara replied.

Miss Dodd seemed to have expected as much.

"I wish Mr Kemp had talked to us more. Something was obviously bothering him, that is why he drank so much. Perhaps I should have been more insistent in asking him? I don't know. He was so private that it felt wrong to push him, but perhaps if I had then he would have stopped?"

"Alcoholism is a complicated business," O'Harris interjected. He had not spoken before and Miss Dodd jerked her head to the side to look at him. "Talking to him might have explained the problem, but it is unlikely it would have changed anything. You are not to blame, Miss Dodd."

"That is kind of you to say," Miss Dodd replied. "But I worked with Mr Kemp every day, I saw him every morning. I watched him slipping away from us and I did nothing. I told myself I couldn't do anything, that he would not want to talk about it. In truth, I was closing my eyes to the matter. It was easier to pretend nothing was wrong and I have to live with the knowledge that I ignored a man in need."

Miss Dodd fell quiet, her body seemed to have become rigid.

"I didn't want to become involved. I know that to be the truth. Perhaps, if I had made the effort, I could now say to you who had killed him, who hated him so much as to take his life. Only, I didn't."

Clara knew better than to try and correct the woman again. She knew she would have felt the same and it would take time for Miss Dodd to realise she could not have changed the things that had happened, that fate had intervened and everything else was out of her control.

"Did you know Mr Kemp was afraid of small boats?" She asked instead.

"No," Miss Dodd hefted her shoulders. "It was not something that had come up. He was very belligerent about getting in a lifeboat. I have never seen him so irate and aggressive. That was not the man I knew. I am sorry,

Miss Fitzgerald, but I really have been of no use to you."

"You have been more use than you imagine," Clara reassured her.

Miss Dodd seemed unconvinced.

"One last question. Did you know any of the other guests aboard the Mary Jane tonight?"

Miss Dodd was surprised at the question, but she quickly replied.

"I recognised a few as customers of ours. Naturally, we don't often have people come to us in person. They send in their orders, but we have special events for our top customers. Tasting evenings and so forth."

"Would Mr Kemp have known these same people?"

"I suppose," Miss Dodd gave the question her usual careful attention. "Mr Kemp, as senior manager, attended those special events also. But if he was aware that some of the guests here tonight were also customers of ours, he made no indication of it."

"He showed no signs of being upset or concerned about someone else's presence on the ship?"

"No," Miss Dodd almost looked exasperated. "Besides, why would one of our customers want to harm him?

"This all seems so preposterous!"

Chapter Eleven

Miss Dodd returned to the sun deck. Clara now faced her toughest challenge, separating and persuading to talk Simon and Elias Noble. While there was no indication that either was an actual suspect – in fact, they had perfect alibis – she hoped they might be able to offer her insight into Henry Kemp's character and why anyone would wish him harm. So far no one appeared to have a motive to kill him. Clara was struggling to think of this as a spur-of-the-moment crime; the whim of a violent argument, for instance. She was certain someone had been prowling around looking for Henry Kemp, probably they had left a lifeboat after seeing that Henry had refused to leave the ship. If, that is, the person looking for him was a guest.

Yet, no one appeared to have a reason to harm him, very few people seemed to have known him well enough to harbour a grudge. Considering the ship was effectively a closed crime scene, and all the potential suspects were near-to-hand, Clara was struggling to get a grip on the case.

"How do you wish to approach Simon and Elias?" Captain O'Harris asked her.

The two brothers were leaning on the ship's rail,

halfway between the band and the buffet tables. Their father had fallen asleep in his chair, an empty plate in his hand.

"Divide and conquer," Clara said. "Elias first, I think, from what little I have learned, he seems the quieter of the two. Simon we will save to last."

"Just ask them politely for a chat?"

"How else can we do it?"

O'Harris nodded at this logic.

"I'll play my customer card again, if necessary," he winked.

They wandered over to the brothers. Simon was nearest, and he glanced up as they approached. Clara had thought him no more than a mute statue earlier on with his father present, now, away from him, he seemed to have developed a personality. Clara reflected that it was not a pleasant personality, at least from first appearances. Simon narrowed his eyes at her and his mouth turned into a thin, unhappy line. He radiated indignation and surliness, even if he did continue to lean on the rail of the ship. Clara wondered how she had caused such consternation, but perhaps Simon was merely displeased about having his evening interrupted. Not that it seemed he was enjoying it much anyway.

"I hoped I could have a word," Clara aimed to speak to them both, but Simon turned his body to face her, which effectively blocked Elias from view. The younger brother seemed to sink down to hide behind Simon's bulk. "If I could speak to you individually, it would be most helpful."

Clara had aimed for polite and non-offensive. It failed to work.

"Why? You spoke to our father," Simon snapped at once.

"Everyone has a different perspective on a person they know, and it is useful to hear it."

"Oh, for crying out loud!" Simon snorted. "I barely knew the man, nor did Elias."

Clara's first impressions – that Simon was the

dominate brother and Elias would agree with all he said – were now confirmed. Simon was their spokesman, and if she did not get Elias on his own she would never learn anything other than Simon's own opinion regurgitated through the lips of his brother.

"I would appreciate it if you did not query my methods," Clara became a little sterner, she wasn't going to be bullied. "After all, this is my business. I would not like to tell you how to import wine, for instance."

Simon was unimpressed.

"What nonsense! A woman detective? Not that I would have time for you if you were a man either. I don't intend to participate in this idiotic performance."

O'Harris was about to bark, angry on Clara's behalf, but Clara stepped in faster.

"That is a shame, as the alternative is the police, Mr Noble, and a long time sitting in a police station being interviewed and drawing up a statement. I thought your father wished to avoid such publicity for his company," Clara lowered her voice. "Rather bad for business, a senior manager being murdered. Noble and Sons' name will be in every paper, can't be helped if the police get involved. I had aimed to keep this discreet, so that it could all be resolved before we returned to port. But if it is your wish to make things public…"

Clara raised her hands, indicating she could do nothing to help him if that was his desire. Simon noticeably hesitated. No one likes bad publicity, especially sons who are due to inherit a prestigious and thriving business that enables them to live luxuriant and idle lives. Money talked, Clara knew that well enough when it came to men like Simon. She could almost see the cogs in his mind whirring as he processed what she had said. Hopefully he would realise that talking to her, and allowing Elias to talk to her alone, were the best ways of avoiding further scandal.

Eventually Simon gritted his teeth and conceded;

"Fine. You can talk to me."

"I would like to speak with Mr Elias Noble first, alone," Clara told him swiftly.

Simon was ready to argue, his mouth open as he went to form the word 'no'.

"It would be best," Clara interceded before he could speak. "I will not speak with you together. It would be improper, as you may accidentally influence each other."

Clara did not think Simon was smart enough to realise she was jibing at him and indicating he was making Elias sing to his own tune. She was right.

"This is so ridiculous," Simon grumbled, but his fire had gone. "Elias, go talk to her and get her out of our hair."

He pointed a thumb at Clara and O'Harris nearly wrenched it off his hand. He looked fit to explode, but he restrained himself, glancing at Clara for her opinion. She winked at him again. Simon was only left with derisive gestures against her, which she found amusing.

Elias emerged from his brother's shadow. He might be Elias' agent and subordinate in all things, but that did not mean he was a weak person. He had the same look of indignation and stubbornness about him as his brother.

"This way," Clara told him with a smile. She had won, for the moment, and could happily endure Simon's sour glare burning into her back as she led Elias down to the captain's cabin.

She did not offer Elias a glass of water as she had Charles. She asked him to sit and then took a seat opposite. O'Harris sat to one side.

"Let's start with something straightforward," Clara said. "You climbed into a lifeboat with the others, but Henry refused to get in?"

Elias shrugged his shoulders and said nothing.

Clara sat back in her chair and gave a deep, disappointed sigh.

"Really? You want to make this that hard?" She declared to Elias, her gaze now stern. "I thought we had already agreed on this? Talking to me is a lot more comfortable and private than talking to the police."

"Who do you think you are?" Elias demanded of her sourly.

"Clara Fitzgerald," Clara answered promptly. "Private detective and not someone to be trifled with. One of your employees has been murdered Mr Noble, that is a serious matter and yet you seem to think it is a minor mishap. You realise that you have wasted more of your time by arguing with me than if you had just talked to me in the first place?"

"Let me put it another way," Clara glanced at Captain O'Harris. "You won't be leaving this room until you speak to me."

Captain O'Harris understood her sly look, he rose from the table and walked over to the cabin door, which he locked, removing the key to his own pocket.

"You can't keep me prisoner here!" Elias shouted, a sudden panic coming over him.

"You can complain to the police," Clara replied. "In the process, you can explain how you refused to help in the investigation of Henry Kemp's death. However, as the only radio is on the bridge, you will first have to endure the next several hours locked in this room, until we return to port tomorrow. Your choice."

Elias looked at the locked door, a degree of alarm coming over his countenance. He was processing all his options and realising that, even if he remained surly, it was only going to result in his own inconvenience.

"All for the sake of just answering a few questions," Clara addressed this to O'Harris. "It's not even as if I suspect the man of murder."

"Some people make being obstinate a habit," O'Harris replied. "And yet, nearly always it makes life harder for them not better."

"I had just about finished talking to Mr Walsh, by now," Clara pointed out. "He was returning to the party."

"If people want to waste their own time…" O'Harris shrugged.

"True," Clara looked back at Elias who had a face like thunder. "But, presumably it makes you feel better to act so stubborn."

"You two think you are funny," Elias growled.

"No, Mr Noble, what is funny is you sitting there when you could be up on deck sipping champagne. I do believe that in the next few minutes," Clara checked her watch, "the cook will be serving the main course of his feast. Pheasant in port with crisp roast potatoes and buttered peas."

Clara had remembered the evening's programme from the card they had all been given when they boarded. The main course was to be presented at 8.30, following by a range of desserts at ten o'clock. For a man like Elias, who clearly enjoyed his food, missing the feast was paramount to torture. Clara was convinced she saw his lip tremble.

"Ask me these damn questions then!" He snapped.

Captain O'Harris returned to his seat and Clara began again.

"You were in the lifeboat when Henry Kemp refused to get in?"

"Yes," Elias said.

"Were you aware that Henry was drunk?"

Elias started to shrug, then thought better of it.

"We had all been drinking. I hadn't been keeping track of Henry. He did seem to have consumed a lot for so early in the evening."

"How well did you know Henry?"

"Hardly at all."

"You mainly saw him during business hours?"

"Yes," Elias meant this to be his sole answer, but when he saw Clara's expression he elaborated. "I've been spending a few hours each week at the office. Simon is going to take over from father, so really I am surplus to requirements, but I go along anyway. Father wants me to learn too. Henry used to take us around and show us how things worked."

"What did you think of him?"

"He was polite, efficient," Elias frowned. "He explained things well and was very patient. I always assumed he would be senior manager when Simon took over. He was younger than us. I thought he would outlast us."

Which had no doubt made Simon and Elias feel very comfortable, knowing that there was someone they could rely on without having to expend themselves.

"You had no reason to be concerned about him or his habits?" Clara asked.

Elias shook his head.

"Henry was always very proper. Simon liked him, and Simon rarely likes anyone."

That was quite a confession, but Clara did not pursue it. She sensed it was a slip from Elias and didn't want to pull him up on it in case he became more cautious. The slip, in itself, was not revealing, but another might be more relevant.

"Were you concerned when you returned to the ship and could not see Henry?"

"I think Miss Dodd noticed his absence," Elias replied. "She had been worried when he didn't get in the lifeboat. She had been trying to see into the other boats, in case he was in one of them. Miss Dodd had a soft spot for Henry."

"Really?" Clara remarked, recalling what Jane Dodd had said about her first meeting with Henry.

"Miss Dodd took a shine to him," Elias answered. "She has dedicated her life to the company, but that has meant she never married. I think she had hoped Henry would take a shine to her."

"But that never happened."

"No," Elias had mellowed as he talked. "Miss Dodd is a good person. I have always liked her. She deserved to get married and have a family, I always thought that."

Elias' voice had taken on a sentimental tone. Clara paused just a beat, before asking;

"You are fond of Miss Dodd?"

Elias almost startled at the question, which was answer enough for Clara.

"She is older than me," he stated, as if that precluded any possible feelings towards her.

Clara didn't push the matter. She secretly smiled to herself. Elias' slips were becoming more intriguing, though, as yet, they did not relate much to Henry Kemp.

"When you learned that Henry had been murdered, what did you think?"

"I was stunned, naturally," Elias said quickly.

It was the answer that he felt was expected of him.

"You were surprised then? You had not had concerns for Henry before?" Clara pursued a new line of questions that she felt might be more prudent for the future joint owner of Noble and Sons. "There had been no threats against Henry? Through the business perhaps?"

"Father had not mentioned it."

"No trouble that could have reflected badly on Henry?"

Elias frowned, the question had thrown him.

"No one had said anything. As senior manager Henry did bear the brunt from any difficult decisions."

"Had there been difficult decisions recently?"

Elias became uncertain, and this time it was not because he was being obtrusive, rather he genuinely didn't know.

"We changed one of our shipping contracts," he said at last. "It was the oldest one on our books, but we were concerned that the cargoes were not coming in as swiftly as they should and had been more breakages than we would have expected. Henry told me and Simon about it all."

"Henry was the one who cancelled the contract?" Clara asked.

"Yes," Elias nodded.

"It was rather awkward, actually. The skipper of the ship is here tonight. Henry was avoiding him."

Clara wanted to jump up in delight at this news – at last someone with a grudge against Henry!

"What is this skipper's name?" she asked.

"Patrick Wainwright," Elias muttered, he did not seem to realise the significance of what he had just told them. "Can I go now?"

Clara was only half-listening. Patrick Wainwright had a motive to be angry with Henry Kemp, could it be he was the killer?

"Miss Fitzgerald, can I go?"

"Oh," Clara glanced up, "yes, go enjoy dinner."

O'Harris unlocked the cabin door. After he had let Elias out, he looked to Clara.

"Patrick Wainwright?"

"Let's find him!" Clara joined him at the door, a new surge of enthusiasm coming over her.

At last they had a lead!

Chapter Twelve

Clara sought out Captain Pevsner first and asked him to point her in the direction of Patrick Wainwright. She had a hunch that, as a fellow captain, he would know the man. He did and looked surprised when Clara asked.

"Skipper Pat?" he said. "Why do you want to know about him?"

"He appears to have been one of the few people aboard the Mary Jane who knew Henry Kemp and might have a reason to be angry with him."

"Pat would never hurt someone," Captain Pevsner hesitated. "Not badly, anyway."

Clara thought that an interesting statement.

"Does he have a temper?"

"Most skippers do," Pevsner shrugged his shoulders. "It's a hard life out at sea. To be a captain you have to be tough, not just physically, but mentally. You are always battling the elements."

"Being tough does not necessarily mean you have a temper," Captain O'Harris countered. "It means you are resilient and, at sea, I would think being level-headed a necessity."

"Pat is all those things," Pevsner hastily agreed. "Just, he can lose his head when he drinks. Never seen him out of line when aboard his ship, but sometimes in port you can find him in a dockside brawl."

"He is a fighter, then?"

Captain Pevsner was clearly regretting his statement.

"He can throw a punch or two. Never seen him use a knife, however, that is not his style."

Clara said nothing, there was no knowing what a man might do when his temper was up.

"I think I best have a word," Clara said. "I won't get Simon Noble to talk to me while he is eating pheasant, anyway."

Captain Pevsner walked with them onto the sun deck and pointed out a dusky-skinned man wearing a smart, but clearly old, dress suit. Skipper Patrick Wainwright was in his late fifties or early sixties and had the weathered appearance of a man who has spent all his years out in the elements. His face seemed cut by lines of deep wrinkles, his forehead, in particular, bore distinctive worry lines even when he was not frowning. The corner of his eyes bore dozens of tiny creases that looked like the frantic work of a poor seamstress. His was a face you could imagine protruding from an oilskin, the wind whipping salt water over him as he fought to keep his ship on track. It was not a face you expected to associate with a dress suit, even an old one.

"Skipper Wainwright?" Clara asked politely as they drew near.

Captain Pevsner had departed, not wanting to be around. He seemed upset at the thought of a fellow seaman – a skipper, no less – murdering one of his guests. He didn't want to be associated with the interview, at the very least.

Patrick Wainwright looked at Clara with a curious twinkle in his eye. He had a plate in his hand, but it was empty. Unlike some of the guests (namely the Nobles), Wainwright did not feel the need to eat until he burst. He had enjoyed a modest plateful of pheasant and potatoes and was now satisfied. At least Clara would not be interrupting his meal.

"I am," Wainwright said at last. "Who are you?"

"Clara Fitzgerald," Clara introduced herself. "And this is Captain O'Harris."

Wainwright raised an eyebrow at O'Harris' title.

"RFC," O'Harris quickly interjected. "I flew in the war."

"Braver man than me!" Wainwright said with a laugh, some of his caution lifting. "I think the sea is bad enough."

"Would you have a moment to talk to us?" Clara said, hoping to catch him while he was distracted.

Wainwright was not so easily caught off-guard.

"What for?"

"It is a private matter," Clara lowered her voice. "I wanted to ask your opinion on a certain person who has, unfortunately, caused Captain Pevsner some trouble this evening."

Clara felt that was vague enough to not only alleviate any concerns Wainwright might have about whether he was in trouble, but also to play on his camaraderie towards a fellow ship's captain.

"It won't take long," Clara promised.

"Pat, what is this all about?" The question had been posed by a woman who was stood beside Wainwright and who Clara assumed was his wife. She was the same age as Wainwright and almost as tall. She looked worried.

"It is just a minor thing," Clara reassured her. "Someone has caused a spot of bother. I am a private detective, I have been asked by Captain Pevsner to resolve this matter discreetly and quickly. He doesn't want tonight disrupted for his guests. It has already been eventful enough."

Throwing in Captain Pevsner's name had been a deliberate attempt to stir up Wainwright's empathy, once again, for a fellow captain.

"All very cloak and dagger," Wainwright observed, without apparently knowing the irony of that statement. "I can spare you a moment or two."

Skipper Wainwright handed his empty plate and his champagne flute to his wife.

"I shan't be long, my dear, I wouldn't like to think of Pevsner in trouble, especially as this is the last sailing of the Mary Jane."

His wife gave him a look and then positively glowered at Clara, but she did not argue. Clara decided not to take Wainwright down into the bowels of the ship, instead she showed him up to the bridge. A much shorter walk, which would mean he could get back to the party sooner, all being well.

"You knew that this was Mary Jane's last voyage?" Clara asked as they walked.

"Skippers talk," Wainwright answered with a smile. "We know each other inside out. We are the only ones that understand how it is to give your life to a vessel and the sea. It's a tough existence and there is no certainty of how it will end. Old skippers congregate, like sea birds on a wall. We are a separate species, and we know it.

"Pevsner told me the Mary Jane was on her last legs a few weeks ago. She needs more repairs than she is worth. He is heartbroken, I know how it is. These ships get under your skin. They are your safety as well as your responsibility. Sometimes they are also your coffin. Your life becomes indelibly linked to them. Landlubbers can't always understand it. It's just a lump of steel and rivets to them. But to us, well, they are like a good woman. After all, we spend more time with them than our wives. It's why many ships have feminine names."

"It must be awful then, to think of losing them?" Clara said.

"Oh yes, it kills you a little inside. I know many a skipper who lost his vessel in the war who grieved for that ship or boat as much as if she was his sister or wife lost at sea," Wainwright shrugged his shoulders. "I was lucky, as was Pevsner, our vessels survived the war."

"Will Pevsner retire from the sea now?"

"Hard to see him doing anything else," Wainwright

glanced wistfully about him at the struts and ropes of the Mary Jane. "I don't suppose he can afford to buy another vessel. He'll sell Mary Jane for scrap and use the money and any he has been smart enough to save to live out his days ashore. It's not the way he would have wanted it, not yet at least."

They had reached the bridge. Stepping inside and closing the door deafened the noise of the party and it was almost as if they were alone. Clara offered Wainwright the sole seat in the room, but he waved it away. He stood at the rear window instead and looked down on the party-goers.

"What of you, Skipper Wainwright?" Clara began. "How will you cope with retirement?"

"I'm not retired yet," Wainwright laughed. "Not by a long shot."

"Oh," Clara feigned surprise. "I was under the impression that you were no longer operating? That you and Noble and Sons had parted ways. I assumed that meant you were retiring."

Clara had offered him a way out, if he wanted to take it. He had been amenable and she didn't want to get his back up by accusing him directly of murder.

"Who told you that?" Wainwright's humour had left him. He turned towards Clara.

"Elias Noble. You see, the person who has caused bother to Captain Pevsner is Henry Kemp, I believe you know him?"

"I do," Wainwright was becoming suspicious. "What has he done?"

Clara sighed and smiled.

"He has managed to get himself stabbed and, unfortunately, is dead."

Wainwright blinked and took a step back. His shock seemed genuine.

"When?"

"It appears it was while everyone was in the lifeboats. You boarded a lifeboat, I assume?"

Wainwright pulled a face.

"I did not. I offered my assistance to Pevsner, knowing what blighters these mines can be like. He appreciated my help and, I should add, I was on deck the whole time."

"In sight of others?"

"Not necessarily," Wainwright admitted without hesitation. "I participated in locating the rifles on the ship and also doing other tasks that involved me being out of sight. What is this all about?"

"I shall be honest with you, Skipper Wainwright, as you have been most forthcoming. It has been suggested to me that you had a grudge against Henry Kemp. I am trying to find someone with a motive to wish him harm. So far, only your name has been offered as a possibility," Clara explained plainly. "I have been told that Henry Kemp cancelled the Noble and Sons contract with you. I imagine that was a significant blow to your business."

"It was," Wainwright replied immediately. "And I will be honest with you too. I was angry about it. I had a few bad voyages, that was all. Rough seas made the passage difficult and delayed me, then I discovered the cargo had not been packaged as well as it should have been and bottles had smashed. I explained to Mr Kemp that that was not my fault. Whoever had packed the crates of wine had not made the effort to fill them sufficiently with wood shavings to prevent the bottles clattering about. He wouldn't hear of it."

"He withdrew the contract after one bad delivery?" Captain O'Harris said in astonishment.

"I had been late a handful of times, all due to the weather," Wainwright explained. "It was a very bad spring. It was the last voyage when the bottles were smashed. Mr Kemp said that was the last straw."

"You can't have been happy," Clara pointed out.

"After fifteen years serving Noble and Sons, excluding the four years of the war? No, I was not happy. I felt he didn't appreciate the difficulties of being at sea," Wainwright paused. "You think I lost my temper with him tonight and killed him?"

"I haven't decided," Clara confessed. "The problem I have is no one seems to have a motive for disliking Henry Kemp."

Skipper Wainwright made a rough noise in his throat, it sounded part way between a laugh and a snort of derision. Clara picked him up on it.

"You think there are more people with a reason to dislike Henry Kemp aboard this ship than I know about?"

"I think whoever is telling you no one had reason to dislike him is being very selective with the truth," Wainwright replied bluntly. "I'm a bluff man, Miss Fitzgerald, I tell things as they are. Henry Kemp was a good businessman, when he joined the Noble and Sons company he was both efficient and forward-thinking. But he changed. Maybe it was the war, I don't know, a lot of men were changed by that, but he was no longer the star manager that Noble and Sons had hired. I know he was losing the company trade, because of his own heavy drinking."

"You knew about that?"

"Hard not to. He would come to the dock to see a new cargo being unloaded and it was plain he was tight. I have been at sea all my life, I know what heavy drinkers look and act like, I know a few sailors and more than one captain who were prone to hitting the bottle. Henry Kemp was doing his best to mask it, but he was drunk nearly all the time. I suspected that was why he over-reacted to the damaged cargo."

"Did you say anything to anyone?" Clara asked.

Skipper Wainwright for a moment looked sheepish. Then he nodded his head reluctantly.

"I was angry about the whole thing," he said. "I probably should have let it go, but I lost my rag a little. I told Mr Noble. I happened to see him at a fundraising evening for the Brighton and Hove lifeboat. I pulled him to one side and mentioned the whole affair. I have known him for years."

"How did he react?"

Wainwright looked even more embarrassed.

"I didn't mince my words. I was so angry with Mr Kemp. I put it to him plain, that I thought Mr Kemp had been drinking and had not considered the consequences of his actions. I really wanted the decision overruled."

"What was Mr Noble's response?"

"He wouldn't hear of it," Wainwright shrugged again. "He said Kemp was the best thing that had happened to the company. He knew about the decision to cancel my contract and he had heard all the reasons why. He said he agreed with it too. I started to protest, but it was of no use. He said Mr Kemp had already arranged a new shipping contract and I was wasting my breath. That was it, really."

Skipper Wainwright had said all this rather mildly, as if it was a very minor thing, Clara guessed that at the time that had not been the case at all.

"You must have been furious," Clara said.

"I was, but, here's the thing, a month later a new contract came up with a company that imports olive oil. I got that contract and it filled the gap left by the Noble and Sons fiasco. So, you see, even if they had offered me my old contract with them back, I could not have taken it up," Wainwright smiled, knowing he had just delivered the ace up his sleeve. "I have no further grudge against Mr Kemp. I have moved on. I saw him here tonight, exchanged pleasantries and went on my way. He was drinking faster than a man dying of thirst who has just been offered water. I remember seeing him shouting about going in a lifeboat too. But I was far too busy dealing with that mine to be worried about what he was doing."

Wainwright looked very pleased with himself.

"Henry Kemp had no reason to fear me. You need to look elsewhere for the person who killed him."

Chapter Thirteen

"You don't think Captain Wainwright is the killer?" Captain O'Harris leaned on the chart table in the bridge. Captain Wainwright had returned to the party on the sun deck and they were alone again.

"He had the opportunity," Clara admitted. "But, if he is telling the truth about the new olive oil contract, he really does not have motive. He didn't strike me as a man to hold a petty grudge, especially when life has improved for him."

"No, that is true," O'Harris agreed. "Where does that leave us?"

Clara paced over to the window at the back of the bridge and stared down at the guests eating their pheasant and potatoes. The band was taking a break and the only noise was the jabber of dozens of voices.

"Someone was down below decks during the mine crisis. Ronnie glimpsed them and they have not come forward to reveal themselves. That makes me suspicious. Captain Pevsner, I am sure, would have made it plain to his crew that they should afford us all the help they could."

"Which means that person has a reason for not coming forward?"

Clara looked up at O'Harris, her expression answering his question. Whoever was below decks at the same time as Henry Kemp – the shadow in the corridor – it seemed likely they were the killer and were keeping quiet, not realising their presence had been noticed. But who? If all the guests were on the lifeboats, then that left only the crew and none of them had so far revealed a connection to Henry Kemp, let alone a motive.

Clara narrowed her eyes as she scanned the party-goers. She spotted the person she wished to see.

"It appears that Simon Noble has finished his supper," she said. "Let us invite him for a little chat in the captain's cabin."

Simon Noble was stood by the rail, once again, observing the other guests with a frown on his face. He seemed perpetually miserable. His brother was sitting with his father, though it did not look as though he delighted in the company, more that someone had to sit with the old man and he had drawn the short straw. Simon was alone, for the moment, an empty plate still held in one hand, a champagne flute in the other. Clara wondered what, if anything, made the man smile.

"Mr Noble."

"You again," Simon Noble grumbled. "Here, take my plate back to the buffet table will you?"

He thrust the plate at Clara. She ignored it completely.

"If you would accompany us down to the captain's cabin, please, for a chat about Henry Kemp?"

"No, I don't think so," Simon Noble said as if he was turning down a second helping of dinner, not that it looked like he ever turned down second helpings. "I have no interest in continuing this charade. Elias told me you asked him a lot of silly questions. I don't see the point in wasting my time."

"You don't see the point in helping to discover who killed the senior manager of your father's company?" Clara said, not entirely surprised that Simon was being so obnoxious.

"I think that is a matter for the police, not for a woman."

"Steady on, old son," O'Harris stepped out from behind Clara. He was a good head taller than Simon Noble and certainly fitter. He stood before the fat man and crossed his arms over his chest. "I have just about had enough of your attitude and the way you talk to my friend."

Simon Noble scowled at O'Harris, but he had some sense at least, he knew O'Harris was a good customer of the company and not someone to upset. He also could not guarantee O'Harris might not decide to do more than just take his business away. Bullies are cowards, and Simon Noble was most certainly the biggest of both. He gave a small cough.

"Attitude? You are mistaken. You are taking my words the wrong way," he said, dropping his eyes.

"Look me in the eyes and tell me I am taking your words the wrong way," O'Harris' voice had dropped an octave.

Clara decided to intercede.

"You see, you really are doing yourself down, Mr Noble. Half an hour down in the captain's cabin would not only go a long way to warming you up on this cold night, but it would get us to leave you alone. As it is, I am afraid I shall just have to pester you all night until you speak with me."

"You can't do that," Simon Noble snorted in indignation.

"Why not?" Clara asked. "Who is to stop me? I shall be as polite as an old dame, but I shall also be talking to you the whole evening, never letting you be. Until the police arrive, naturally, but that is many hours away."

"You will be spoiling your own evening!" Simon Noble countered, clearly thinking this was a winning move.

"Trust me, old man, she'll take detective work over dancing any day of the week," O'Harris said in a droll tone, he had a smirk on his face which Clara glimpsed. She almost blushed, but restrained herself.

"Do you feel the need to be so contrary just because you can be, or is there another reason?" Clara asked Simon politely.

"Contrary?" Noble barked. "I am being no such thing!"

"And yet you are. Most people would like to help me find the killer of someone they knew. Not nice to think of a murderer walking around with blood on his hands, figuratively speaking," Clara cast a pointed glance over the guests. "Why don't you want to help me?"

"Because I know nothing!" Simon snapped again. "I can't help you, and I just want to get on with my evening! I was on the lifeboat when everything happened. I don't know why Henry was killed, bloody shame that it is."

"Did you know about his drinking problem?" Clara had decided she was not going to get Simon downstairs, but she might get some answers on deck now he was talking.

"What? No," Simon Noble looked away and his answer was not entirely convincing. "I mean, we all like a tipple or two."

"Henry was drinking much more than two glasses of alcohol a day," Clara said. "I'm surprised that an astute man like you had not noticed."

One thing Clara knew, bullies were egotistical and easily flattered. Simon Noble shuffled his feet.

"Now you mention it, I was having concerns," he sniffed. "However, I only saw Henry at the board meetings."

"Had you any doubts about Henry's abilities? Perhaps, being a businessman yourself, you wondered if he was making the right decisions?"

Simon gave another sniff. The flattery was working. He was mellowing and starting to talk.

"I had cause to mention to father a couple of things," he said. "I saw you talking to Captain Wainwright. I queried Henry's decision to take the import contract away from him."

Clara did not for one moment think that was true, but

she said nothing, instead feeding Simon's ego with more fuel.

"I guessed you would have had your uncertainties about that move. I said to Captain O'Harris that I felt you were the one in the family with your head screwed on."

Simon Noble actually smiled a fraction, although it could have been a grimace.

"I do try," he said with feigned modesty.

"How did Henry Kemp seem tonight, at the party?" Clara asked him. "You seem to have been alert to his mood."

Simon Noble shrugged.

"He was not at his best," Simon told them. "I noted that at once. No one else was much paying attention, but he seemed tired and beaten to me. He started drinking as soon as we were aboard and, before long, he was considerably drunk."

"He didn't get on the lifeboat because he had been drinking?"

"I don't know why he was so cross about the lifeboat," Simon remarked. "I thought it was foolish. No one wants to die over a New Year's Party, do they?"

"No, not really," Clara agreed with him. "That was the last you saw of him?"

"I wasn't going after him," Simon's belligerence had returned. "I wasn't risking my life for him."

It was hard to imagine Simon Noble risking his life for anybody.

"Can you think of any reason someone would wish Henry harm?" Clara asked him.

Simon seemed to find the question amusing.

"Henry was such a loner I don't know anyone who knew him well enough to want to kill him. I don't think he had any friends."

"No one?" Clara said in some surprise.

"If he ever attended anything where he was allowed to bring a guest, he always brought his mother. There was no woman in his life, though," Simon raised an eyebrow.

"I rather fancy Miss Dodd would have liked to have changed that. Woman are not meant to be unmarried, are they?"

He addressed this to Captain O'Harris, a conspiratorial statement between two men, or at least that was what he was attempting. O'Harris did not respond.

"Is there anyone on board who Henry Kemp knew, aside from Skipper Wainwright?" Clara asked, directing his attention back on her.

Simon Noble made a show of examining all the guests dotted about the sun deck, then he shook his head, making his jowls wobble like he was some great saggy-jawed dog.

"I can't help you there. I don't know what a lot of our customers look like. Many go through agents, or only ever direct their orders through letters and never in person. I did not, for instance, know that you were a good customer of ours, Captain O'Harris," he broke into a smile, Clara was amazed as well as amused. "I rarely meet our customers face-to-face. Maybe there are some here tonight, though, I can assure you Captain Pevsner is not among them."

He looked gloomily at his champagne flute. Clara felt they were achieving nothing. Simon Noble was as much a dead end as the others and she was beginning to feel slightly despondent about the whole affair. No one had motive, no one had opportunity. It was as if the killer had been a ghost, a phantom that had slain Henry Kemp for no better reason than that he was there.

She was about to end the conversation when she felt a tug on her hand. She glanced down and saw Bert at her side.

"Apologies!" Bert's mother was hurrying over to catch up with her son. "He wants to show you how he completed that puzzle the captain gave him."

Bert held up the bottle in one hand and opened the other to reveal the nail now sitting in his palm.

"Oh, well done!" Clara declared, smiling at him.

Bert grinned.

"I wanted to show you before I gave it back to the captain," he said, then he turned around to show Captain O'Harris.

"Not bad, old man," O'Harris praised him. "First rate puzzle solving!"

Bert was beaming with delight now, enjoying the praise. He turned towards Simon Noble, holding out the bottle and nail for him to see. Simon Noble was pretending he did not exist.

"Oh, hello again," Bert said. "Is your friend feeling better?"

Simon Noble seemed to start, but when he spoke it was with his usual bluster.

"What is a child doing here? Someone take him away."

Clara was not listening to him. She crouched down by Bert.

"You've met Mr Noble before?" She asked him.

"Yes," Bert said, some of his jubilation ebbing.

"What? The child lies! Liars have their bottoms smacked, young man!" Simon Noble squawked.

Captain O'Harris loomed over him again.

"Shut up," he hissed in his ear.

Clara edged Bert away from Simon Noble. The young lad was looking anxious. His mother was getting upset.

"He can't talk to my son like that!" She said to Clara, then she turned on Simon Noble. "My son is not a liar!"

Clara had Bert face her and put aside the noise of Mrs Nightly and Simon Noble arguing.

"When did you meet Mr Noble before?" she asked him.

"When I was looking for my mum," Bert said quietly.

"After you returned to the ship?"

Bert nodded.

"Where did you see him?"

Bert frowned.

"It was a big room downstairs," he said. "There were lots of pots and pans about. I think it was a kitchen."

"And he was with someone?"

"Yes."

"This friend, he was unwell?"

"He was lying on the floor," Bert explained. "I asked that man if he had seen my mum."

He pointed to Simon Noble.

"What did he say?" Clara asked.

"He said no and that I should be on my way. I asked why the other man was lying on the floor, and he said he felt unwell and it was nothing to bother about."

"What happened then?"

"I went to keep looking for mum."

"There was no one else around?"

Bert shook his head.

"Bert, you have been most helpful, thank you," Clara squeezed his shoulder.

Then she rose and Mrs Nightly approached to remove her son from Simon Noble's presence.

"What a nasty man!" She remarked to Clara, before she took Bert away.

Clara turned back to Simon Noble. Her face had become very serious.

"You don't believe that little imp, surely?" Simon Noble cried out. "The child is clearly mistaken or lying!"

"All this time I was working under the impression that Henry Kemp was killed while the lifeboats were away," Clara spoke perfectly calmly. "I thought there would not have been time afterwards. Now I see I was wrong."

"Why would I kill Henry?" Simon Noble laughed at her. "He was nothing to me, just our senior manager!"

Clara did not have an answer for that and, in truth, the case against Simon Noble was weak if all it hinged upon was one small boy seeing him standing over the dead man.

"Where is the evidence for it?" Simon Noble demanded. "If I had stabbed Henry, then why is there no blood on my shirt cuffs?"

He revealed his perfectly white cuffs from the sleeves of his jacket. Clara was beginning to feel her own doubts.

The timings did not add up, there would have been such a slim window of opportunity. There was no motive and no real evidence. Yet she had seen Simon Noble's face when Bert had recognised him. She was sure that, just for a moment, he had been scared.

"I've had enough of all this," Simon Noble barged past her, heading for the buffet table with his empty plate.

Clara let him go.

"Do you think he did it?" O'Harris asked her.

"I think he was there," Clara replied. "I don't think Bert was mistaken on that. Whether that means he found Henry Kemp's body or actually was the one to murder him is harder to say."

"But there is no proof," O'Harris sighed.

Clara pursed her lips.

"There was someone else down below. Ronnie saw them. Maybe there is another witness to this crime and they have not come forward for some reason."

"And the motive?"

Clara grimaced. That was the sticky question – what was Simon Noble's motive to kill Henry Kemp?

Chapter Fourteen

Clara found Captain Pevsner and asked that they might have a word in private. They retired to the bridge and Clara revealed what she had learned. Pevsner became grim-faced as she explained.

"The lifeboats returned to the Mary Jane one at a time," Clara said. "I have to assume that the lifeboat containing Simon Noble arrived back before your kitchen crew. Mr Noble came aboard and went in search of Henry Kemp, we don't know quite why he did that, but he did. By luck, he went down below and came across Henry in the kitchen. Now, what I can't say for sure is whether Henry had already been stabbed or whether something then occurred that caused Simon Noble to stab him.

"However, it seems somewhat odd that if Simon Noble merely found the body, he did not then raise the alarm himself. There is still a shadow of suspicion hanging over him."

"This is not what I had hoped for," Captain Pevsner said solemnly. "I will admit that I had hoped it was some accident involving a crew man, not a guest."

"I had thought that a logical assumption too," Clara agreed. "Until it came to my attention that there was a narrow, but highly possible, window of opportunity for someone to have committed the crime after the lifeboats had returned."

"But you cannot prove anything?"

"My only witness is Bert, a sweet child, but not someone any court would take seriously. In any case, he did not see the murder committed. And Simon Noble was correct when he said that had he stabbed Henry Kemp there would have been blood on his sleeves," Clara pulled at the sleeve of her dress to highlight her words. "The only possibility I can see to explain such a thing is that Simon Noble changed his shirt after the crime. It is not unknown for people to bring spare clothes to an event like this, especially when they expect to spend the night. Captain Pevsner, I would like to take a look in Simon Noble's cabin."

Pevsner looked as though she had just suggested he scuttle his ship. He ran a hand over his face.

"I cannot authorise you to invade a guest's privacy, I am sorry."

"I understand," Clara nodded. Her powers were not as great as those of the police, after all. "I am not sure what else I can do. We believed there may have been another witness to the crime, but we have not been able to identify them. The evidence I have is also far too flimsy to present to the police. I can tell them my views, but they won't arrest a man on them, I can guarantee that."

Captain Pevsner's shoulders sagged. The situation looked unresolvable.

"Thank you for all your assistance, Miss Fitzgerald, I cannot fault your diligence. I shall allow the party to proceed and then, when we dock tomorrow, I must bite the bullet and summon the police. I cannot avoid the scandal any longer," the unfortunate ship's captain looked truly defeated. "Please, carry on with your evening. I have inconvenienced you too long already."

"It was no inconvenience," Clara reassured him. "I am sorry I could not have been of more use."

"On the contrary, you have given me something to

report to the police," Pevsner smiled weakly. "Please, go and enjoy yourselves."

Clara and Captain O'Harris strolled back onto the sun deck. Dessert had at last been served and there was an array of sweet things on the buffet tables. Clara's stomach gave a rumble. They had missed out on the main course; she was determined not to miss out on dessert. She approached the buffet table, behind which stood several servers dressed in crisp white jackets. There were so many delightful things to eat, and she was so ravenous, that picking just one was difficult. She opted in the end for a large bowl of raspberry trifle, not that there was much in the way of natural raspberries in it, as they were out of season. But these days manufacturers could produce all manner of artificial flavours.

Captain O'Harris chose a serving of Spotted Dick and custard, and warmed his hands on the bowl as they walked to a couple of free chairs and sat to eat.

"This is reminding me of an incident that happened during the war," Captain O'Harris carefully cut a portion of his pudding with his spoon and dipped it in the thick custard. "This fellow was murdered, a sergeant. He was killed in a dug-out when other men were in there sleeping and not a single one could say who had done it. It might have been one of them, but they all declared they had been asleep and no one could suggest a motive. It was very mysterious."

"I don't like leaving a case unsolved," Clara said, her enthusiasm for her trifle waning as she considered the possibility of failure. "I am almost certain Simon Noble is the culprit, I can't think why he would otherwise not have reported Henry's death."

"He might be covering for someone."

"You mean he stumbled on the killer, recognised them and then let them escape all before Bert spotted him? The timing would not only be very tight, but what would be the odds of him knowing the killer and being so inclined to protect them?"

"Maybe he did not go after Henry Kemp alone?" O'Harris postulated.

"Which brings us back to the first question, why? What motive did Simon Noble or anyone he was with tonight have for killing Henry Kemp?"

That was becoming the impossible question. Without a motive, it was going to be hard to convince the police to arrest Simon Noble on suspicion of murder. Even Clara's friend, Inspector Park-Coombs, would need more than her guesses and assumptions. Simon Noble was a powerful man, that could not be ignored. His father could command expensive solicitors. Park-Coombs would not touch the man without strong evidence that he was the killer, he would be risking his job otherwise.

"Miss Fitzgerald?"

Clara glanced up and saw that Miss Dodd was hovering near her. She had emerged from the group of guests silently, creeping up on Clara without her noticing. Clara wondered how much she had overheard.

"Are you any closer to knowing who killed Mr Kemp?" Jane Dodd asked with such desperate hope in her voice that Clara felt quite dreadful.

Clara wanted to offer her something.

"I have a theory, but I cannot prove it," she said.

Miss Dodd looked disappointed.

"Is there anything I can do, anything at all?" She asked pathetically.

Clara could see that what the others had implied about Miss Dodd – that she had a soft spot for Henry Kemp – was not just male gossip.

"Please, sit down," Clara motioned to an empty chair beside her. "Maybe you can help me. Tell me again, in as much detail as you can, what happened when you returned to the liner from the lifeboat?"

Miss Dodd was frowning as she sat down.

"We were helped back aboard the ship," she began.

"Out of your party, who climbed back aboard first?"

The frown deepened. Miss Dodd pulled back the

curtains of her memory and tried to think.

"I was sitting with Mr Walsh," she said, painting herself a picture of the moment. "The two Mr Nobles were ahead of us. But I can't say which of them climbed aboard first."

Clara restrained the sigh that almost escaped her lips at this news. She took up another spoonful of trifle.

"I remember Mr Walsh was very insistent on finding Mr Kemp, he was most concerned that he did not appear to be on the other lifeboats," Miss Dodd continued.

"Were you concerned?" Clara asked her.

Miss Dodd blushed.

"Yes. I was most concerned," she clasped her hands together, the fingers deeply intertwined. "Mr Walsh said we should all look for Mr Kemp, I agreed with him. Mr Simon Noble actually agreed with us. Said he would like to have a few words with Mr Kemp about his behaviour."

"He was angry with Henry Kemp?" Clara asked. This was new information.

"Not so much angry, as annoyed," Miss Dodd replied. "He felt that Mr Kemp had behaved inappropriately and that would reflect badly on Noble and Sons. Now I think about it, he must have climbed up first. Yes, because he said he was going to find Mr Kemp and when his brother protested a little, he told him to hold his tongue."

Clara was getting a better idea of those few moments before Henry Kemp met his fate. There would have been just a few minutes leeway, during the time it took for the kitchen crew to be returned to the ship. Simon Noble could have found Henry Kemp and killed him.

"Did Simon Noble have any reason to dislike Henry Kemp?" Clara asked Miss Dodd.

The woman looked immediately surprised.

"Well, no. They hardly saw each other, certainly not outside the board meetings. I always took notes in the meetings and there was never anything uncivil. Mr Noble might have been cross that Mr Kemp had been rude to the crew when they wanted him to get into a lifeboat, but to think he disliked him is too strong a term."

Miss Dodd stared across the deck to where Simon Noble was stood once more with his brother Elias. They both had bowls piled high with pudding.

"Miss Fitzgerald, I feel you are getting at something?" Miss Dodd turned sharp eyes on Clara. "Why are you interested in who climbed out of our lifeboat first?"

The woman was clever, Clara had never doubted that. She had made a career for herself in a male dominated world, and she was good at it. She was wily enough to see through Clara's indelicate attempts to get further information about Simon Noble's activities.

"You think Mr Simon Noble was responsible?" Miss Dodd filled the silence that had followed her last question.

"I only can say that I know Simon Noble was seen near Henry Kemp's body before the alarm was raised."

"And he did not raise the alarm himself," Miss Dodd could guess the rest. "He acted as if he had no knowledge of where Mr Kemp was. He lied to us. You are absolutely certain he knew Mr Kemp was dead before you approached us?"

"Yes. I am certain," Clara told her. "There is a witness. That does not mean Simon Noble is a killer."

"But it begs the question why did he not call for help or alert the captain," Miss Dodd's hands were knotting together tighter and tighter, her face growing hard and stern. "Why did he lie to us all and pretend he had not found Mr Kemp? That does not seem like the actions of an innocent man."

"I can't answer those questions, just as I can't explain how Simon Noble's shirt sleeves are unmarked by blood or why he would want to seriously harm Henry Kemp."

Miss Dodd's soft gaze had turned savage as she stared across the deck at the man who would one day be her employer.

"He could have changed his shirt."

"Yes," Clara agreed. "But I can't prove he did."

"You would need to find the shirt he wore," Miss Dodd

was rushing on.

"Supposing he has kept it and not thrown it into the sea."

Miss Dodd was silent a moment, then she opened her handbag and fumbled around inside it. After a moment, she withdrew a cabin key.

"I was given charge of the spare keys to all the rooms," Miss Dodd said. "Mr Noble insisted. He values his privacy and he does not like the idea of a key to his room being left in charge of a steward. He doesn't trust anyone, you see, except for me. I have the spare key for all the Noble rooms."

She pressed the cabin key into Clara's hand.

"This is the key to Simon Noble's cabin. Search it, for the sake of Mr Kemp," Miss Dodd almost choked on her emotions. There was no doubting now that she had strong feelings for Henry Kemp. Suggesting she had loved him might be going too far, but she was certainly extremely fond of him.

"This could get you into a great deal of trouble," Clara pointed out to her.

"Is there any worse trouble that can befall you than being dead?" Miss Dodd asked her, the determination in her face etched into every line. "I am not a fool, Miss Fitzgerald, the moment I learned that Mr Kemp had been stabbed I came to the conclusion that it must have been one of our party. I could not say who, but it was far too obvious. There was no one else on this ship who had such a grudge against Mr Kemp to want him dead. Mr Noble mentioned the possibility of Mr Kemp getting into a fight, he seemed to think that a plausible explanation for his death, but I never believed that.

"Mr Kemp was never a violent man, even when he was drunk. I knew he was drinking heavily, I edited the truth to make it seem less than it was when I explained that to you, but the truth is I think these last few weeks he has been nearly constantly intoxicated. But he did not start fights. He could be moody, and would say sharp things, but he was not a man to become violent. That was not in his nature."

Clara felt there was nothing that was not in the nature of a man who drunk to excess and lost his inhibitions as a result, but she did not say that. The fact of the matter was, there was no real evidence that Henry Kemp had been in a fight or even a struggle, something that could have become violent enough to cause someone to grab up a knife to defend themselves. The more she thought about it, the more Clara was convinced someone had come upon him and deliberately stabbed him.

"You will search Mr Noble's room?" Miss Dodd pressed her.

Clara folded her fingers about the cabin key.

"I shall. Thank you for your assistance."

"It is the least I can do for Mr Kemp," Miss Dodd's face twisted in sorrow. "He was a good man who did not deserve to die, and if one of them…"

She caught herself, but her eyes reached across the deck and glared daggers at Simon Noble and his brother Elias.

"Poor Henry," she whispered to herself. "Poor, poor Henry."

Chapter Fifteen

Clara and Captain O'Harris slipped away from the sun deck as discreetly as they could. Clara weighed the cabin key Miss Dodd had given her in her hand. She was about to trespass onto someone else's personal space, she had to wonder if she was doing the right thing. Clara could be quite lenient with herself when it came to solving a case, she would allow herself a fair amount of latitude in the course of catching a killer. She didn't often, however, sneak into a suspect's room, especially when that suspect was still wandering around as a free man.

She toyed over what she was doing as she walked down below. Without searching the cabin she might never prove that Simon Noble had harmed Henry Kemp. She still might not even with searching the cabin. Simon Noble might have been clever enough to throw his bloodied shirt overboard. Then again, if he thought it was safe in his cabin, why dispose of an expensive item unnecessarily? Clara was torn, but the closer she came to Simon Noble's cabin door, the more she knew that, even with her doubts, she was going to enter his cabin and search it.

Captain O'Harris had been walking by her side, he paused as they reached the correct cabin.

"Want me to keep a lookout?" he offered.

"You read my mind," Clara smiled at him. "Sorry that this is not quite the evening you were expecting."

"Don't worry about me," O'Harris grinned back. "I'm enjoying myself. The subterfuge, the sneaking about."

He chuckled.

"It's rather like an adventure novel!"

Clara was relieved he was not cross at their evening being interrupted. She tried the key in the cabin door and heard the lock click. She took a breath and paused.

"What's the matter?" O'Harris asked.

"What if I am wrong?" Clara said. "What if I have trespassed into a man's cabin who is not guilty of murder?"

"Do you think you are wrong?" O'Harris asked.

Clara paused, giving the question due thought.

"No."

"Then there is nothing to worry over."

Clara tilted her head as she looked at Captain O'Harris' broad grin. She found herself returning the smile.

"Right then!"

She opened the cabin door and stepped inside. The cabins were all fairly uniform, they were of another age and what had been considered luxurious in the 1880s now seemed rather cramped and inconvenient to a modern mind. The beds were fitted against the wall on Clara's right. There were two bunk beds, one above the other. The top bed was still neatly made, the bed sheets tucked firmly down the sides of the mattress, the lower bed was rumpled, as if someone had sat on it recently. Straight ahead of Clara was a large porthole, firmly bolted in place and with a pair of plain curtains to pull across it. To the left of the porthole was a built-in wardrobe, the doors shut. Just beneath the porthole stood an overnight bag.

The room had barely been lived in and there was a dearth of personal belongings. A starched collar, the sort of removeable one men sometimes wore with their dress shirts had been discarded on the bed, along with a box that proved to contain a spare pair of cufflinks. Clara examined the cufflinks carefully, in case they had been splattered by blood, but they looked clean. She crouched by the overnight bag next and flicked it open. It proved to be empty, except for a novel about spies in the war and a tooth cleaning set. Clara was not entirely surprised. The natural thing to do would be to hang the clothes in the wardrobe, to prevent them getting unnecessarily creased.

She opened the doors of the cupboard and found a fresh set of trousers, casual jacket and bowler hat. The trousers and jacket were on a hangar, the bowler on a top shelf. At the base of the wardrobe was a pair of brown leather shoes. These were the clothes Simon Noble would dress in tomorrow when he left the ship. Casual attire, but still smart. However, she instantly noticed one thing that was missing. There was no change of shirt. Clara shut the wardrobe and looked around the room once more. There was no sign of the spare shirt anywhere, but there was one place further to look.

There was a door next to the wardrobe, it led into an adjoining bathroom. The bathroom itself, as Clara knew from her own cabin, was not large and contained a small sink and a toilet. A cupboard mounted on the wall could be used for storing toiletries. Clara entered the small space and the first thing that caught her eye was that the sink was full of water. Draped over the edge of the basin was what first appeared to be a white cloth. Clara pulled its edge and realised it was a shirt. Her heart started to pound. In the sink the water had a pink hue and was scummy with soap. She pulled the plug and drained the water.

A sodden shirt, the sleeves deep in the sink, emerged. Simon Noble had tried to scrub clean the shirt. He had used a nail brush and a thick bar of soap that each cabin was supplied with. His attempts had proved in vain; the cuffs of the shirt remained stained with rusty red marks. He had left the shirt to soak, in the hopes of salvaging it.

Simon Noble had never washed his own shirt in his life, Clara was certain of that. If he had, he might have known that trying to get blood stains out of white fabric was one of the toughest things possible. Blood is remarkably resilient. Any washerwoman would have told him that. It needed vigorous scrubbing and a caustic agent if any attempt was to be made; certainly ordinary soap would not be sufficient. Even with the right materials very often a mark remained, a slight discoloration which revealed where the stain had once been.

Simon Noble would have been far better off tossing the shirt overboard, but that too would have held risks. On its own, the shirt would not have sunk, but would have drifted and perhaps been spotted by an observant crewman and rescued. It certainly would have aroused attention as being out-of-place. It might even have raised fears that someone had fallen overboard. If he had sufficiently weighted it and tossed it into the sea, then probably it would have sunk and all trace of his crime would have been lost. But Simon was not that clever, and he had clearly thought he could wash the shirt and continue to use it.

Clara noted that the tailor's label in the neck of the shirt indicated it was indeed a very expensive piece of clothing, the sort of thing even wealthy men think twice about disposing of. She was delighted to also note that the initials S. N. had been stitched into the bottom edge, just above the hem. Clara guessed that Simon was precious about his shirts and did not want them accidentally being returned to his brother or father. The initials would be for whoever did the Nobles' washing, ensuring they all received the correct belongings. For Clara, it pinned Simon Noble into a corner, providing her with damning proof that he had stood over Henry Kemp and come close enough to stain his cuffs.

And there was a lot of blood on the cuffs. Even with Simon's attempts to wash out the stains the marks were plain. One cuff, the left, was more bloodied than the other, and Clara recalled that Henry Kemp had been stabbed in the left-hand side. She whistled through her teeth. Clara had her killer.

"Any luck?" O'Harris called from outside.

Clara emerged from the cabin and showed him the shirt. It dripped water onto the floor as she walked into the corridor.

"Is that it?" O'Harris said, somewhat incredulous. He lifted up the left sleeve and looked at the dull, rusty stains on the cuff. "He can't deny that he was with Henry Kemp's body now."

"He can still protest that he did not kill him," Clara hesitated. She was beginning to feel her doubts creeping in. "He could say he came across the body and stained his cuffs while checking to see if Mr Kemp was alive."

"Then why lie about it and hide the shirt?"

Clara shrugged. She did not think Simon Noble innocently stumbled across the dead Henry Kemp, but she knew enough about courts of law to realise the evidence she held was circumstantial only. A clever solicitor – and the Nobles could hire the best and cleverest – could argue that there was too much doubt to convict Simon Noble of murder. They could employ all manner of excuses; Simon had been in shock, he had been scared of being accused, he had been frightened of the killer, etc, etc, to explain why he had not raised the alarm and had hidden the shirt.

In fact, a good solicitor could even argue that the shirt was not hidden. That he had merely, and quite naturally, changed it as it was soiled. He could hardly return to the party with blood on his cuffs. He had not made real efforts to hide it, other than leaving it in his cabin. The more Clara thought about it, the more she feared that she had very little to use against Simon Noble. Without a witness to the killing, and without a clear motive, Simon Noble could wrangle his way out of any charges brought against him.

"It's a start," O'Harris said, reading her expression

accurately.

"Let's take it to Captain Pevsner," Clara said. "And see what he wants to do."

Not knowing where Captain Pevsner was at that moment in time, and not wishing to traipse about the ship with the damp shirt on view. Clara went to the captain's cabin, while O'Harris went to find the good skipper.

Clara hunted through the cabin and eventually found a large towel in a drawer. She threw this over the table and spread the shirt out on top of it. She took another good look at her find. No one could argue with the blood on the sleeve cuff or suggest it had come from something minor like a shaving accident. But why had Simon Noble slain his employee? No one had hinted at a suitable motive and Miss Dodd seemed certain Henry Kemp would not have become violent enough to suggest they had argued and Noble had raised the knife in self-defence. No, there was something Clara was missing. But a stained shirt was not going to tell her what that was.

Captain O'Harris returned half an hour after leaving Clara. Captain Pevsner was following him. He looked at the shirt and said nothing. The stained cuffs spoke for themselves.

"Where did you find it?"

"In the sink of his cabin," Clara pulled the spare key for Simon Noble's cabin from her pocket. "I didn't break in. I was offered the key."

She did not mention who had offered her the key.

"He was trying to wash the stains out and clearly failed."

"So, he did it?" Captain Pevsner breathed sharply, relief and horror mingled on his face. "He killed Henry Kemp."

"I think so," Clara said. "But the evidence is circumstantial. We can present this to the police, however, and I think we ought to confront Simon Noble with what we have found. We might just shake him enough to get a confession."

Clara knew that was a real last ditch hope, but she was running out of options. Captain Pevsner did not share her uncertainty, he nodded.

"I shall fetch him myself," he said. "Please wait here for me."

He departed the cabin. Clara took a seat in a chair and glared at the shirt. Proof, and yet no proof. O'Harris smiled at her sympathetically.

"He will wriggle out of it, won't he?" He said.

"I doubt they will even be able to get him into court, not with such a flimsy case against him. They won't risk it. The Nobles have money, and you don't go around charging wealthy men with murder unless you can jolly well prove it without doubt."

"Poor Henry Kemp," O'Harris repeated Miss Dodd's words. "What could he have done to incur Simon Noble's wrath?"

Clara shrugged, that was what was bothering her too.

The said nothing while they waited for Captain Pevsner, finding it hard to know what to say to each other. The shirt had become the focal point in the room, yet it was also the source of their silence. It starkly reminded them that a man had died and they were battling the odds to bring his killer to justice.

"Simon Noble is going to get away with murder," Clara said miserably.

O'Harris frowned, but he could not offer any consolation. They were distracted from their thoughts by the return of Captain Pevsner. How he had managed to persuade Simon Noble to join him Clara could only guess. But the man walked into the cabin willingly enough, then he saw O'Harris and Clara. He scowled, for a moment not noting the shirt laid out on the table.

"Hello again," Clara said. "Apologies for disturbing you once more, but there has been a problem with the laundry."

Clara wafted a hand towards the shirt on the table. Simon's eyes slowly followed. Clara was convinced they

124

widened as he spotted what was laid out before him. But she had to give him credit, he did not crumple, rather he went on the defensive.

"You've been in my cabin! This is a disgrace Pevsner!"

"I was not responsible," Captain Pevsner hastily protested. "They were given a key."

"Not by me!" Simon Noble snapped and then he realised who must have given them the spare key to the room and he hesitated for just a fraction of an instant. "What lies have you been spinning to Miss Dodd?"

"Mr Noble," Clara rose from her seat. "I have spun no lies, I merely have presented the truth to you. Here is your shirt, from your cabin. The initials alone mark it as yours. And the cuffs are stained, I think it likely an expert could verify those marks are blood and a great deal of it. This is the shirt you wore when you killed Henry Kemp. You tried to wash it clean, but it is plain you failed. Do you wish to say anything?"

Simon Noble glowered at her, then a thin grin crept onto his face. It was a nasty, evil grin, one that indicated that he was clever enough to see through Clara's bluff.

"Do I wish to say anything? Yes, tell me Miss Fitzgerald, why would I kill Henry Kemp? What reason could I possibly have?"

Clara clenched her fists as he sneered at her. There was nothing worse than knowing she had no reply to his question.

Simon Noble grinned.

Chapter Sixteen

There was nothing else for it. Simon Noble was not going to confess to anything and the case against him was becoming flimsier and flimsier. He tried to take back his shirt, but Clara refused. That had to stay with them else they had nothing. Noble argued the discoloration was meaningless, trying to suggest the stains were caused by rusty water in the lifeboat and not by blood. Clara replied that that meant there was no harm in her retaining it to give to the police. There was a potential for the situation to dissolve into an argument, but the presence of Captain Pevsner and Captain O'Harris kept matters from over-boiling. Reluctantly, Simon Noble allowed the captain to lock the shirt in his safe. It was out of all their hands now and could be given to the police in due course.

"And what will they do with it?" Simon Noble huffed.

"That is up to them," Clara answered. "You may think you have won, but things are far from over. If you really did kill Henry Kemp I shall learn why."

"You really think a stained shirt will lead to me being arrested?" Simon Noble was amused.

"I think it is a start," Clara replied.

"You really have nothing," Simon Noble scoffed, he threw back his shoulders and grinned arrogantly.

Clara wanted to slap him. He thought they had nothing, and he was more than a smidge right.

"I'm getting back to the party," Simon Noble snorted. "I am bored with your games. I'll take my spare cabin key, too."

He held out a fat hand. Clara hesitated for a moment, but she could not deny his request. She handed over the key.

"I'll be having words with Miss Dodd about this," he said as he clasped his fist about the key.

"She thought she was helping you," Clara lied boldly. "She knew we thought you had something to do with the murder of Mr Kemp. She thought by letting us search your cabin we would find nothing and so be forced to reconsider our suspicions."

That statement clearly threw Simon Noble. His arrogance faded a fraction and a frown crept onto his forehead. He wasn't sure what to believe.

"Miss Dodd has always been very loyal to the family," he said uneasily.

"She thought she was doing you a favour," Clara insisted. "She was convinced you were innocent and wanted to prove it. It is not her fault she was mistaken."

Simon Noble's scowl returned, he puffed out his cheeks and looked ready to explode. Clara had deliberately goaded him, to turn any anger he might have at Miss Dodd onto herself. She did not want the woman losing her job because she had cared about finding the truth.

"You used Miss Dodd," Simon snapped. "You tricked her into thinking she was being helpful. Shame on you."

Clara did not care if he belittled her, as long as it protected Miss Dodd from his wrath.

"I'm getting back to the party. I've had enough of all this nonsense," Simon Noble turned on his heel and stormed out.

Clara felt her shoulders sag as soon as he was gone. She had been standing rigid, like a sentry on duty, her muscles tense with defiance towards Simon Noble. She would not let him see that he had the advantage and that she had... well, a damp shirt with stained cuffs. Once he had gone she could drop the pretence and her shoulders not only sagged with relief, but also with despondency.

"Once again, thank you for all your help Miss Fitzgerald," Captain Pevsner spoke. He had a wane smile on his face. "I know you have done everything in your power. I believe we know who killed Henry Kemp, but we shall never be able to prove it."

"Never is a strong word," Clara said, though she could not master her usual conviction. "I still hope to prove my case. Please keep the shirt safe."

Captain Pevsner picked up the safe key. After a moment, where he looked at the key thoughtfully, he gave it to Clara.

"There is only one key," he told her, "you take care of it."

Clara was touched by the gesture, both one of trust and of deference. She took the key and thanked him, before slipping it into the small handbag, no more than a purse on a chain, that she had brought with her that evening.

"Now, both of you return to the party," Captain Pevsner instructed. "Tomorrow I shall send word out to the police of what has happened and they can meet us in the harbour. Until then, go and enjoy yourselves."

Captain O'Harris caught Clara's eye, then he held out his arm. She smiled as she slipped her arm through the crook of his. Saying polite 'good evenings' to Pevsner, they left the cabin and went back onto the sun deck.

"I'm cold," Clara remarked at once.

The evening had grown dark and snow drifted in light flakes about the ship. It was too little to lay, at least for the moment. The crew had started to serve hot totties to the guests, along with hot chocolate, tea and coffee. O'Harris fetched two warm drinks for himself and Clara and they wrapped their hands around them, seeping the warmth of the liquid into their bodies. The band looked weary, their fingers cold and stiff. They were being offered hot drinks too. Their breath was coming out in clouds.

"Time for some livelier numbers!" The band leader announced. His musicians did not look impressed, but obeyed nonetheless.

"Care to dance?" O'Harris asked Clara.

"I'll probably step on your toes my feet are so cold!"

"I'll survive," O'Harris laughed.

Depositing their drinks on a nearby table he escorted Clara onto the middle of the sun deck and, as a fast-paced tune began to be played, they picked up the rhythm and started to dance. Clara found her laughter returning. Being with Captain O'Harris always made her smile. His arm around her and the warmth of his body as they danced filled her with delight. His eyes shone with pleasure and energy; this was the old O'Harris, the one that had vanished for a short time, but who was now returning. Clara could not help but feel happy. A part of her was insulted by the emotion, reminding her that down below a man lay dead. But she could not change what happened to Henry Kemp and moping about, spoiling her evening with Captain O'Harris, would neither solve the case faster or bring Kemp back to life.

They danced in big sweeping circles. Clara lost track of everything; blissful oblivion enveloped her and she was glad for it. When the music suddenly ended and they came to a halt to clap the musicians, she found herself near the rail, not far away from Miss Dodd. Clara met the woman's eyes without meaning to. Miss Dodd looked sad. Her eyes quietly rebuked Clara for disregarding her duty so she could dance. Clara's happiness was tempered. She looked away, feeling Miss Dodd's silent accusation following her.

"Well, I am lot warmer now!" O'Harris remarked, not noticing the woman.

He tracked down their drinks and handed one to Clara.

"Have you seen the time, a quarter to midnight!"

O'Harris showed Clara his wristwatch which was marking down the final minutes of 1921. "I am looking forward to 1922, Clara."

Clara had been distracted by Miss Dodd, now she brought her full attention back onto O'Harris.

"I plan on making it a very good year," Clara agreed with him. "Now I have you back, I intend to make the most of it."

She reached out for his hand. O'Harris squeezed her fingers.

"And the plans for transforming the old hall into a convalescence home for veterans of the war are going well. The winter has interrupted work, but it shan't be long before the place is ready. I hope to receive my first guests in the late spring."

Captain O'Harris had witnessed first-hand the limited care that was generally offered to men suffering from psychological problems caused by the traumas of war. In response, and looking for something new to do with his life rather than flying aeroplanes, he had decided to turn the great mansion he had inherited into a place of peace and restoration for those who had served in the war. His plans were in full swing and he was in the process of securing local patrons and supporters to ensure its success. He was excited about the future; a far cry from the man who had first returned to Brighton.

Clara was distracted by the arrival on deck of Captain Pevsner. He did not look as jolly as the evening should have decreed. He seemed to hunch a fraction and his smile had the appearance of being a touch forced. His guests, if they noticed at all, would probably blame his reticence on the quietly whispered rumour that this was the Mary Jane's last voyage. Only the Noble party and the crew knew the shadow hanging over him was due to the murder that had taken place on his ship.

"Ladies and gentlemen!" Captain Pevsner began as he stood before the bandstand. "I want to thank you all for coming on this very special evening. Over the years I have conducted many New Year's Eve parties at sea, each has been special, but tonight is more so than all those others. Tonight the Mary Jane says her own farewell to the waves. She has seen times of peace and times of war, she has served her country valiantly and defied the enemy who would have gladly put a torpedo in her bows. Now it is time for the old girl to rest.

"Ship's captains are born to the water and don't retire well to the land, but as I say goodbye to 1921, I must face 1922 as a landlubber. The Mary Jane has been my home, my workhorse and my friend these last forty-odd years. I'll miss her. I'll miss her creaks and groans, her rumbling engine and her rattling pipes. I'll miss her quirks, as much as I will miss her charms. I will also miss my crew who have served me and Mary Jane loyally. Some have been with me for decades, others only a matter of months, but all of them are fine, fine men, who I wish the very best for the future. Could I politely impose on my guests to offer a round of applause for my good crew who have made tonight, and all the nights aboard Mary Jane possible?"

The guests obediently applauded the crew. The clapping was fairly vigorous, encouraged by the copious amounts of champagne everyone had drunk.

"Thank you!" Captain Pevsner smiled at his audience and some of his gloom lifted. "I would also like to ask for a toast to the old gal who has made this evening possible. Please, raise your glasses to Mary Jane, who has carried her many passengers safely all these years and has not let me down."

Glasses were raised and there were a few cheers from those already quite drunk. Pevsner smiled, then he removed a pocket watch from his jacket and checked the time.

"My friends, it is one minute to midnight, please, assist me to count down the last moments of 1921!"

Together the guests began a sixty second countdown. Clara glanced at her own watch and smiled; Captain Pevsner's little speech had gone on too long, the time was really a minute past midnight, but no one else had noticed and the countdown revved up the crowd. As the final ten seconds was reached, voices raised higher and there were giggles of excitement. O'Harris was already counting, Clara joined in. She had forgotten all about Miss Dodd.

"Four! Three! Two! One!" Captain Pevsner took a dramatic step away from the band and waved his arm at them like he was a compere at the music hall. The band obeyed and instantly started to play 'Old Lang Syne'. People started to sing – it was out of tune and many did not know the words, but they sang. They crossed their arms and took the hands of those nearby, shaking them up and down as heartily as they could. Clara and O'Harris found themselves swept up into a small group of enthusiastic singers, grabbing hands and shaking them as hard as they could. Clara was struggling to sing as she was laughing so loud. She glanced at O'Harris and was delighted to see he was in stitches too, his face red with intoxicating merriment.

The music came to its climax, everyone threw up their arms in the air and cheered.

"Happy New Year!"

More champagne was handed around. The crew were hastening to refill peoples' glasses. Toasts were being shouted out over random things, just for the sake of it all. O'Harris collected two champagne flutes from a passing waiter with a tray and handed one to Clara.

"A toast to the future, of which I am now certain I have one," he said.

Clara gladly raised her glass to that.

"And a toast to old friends rediscovered," she responded.

They tapped their glasses together, making a pleasant clinking sound.

"I hope we have many more years together to enjoy our friendship," O'Harris had a glint in his eye as he took a sip of champagne. "Oh, gosh! This stuff doesn't improve the more you drink it!"

Clara laughed loudly and then felt a bit embarrassed. It was not like her to be so carefree, but the party atmosphere had become infectious. From behind her, Clara became aware of a noise, as if a commotion was occurring, but she was so busy with toasts and laughing with O'Harris that the sound failed to register at first. Then there was a cry; not a cry of delight or excitement, but a cry of almost surprise. Clara started to turn her head, though she was still really paying little attention.

"A toast to you," a drunk man stumbled over to Clara and O'Harris and presented his champagne flute. "And to me and to us, oh, and to them over there."

He wobbled away to another group of people before they had a chance to clink his glass. Clara was just starting to laugh when she heard a splash. The noise startled her enough to make her jump and turn in the direction of the starboard rail. O'Harris turned too. No one else seemed to be taking heed, until Clara caught sight of Charles Walsh by the rail. He was looking around him, his voice raised in horror.

"Help! By God, help!" He cried to the crowd. "She has jumped overboard!"

Chapter Seventeen

"Who is it? Who went overboard?" Clara ran to the rail where Charles Walsh stood.

She was not alone, a number of people, most just drunken gawkers had reacted to the splash and Walsh's cry for help. They were hovering by the rail, gazing over into the sea below without offering any assistance. Clara pushed through them, Captain O'Harris just behind her. Captain Pevsner arrived moments later.

"It's Miss Dodd!" Charles Walsh declared breathlessly. "She just… tipped over!"

"Bring me a light!" Captain Pevsner called to one of his crew.

They all looked at the dark water, the wavelets lapping lightly at the side of the Mary Jane. They seemed like some sort of tar rather than ocean water. They looked hard and rigid, capable of sucking a person beneath them, never to return them. Clara felt uneasy, the calm sea seemed all the more sinister for its placidity.

A crewman handed Captain Pevsner a big electric lantern. It was like the big bulls' eye lanterns that used to contain oil or a candle, but this one was modern. When he switched it on it cast a large beam of light across the water. He shone it steadily back and forth, looking for

Miss Dodd.

The water seemed to have utterly absorbed her. There was no sign in the inky black of the night. Clara bit her lower lip, a sensation of dread sweeping over her.

"There!" Charles Walsh shot out an arm and pointed to a spot that seemed far too distant from the ship to possibly contain Miss Dodd.

The location was just outside the sweep of Captain Pevsner's beam of light, a snatch of movement had attracted Walsh's eye. Pevsner now raised the lantern and Miss Dodd appeared in the beam. Her head was just above the water and her arms were outstretched, but she did not appear to be making a great deal of effort to stay afloat.

"She won't last long out there," Captain Pevsner said, mostly under his breath, but Clara heard him and knew what he meant.

The ocean was freezing this time of year and a person could die of cold before they ever drowned. Miss Dodd was in evening wear, not designed to protect her from the wintry temperatures and certainly not icy water.

"Lower a lifeboat!" Captain Pevsner called out again, then he grabbed a round lifebelt from the rail. He made sure it was attached to a sturdy long cord, then prepared to throw it. "Please stand clear!"

Not everyone at once moved, too intoxicated or tired to react immediately. Clara and O'Harris shuffled them back, freeing up space for Captain Pevsner to swing back his arm and hurl the lifebelt in the direction of Miss Dodd. It was an impressive toss, Pevsner put his all into it, but it still landed several feet too short.

"Swim to the lifebelt!" Captain Pevsner cupped his hands around his mouth and shouted.

Miss Dodd did not move.

"It's the cold, it's numbed her," Captain Pevsner declared, then he turned and shouted. "Is that lifeboat ready?"

"Yes Captain!" A voice called back.

Pevsner began to head for the lifeboat.

"Can I be of any help?" O'Harris asked.

Pevsner smiled at him.

"My men have all done this before and I would not be a good captain to put another of my guests needlessly in danger. But, thank you."

He hurried away. Clara did not watch him leave, her eyes were on Jane Dodd. The lantern had been left perched on the rail, it had a clamp on the bottom to enable it to be fixed in place. It now operated as a beacon for the rescuers. Clara winced as the light glimmered on the water and highlighted the shoulders and head of Miss Dodd. It was hard to say if she was conscious; she did not seem to be moving a great deal. Might she already have succumbed to the cold?

"What is going on?" Arthur Noble had finally managed to wobble towards the rail to investigate matters.

He was stuffed full of food and more than a few glasses of champagne. He looked slightly pained, as if even a man of his proportions could over-indulge. He pushed aside a guest or two who were blocking his path to the rail. Just behind him were his sons. Simon looked as foul-tempered as always, Elias bore a worried expression.

"Miss Dodd has gone overboard!" Charles Walsh repeated in the same tone of horror he had cried out in before. He seemed utterly shocked by the experience, and unable to comprehend what had happened.

"Miss Dodd?" Arthur Noble pushed his way to the rail and looked across the water. "By my grandfather's soul, is that her out there?"

He lifted a flabby hand and pointed out to sea.

"Yes," Charles Walsh said mournfully. "She doesn't seem to be trying to swim."

A splash to their left informed them that the lifeboat had finally been lowered into the water and the rescuers were on their way. Oars smacked the water and Pevsner was calling out directions as his men rowed as hard as they could.

"How did she end up all the way out there?" Arthur Noble was still somewhat dazed by the situation, not helped by all the cheap champagne. He was not a man who grasped things quickly at the best of times.

"I imagine it is the current," O'Harris volunteered. "It will have dragged her away from the ship."

"Well, why did you let her fall in Charles?" Arthur Noble turned on his employee now. "What a damn foolish thing to do."

"I didn't let her fall in," Charles replied, utterly appalled by the criticism. "She was stood at the rail as we all toasted in the New Year. She gave a sort of groan, I looked over when I heard it. I asked if she was all right and she looked at me so very sadly. Then she just seemed to step backwards into the rail and toppled over."

"Damn stupid!" Arthur Noble blustered. "She'll catch her death and be off work for weeks!"

Noble did not appear to notice the contradiction in his statement. Clara was not in the mood to point it out to him. His belligerence in the face of what was fast shaping into a tragedy was beginning to try her patience. He was the sort of man who saw human disasters only in terms of how they affected him.

The lifeboat was covering the water quickly, Pevsner was calling for his team of rowers to ease their rate, so as to not make huge waves near Miss Dodd and drown her. He was near enough to the lifebelt to reach out and drag it to him with a boat hook. He tossed it right next to Miss Dodd.

"Dear lady, take hold!"

It was a relief to see Miss Dodd move her arm and rest her hand on the lifebelt.

"She is still alive!" Charles Walsh cried out.

"Silly woman," Arthur Noble puttered. "I don't need to lose two employees in one night. What is Pevsner doing? Why not haul her in?"

Pevsner was having the lifeboat drawn as close to

Miss Dodd as was possible, taking it slowly and carefully so he did not duck the woman beneath the waves.

"Haul her in!" Arthur Noble crowed from the ship's rail.

"She barely has a hold on that lifebelt, she won't be able to cling to it if he tries to pull her in," O'Harris managed to keep his voice reasonable as he informed Arthur Noble of that fact.

Arthur Noble snorted, and now he roared out.

"Miss Dodd! Show willing! You are making such a spectacle of yourself!"

"You pompous, idiotic fool!" Charles Walsh was the first to lose his temper with Arthur Noble, but there were plenty of others not far behind him, including Clara and O'Harris.

"Have some compassion!" Clara barked at him.

Captain O'Harris was more practical in demonstrating his outrage. He grabbed Arthur Noble by his jacket and hauled him away from the rail. Noble was too startled to object and his sons politely moved out of O'Harris' way – though Clara thought it too generous to imagine they were also offended by their father's actions. O'Harris dragged Noble to a chair by the buffet table where he deposited him with a thud. Noble started to rise, but O'Harris placed a hand on his shoulder and pressed him back into his chair.

"You will stay there!" He commanded fiercely.

Elias and Simon wandered over to their father and watched the scene that was unfolding with curious, but cautious gazes. Arthur Noble looked stunned.

"You can't..."

"I can!" Captain O'Harris did not allow his argument any room. "You are an obnoxious old man, who doesn't care about anyone but himself. You have tried my patience long enough. Your unfortunate secretary of many years standing may be on the cusp of death and you bark orders at her from over a ship's rail? What sort of man are you?"

Arthur Noble stuttered out nothing in particular, the noise that came from his lips was more of a burble. He didn't know how to respond. O'Harris had said his piece and now he was done. He glanced at Elias and Simon, stood just to his side.

"Make sure he stays here," he told them. "If he isn't careful, one of the guests he has managed to offend this evening might just help him topple over the rail."

Simon's mouth almost twitched into a smirk at the joke. Elias looked more serious. O'Harris left them and returned to Clara.

The scene in the water had moved on. The lifeboat had been gently manoeuvred until it was almost right next to Miss Dodd's head. Captain Pevsner was leaning over and threading a rope over Miss Dodd's shoulders.

"Slip your arm through it!" He told her, his voice firm but kind, unlike that of Arthur Noble.

Miss Dodd obeyed slowly. It was plain she was struggling to command her body. Her arm went through the rope and Captain Pevsner tightened it. Now she was secure. He gave the rope to one of his crewmen to hold and then reached over the side of the boat once more to lift out Miss Dodd. The rope prevented her from being pushed under by accident. Pevsner slipped his arms under hers and started the awkward task of drawing her body from the water. Miss Dodd flopped like a rag doll and it was obvious she could offer her rescuers no assistance as she was manhandled into the boat. The process seemed to last forever but, finally, Miss Dodd was in the lifeboat and blankets were being hastily thrown around her.

"All haste back to the Mary Jane," Pevsner told his men and the lifeboat was once more being vigorously rowed, this time back towards the ship.

Clara let out a breath she had not realised she was holding. Charles Walsh looked fit to burst into tears. He glanced at Clara, his fears etched on his face.

"She threw herself over," he whispered. "I couldn't tell Mr Noble that. It would shame Miss Dodd, but I know she threw herself over."

Clara touched his arm, trying to express what little comfort she could offer him.

"Because of Henry Kemp?" She suggested.

Charles Walsh seemed to wince, then he nodded.

"She hasn't been right since his body was found. I know it was a shock to us all, but she took it very hard. But I still never thought…" Charles' eyes welled with tears. "Excuse me."

He disappeared swiftly. Clara let him go.

"I hope Miss Dodd is all right," Clara said to O'Harris.

She glanced along the rail to the point where the lifeboat was being hauled up again. Winches were being operated as fast as they could to bring the rescuers and Miss Dodd level with the deck. The ship's doctor was hovering nearby.

Clara walked forward, not wanting to interfere, yet needing to see for herself that Miss Dodd was still alive. If it was true that Miss Dodd had thrown herself overboard, and it was not a tragic accident, then Clara had underestimated the woman's strength of feeling towards Henry Kemp. Clara did not like it when she missed things, especially when it could cost someone their life.

The lifeboat was now slightly higher than the ship's rail and it was possible to swing it inwards and bring it down on the deck. Miss Dodd was a shivering lump in the middle of the little boat, the blankets wrapped so completely about her that only her head appeared. She was white as a sheet and her teeth chattered audibly. The ship's doctor leaned into the boat and gave her a sip of brandy from a flask he had brought with him. Two crewmen were waiting with a stretcher nearby.

Miss Dodd was gently helped from the lifeboat. As the only other woman present, Clara drew close to her for moral support. When she offered Miss Dodd her hand the woman took it at once. She looked at her plaintively, but for the moment could not speak.

Still holding Clara's hand, Miss Dodd was laid on the stretcher and covered with more blankets. The doctor rubbed at her free hand, trying to bring some warmth back to it.

"Let's get her to the sick bay."

Miss Dodd was carried carefully down below. She arrived at the sick bay unscathed, but was drifting into unconsciousness.

"Keep with me," the doctor commanded her urgently.

Clara squeezed Miss Dodd's hand.

"Come now, you mustn't fall asleep. You have to tell me what this is all about."

Miss Dodd wearily opened her eyes and looked at Clara. She seemed exhausted, her hand no longer gripped Clara's firmly. She was slipping away.

"Poor Henry," she whispered so softly only Clara could hear, and even then she had to lean close to Miss Dodd's mouth as she spoke. "I can't... not without him..."

"Miss Dodd, you must remain strong. Henry would not want things to end like this," Clara rubbed at Miss Dodd's now limp hand.

"What... the point?" Miss Dodd mumbled.

She gave a deep sigh.

"You have to help me find Henry's killer," Clara begged her, hoping to resurrect her with her plea. "We must bring justice to Henry, mustn't we?"

Miss Dodd's eyes, now seemingly bleached of colour, fixed on Clara's face and a trembling smile creased her lips.

"You must..." she said softly. "I have faith... in you..."

Miss Dodd took another deep breath and her eyes closed. She exhaled and then stillness came over her.

"Miss Dodd?" Clara rubbed at the woman's hand desperately. "Miss Dodd?"

The ship's doctor walked back over and looked at the prone woman. He felt for a pulse, then produced a stethoscope and listened to her chest for a heartbeat. He glanced up at Clara. He did not need to say anything.

Clara put down Miss Dodd's hand and felt momentarily defeated. What was it about Henry Kemp that had led to this awful chain of events? She left the sick bay feeling hollow inside. She had liked Miss Dodd and the woman had wanted to help. When Clara could not provide the evidence that would place Simon Noble in shackles, had Miss Dodd felt everything was over? Clara felt troubled by it all, but she also felt resolved. She was not going to let this case rest. She would find out why Henry Kemp had to die, and she would make sure Simon Noble faced justice.

Chapter Eighteen

The party was at an end. While most of the guests were unaware that Miss Dodd had passed away, the escapade in the water had dampened their spirits. It was late, and the night seemed to be getting colder and colder. The band had been instructed to play on until one o'clock, but they had lost their enthusiasm too. Without prompting, the party-goers drifted back to their cabins.

Captain O'Harris walked with Clara to her cabin, his was just next door, but he loitered with at her doorway.

"Are you all right?"

"It should never have happened," Clara said softly, her head turned away from him. One hand pressed into the side of the door frame as if holding onto it for support. "I failed Miss Dodd. She had banked everything on my finding proof Simon Noble had killed Henry Kemp in his cabin."

"You found the bloody shirt," O'Harris pointed out.

"Yet it was still not enough," Clara groaned a little to herself. "I do not have enough to warrant arresting Simon Noble. Miss Dodd must have realised that. I doubt he kept his mouth shut when he came back on deck. He would have confronted her over the spare cabin key. Miss Dodd was placed in a position of losing of her job along

143

with losing the man she clearly cared for deeply. I think it all became too much for her and she threw herself overboard."

"That isn't your fault," O'Harris said gently. "You cannot make evidence appear out of thin air, she knew the risks when she gave you the key. There is only one person to blame for all this and he will certainly not be feeling any guilt tonight."

Captain O'Harris pulled a face.

"I know his type. They bludgeon their way through life, unconscious of those they knock down along the way. Simon Noble no more cares that Miss Dodd threw herself overboard because of his actions, than he cares that he killed Henry Kemp."

"I wish I knew why he had done it," Clara's self-pity was slowing disappearing to be replaced by her usual resolve. Clara did not like introspection, she liked action. "That is surely the key to this puzzle; knowing why Henry Kemp had to die."

"I have a feeling the answer to that is not aboard this ship," Captain O'Harris tapped his fingers on the wooden wall of the corridor where he stood, a thoughtful frown coming onto his face. "Are you going to pursue this?"

"I wouldn't be able to live with myself if I didn't," Clara told him firmly. "Miss Dodd put her faith in me to discover the truth. I can't let her down. I can't see a murderer walk free. When I close my eyes I see that horrid smirk on Simon Noble's face again and again. He thinks he has defeated me and that alone makes me determined to prove him wrong."

Clara's words were certain and calm, her melancholy had evaporated. Captain O'Harris was satisfied.

"Best we both get some sleep then Clara, goodnight."

"Goodnight, John," Clara smiled at him. "It's been one heck of an evening."

"I look forward to witnessing the rest of the investigation," O'Harris said with a wink of his eye.

They both entered their cabins. Clara threw herself

down on her bunk, casting off her shoes which had pinched and nipped her feet all night. She drew in a deep breath and then exhaled it slowly. She was going to wipe that smirk off Simon Noble's face. Just let him wait and see.

~~~*~~~

They arrived back in the harbour just after seven the following morning. The police were waiting for them. As the gangplank was dropped and a handful of early bird guests started to descend, Inspector Park-Coombs walked up and ushered them back aboard. Captain Pevsner looked pained.

"Inspector, surely not every guest must remain aboard?" He asked miserably.

"No one is leaving until I know what went on. I shall need statements from everyone. For most of your passengers that will be a mere formality," Inspector Park-Coombs informed him with a look upon his face that indicated he would take no argument on the matter.

He stationed a police constable at the top of the gangplank to prevent anyone leaving.

"What is this Pevsner?" A man in a day suit began to protest. He had his luggage in his hands and his wife at his side. "Why are the police here?"

Captain Pevsner didn't know how to answer. His hope of keeping the matter quiet from the majority of the guests was now dashed. Inspector Park-Coombs looked at him with a hint of sympathy. He was not that hard a man.

"Best you put out a ship-wide announcement," he suggested.

Captain Pevsner looked defeated. He shuffled away the early guests from the gangplank, promising them a full breakfast in compensation for the delay, and explaining in as brief detail as possible what had occurred the night before.

Clara appeared through a door and nodded to

Inspector Park-Coombs. The inspector was a wily and clever detective, and he had worked with Clara successfully in the past. They both knew they benefited from the different styles of investigating they could bring to a case. Park-Coombs twitched his moustache and smiled at Clara.

"Have you not solved it already?" He teased.

"Actually, I have," Clara replied, a slightly satisfied smile coming onto her face. "I know who killed Henry Kemp, I just can't prove it."

"You best fill me in," Inspector Park-Coombs walked towards her. "You have clearly had several hours head start."

"The disadvantage of that is I have barely slept a wink," Clara started to yawn as she spoke. "I woke up at six and couldn't get back to sleep. I've been waiting for your arrival ever since. Captain Pevsner has allowed us the use of his personal cabin and I have something I need to show you."

Clara turned and indicated the inspector should follow. She explained the events of the previous evening as they walked through the ship. The inspector asked questions here and there, but mainly nodded and listened. By the time they were at the captain's cabin he knew as much as Clara did.

"And, as far as you have been able to determine there was no reason for anyone to wish Henry Kemp harm?" He asked, shutting the cabin door behind him.

"No one has offered a reason," Clara agreed.

"But Simon Noble seems the obvious culprit," Park-Coombs ran his thumb over his moustache. "Hard to imagine there was time for someone else to murder Mr Kemp and leave before Simon Noble found him, and then this lad Bert Nightly spotted him."

"Oh, I am certain Simon Noble is the killer. His behaviour makes no sense otherwise. Any innocent person who stumbled over a person they worked with stabbed like that would have summoned help. Simon

Noble did not. He left Henry Kemp where he was and pretended nothing had happened," Clara unlocked Captain Pevsner's safe with the key he had left in her keeping. She removed the shirt, still damp, and placed it on the table in the room. "Any innocent person would surely be horrified by what they saw. But Simon Noble was calculating. He left the scene and changed his shirt. He then attempted to wash the blood stains out, unsuccessfully as you can see. He returned to the party without a hint of what he had witnessed and when I began inquiring about Henry he made no indication that he was aware of what had happened. His attitude and actions speak for themselves. He is also smart enough to know that this shirt alone only proves he was present at the scene of the crime. Without a reliable witness who saw him stab Henry, or a strong reason for him to wish him harm, I am afraid there is nothing to convict him with."

The inspector examined the sleeves of the shirt carefully.

"You are right Clara," he said at last. "You have a bloody shirt and a young boy who saw Simon Noble near the body. It is not enough. A clever solicitor would tear such a flimsy case to shreds."

"I am not finished with Simon Noble," Clara said darkly. "He is a murderer and I intend to prove it. If you are amenable to me continuing to poke around? No one has hired me in this matter. I would be doing it for my own sake and for the sake of justice."

"And because Simon Noble annoys you?" Park-Coombs suggested with a hint of a grin.

"I don't let personal feelings cloud my judgement," Clara said, somewhat affronted. The inspector continued to grin at her. "Oh, all right, so maybe I was rather offended by Simon Noble's attitude towards me. He seems to think he has won and that a woman can't do anything to change that."

"Good for us we know he is very wrong," Park-

Coombs placated her. "Now, this mystery witness you haven't been able to track down, what of them?"

"I thought at first they might have been the killer," Clara admitted. "They were down below at the same time as Henry Kemp. It is only a vague hope that they might have seen something. I've tried to work out the timings, but it is all rather hazy what with the drama of the mine. Ronnie, one of the crew, was trying to keep an eye on Henry Kemp. About the time the mine was being shot at, Kemp headed downstairs. Ronnie followed but became distracted by finding the ship's cat. Now, he also saw a shadow that suggested someone else was down below. Probably a crewman, but I have been unable to confirm that every guest, barring Kemp, was in a lifeboat.

"By the time Ronnie was back on deck the mine had been exploded and the lifeboats were being called back. The lifeboat containing Simon Noble was one of the first to return. He climbed out and went looking for Kemp, who was still in the kitchen down below. I don't know how long that took him."

"And this other person down below may or may not have witnessed what happened next," Park-Coombs saw the problem with this assumption. "But no one is admitting to being that third person down below."

"No," Clara shrugged her shoulders. "All we know is that Ronnie thought he glimpsed someone. He might be wrong."

"Then we are left with one option – find a strong motive for Simon Noble to want Henry Kemp dead. If we have that, then everything else will fall into place."

"Still circumstantial," Clara pointed out.

"I've convicted on less," Park-Coombs was unfazed. "Most murders are not witnessed, after all. You rely on proving the suspect wanted the person dead and some evidence to back up that they were in the right place at the right time. What about this Miss Dodd?"

Clara closed her eyes for a moment. She had dreamed of Miss Dodd in the water. Clara had been trying to reach her in a boat, but every time she drew near Miss Dodd drifted further away.

"She threw herself overboard," Clara said at last.

"And you are sure it was because she was heartbroken over Henry Kemp's death?"

Clara was thrown by the question. She had never doubted the reason for Miss Dodd's dramatic tumble.

"What are you saying?"

"The timings are hazy," Park-Coombs repeated what she had said earlier. "Simon Noble and Jane Dodd were in the same lifeboat. If he went looking for Henry Kemp, then why not her also? And what if she found Henry first?"

Clara had never considered Miss Dodd a suspect. She had spoken to the woman personally and seen her grief. Had that blinded her? Could Miss Dodd have thrown herself into the ocean because of guilt rather than grief?

"I hadn't considered that," Clara admitted.

"We have to keep open all possibilities. I agree that Simon Noble seems the most likely culprit, but I like to work through other options, just in case. I've been in court enough times to know that a good solicitor will dig holes in a case by suggesting other suspects, and if you can't explain definitively why those others could not have committed the crime, you risk the jury starting to consider reasonable doubt."

"I'll need to talk to everyone again who was in the Noble party and ask who they were with when they climbed back aboard. Miss Dodd can no longer provide anyone with an alibi, unfortunately," Clara shook her head. "Instead of narrowing things down, suddenly it seems that everyone could be a killer again!"

"I'll worry about the interviews with the guests," Park-Coombs told her. "You get on shore and begin work on finding a motive. Only lunatics kill for no reason. Somewhere, out there, is a motive for this crime."

"Thank you, Inspector," Clara was relieved to have someone to take the burden off her. "Do you think there any likelihood of someone in your laboratory finding fingerprints on the knife that killed Henry Kemp?"

"Wouldn't that be good?" Park-Coombs smiled. "I like to give the boys something to work with. I'll have Dr Deàth examine the body too. I don't doubt the ship's doctor; a fatal stabbing is not exactly hard to work out, but you never know what a fresh pair of eyes might see."

Dr Deàth was the coroner for Brighton and Clara trusted his judgement. If there was anything more to find concerning Henry Kemp's murder, Dr Deàth would discover it.

"I shall let you get on," Clara said, returning the stained shirt to the safe for the time being. She handed Park-Coombs the safe key. "I warn you now, the Nobles are obnoxious, arrogant and full of their own self-importance."

"Sounds just perfect!" Park-Coombs laughed. "I am sure I shall have a lot of fun interviewing them. No doubt they are heartily fed up of questions by now."

"They are heartily fed up with me, that's for sure!" Clara managed to laugh too. "I hope, before long, they will wish they never heard my name!"

"You find that motive, Clara, and they will definitely regret committing a crime under your nose."

"Don't worry Inspector," Clara smiled. "I shall do exactly that."

Chapter Nineteen

Clara and Captain O'Harris collected their luggage and headed for the gangplank, they were almost descending when Charles Walsh hurried over to them.

"Miss Fitzgerald, are you leaving?"

He looked urgent and upset. He had seen two work colleagues perish in the spate of a few hours, and his employers' reaction to their deaths had not inspired confidence.

"Yes, the police are taking over the investigation aboard the Mary Jane," Clara told him and his face fell further.

"You will not be assisting them?" He asked.

Clara smiled.

"Whatever made you think that? I shall most certainly be continuing," she promised. "But, I think the key to this matter lies ashore. I need to discover why Henry Kemp was killed."

"Will you be going to the Noble and Sons' offices?"

"At some point."

Charles Walsh quickly dug in the pocket of his trousers and produced a slip of card. He looked slightly abashed that he had a business card with him on an evening out.

"Mr Noble insists," he explained hastily. "Never miss an opportunity to do business."

He mimicked Arthur Noble's pompous and bloated voice perfectly. Clara almost laughed, but restrained herself.

"Anyway…" Charles Walsh fumbled in his other pocket. He came up empty-handed. "Do you have a pen or pencil?"

Clara opened her handbag. This was not the fancy one she had worn during the evening's festivities – the one that could only hold a handkerchief – this was her normal, every day handbag. From it she produced several pencils, all freshly sharpened. If Charles was surprised he masked it well. Taking a pencil, he wrote on the back of the card and then signed his name.

"Show this card if anyone is reluctant to work with you at the office," he gave the card to Clara.

On the back he had quickly written 'all assistance to be provided to the cardholder.' Clara thought it could be very useful. She stored the card in her purse.

"Before I go, Mr Walsh, can I ask you a final question?"

"Of course," Charles Walsh said keenly.

"To the best of your recollection, where did everyone go when they returned from the lifeboat?"

Charles Walsh was swift to reply.

"Mr Simon Noble disappeared quite quickly. I helped Miss Dodd aboard and we returned to the sun deck. Elias Noble followed us. Mr Noble arrived a short while later and eventually Mr Simon Noble returned too."

"Miss Dodd and Elias Noble were on the sun deck all the time before you learned of Henry Kemp's death?"

Charles Walsh paused just a moment to consider the question.

"Yes, I am certain of it."

"Thank you," Clara said.

As long as Charles Walsh was not lying, Miss Dodd and Elias Noble did not have an opportunity to murder

Henry Kemp. She felt relieved about that. When Inspector Park-Coombs had opened up the possibility of Miss Dodd being a killer she had suddenly felt her certainty about Simon Noble's involvement shatter. If she could be brought to doubt her conviction, then most certainly a jury who had not been 'on the scene' could be made doubtful. Charles Walsh had provided her with the first testimony that this was not the case. She could no longer confirm it through Miss Dodd, but Elias Noble would surely back him up? Both men had a vested interest in proving they were not the killer. That left Simon and Arthur Noble unaccounted for during the vital window of time when Henry Kemp was murdered.

Arthur Noble's delay to arrive on the sun deck could be easily explained away – he was on a different lifeboat to the others, but that still meant there was a piece of time when he could have gone below decks. Time to move on, without a motive speculation only made things more complicated.

Saying goodbye to Charles Walsh, she headed down the gangplank with O'Harris. The day had started with a promise of sunshine. Now it had become overcast and rain threatened. Stepping back onto dry land, Clara felt a little unsteady, as if she was still at sea.

"What do you want to do?" Captain O'Harris asked her.

"I would like to visit the offices of Noble and Sons before the Nobles get ashore," she answered. "But they are all the way in Hove."

Captain O'Harris grinned, there was a devilish quality to it.

"That actually should not be a problem," he glanced at his watch. "I believe Jones should be here any minute, I asked him to arrive at nine."

"Jones?" Clara raised an eyebrow. "Who is Jones?"

"As you know, after my unfortunate flying mishap and everyone thinking I was dead for a year, my staff for the house were all dismissed. Not such a bad thing, to be honest, as many of them were old retainers from my uncle's time. I've had the opportunity to reconsider exactly who I might need to help run the house. I hired Jones just before Christmas, I haven't had the time to introduce you."

"And what does Jones do?" Clara asked.

Before O'Harris could answer a dark burgundy car swept into the harbour. It was a Bentley manufactured just before the war and it caught the eyes of all the dock workers. You could not fail to miss it with its spotlessly shiny chassis and its purring engine.

"Jones is now my driver and responsible for all my cars," O'Harris beamed with pride.

O'Harris had inherited a passion for all things mechanical from his uncle and had the money to indulge his interest. Between his purchases and those of his late uncle he had a garage full of cars.

"Jones is ex-RFC," O'Harris waved at the car and then hurried towards it with the suitcases. Clara ran behind him, listening to his explanation. "He was ground crew, never flew. Excellent mechanic. I had a letter from another friend telling me that Jones was struggling to find work now he was back in blighty. I hardly had to consider before I offered him a job."

The man named Jones stepped out of the car. He was in a tidy, but slightly old suit. He opened the back door of the Bentley for Clara and O'Harris.

"We haven't organised the uniform yet," O'Harris whispered in her ear as they clambered in.

Jones shut the door and returned to the driver's seat.

"Where to, Sir?"

"We need to get to the offices of Noble and Sons in Hove. I can give you directions. I've been there a couple of times before the war," O'Harris instructed.

Jones had left the engine running, now he drove steadily away from the harbour, guiding his charge around workers and crates of cargo.

"I thought you always drove yourself?" Clara asked

O'Harris, with just a hint of concern.

His accident had knocked the captain's confidence in more ways than one. She was slightly worried that he might have given up driving as well as flying.

"I still drive," O'Harris reassured her. "But there are times when the car needs to be brought to me. Like today."

They made it out of the harbour and were soon on a country road heading to Hove. Jones was a cautious driver, which Clara greatly appreciated. O'Harris might have been more impatient with his relentlessly steady driving, except that he was concentrating on the way they had to go.

Hove was a town just on the outskirts of Brighton. Very often the two were lumped together as Brighton and Hove. Neither the residents of Brighton or of Hove liked that much. They considered themselves separate places, with separate identities. However, they were also very much dependent on each other and interconnected. They therefore had to accept that, from the perspective of the outside world, they were more one place than two.

The rain began to fall and Clara was very glad to be in the dry car. She usually walked everywhere, or caught a bus. She watched the grey clouds drifting overhead and reflected that they were jolly lucky it had not rained last night. That would have made the evening unbearable.

She still felt sorry for Captain Pevsner; his last voyage had proved eventful for all the wrong reasons. Two of his guests had died. That was the sort of thing that haunted a person.

"I believe this is it, Sir."

They had driven into the town of Hove, following O'Harris' directions. As they took a right they came in sight of an old red-brick building. It had white faux pillars attached to the front and pale stones outlining the windows and corners. A large sign that stretched the length of the property declared that this was the home of Noble and Sons. The old building was their headquarters, actual storage of wine would be taken care of in great warehouses on the docks. It wouldn't surprise Clara if the red-brick property had belonged to the Noble firm since the time it was constructed. It certainly had a sense of grandeur to it that only comes with age.

Jones opened the car door again and Clara hurried to the building's entrance, which was sheltered by a narrow porch. O'Harris joined her a moment later, having given Jones instructions to wait for them where he was. Clara tried the door and found it was unlocked. She stepped into a foyer that encompassed the entire right front side of the building. Straight ahead was a staircase and a corridor, with doors leading off it. To her left there was another door, leading presumably into the front room opposite the foyer. The foyer was tiled in black and red squares. A large desk was positioned diagonally across the rear corner and faced a small seating area. A man sat behind the desk. He was dressed in a black suit and looked to be in his mid-twenties.

"Can I help?" He asked as they entered.

Clara approached the desk.

"I hope so," she said. "I am here due to an unfortunate tragedy that has befallen two of the employees of Noble and Sons. Mr Henry Kemp and Miss Jane Dodd both passed away last night."

The young man looked stunned.

"Oh," he said, unable to say more for a moment. "That is something of a shock. They went out for the evening, last night."

"They did, it was during the New Year celebrations that misfortune overtook them. The police are already involved, but I am also assisting the investigation. I have the permission of Mr Charles Walsh to do so."

Clara produced the signed business card and showed it to the man. He read it, his fingers trembling slightly as he held the card, then he gave it back.

"Yes, that seems in order. Please, what happened?"

Clara had anticipated such a question. In the car she

had thought how best to answer it. Lies were never a good idea, but the truth was also difficult. Telling someone a colleague has been murdered can only shock them. In the end, you had to just be honest and hope people did not fall to pieces because of what you said.

"Mr Henry Kemp was murdered last night."

The man behind the desk blinked fast.

"Murdered?" He repeated the word very carefully, as if it was from a foreign language and he had never heard it before. "By whom?"

"That is what I am trying to determine," Clara explained. "I would like to take a look at Mr Kemp's office and I wish to have any details you hold on his next of kin."

The man looked like he might protest, then he remembered the card he had been shown.

"Mr Walsh knows about all this?" He asked, still struggling to comprehend everything.

"Mr Walsh was present last night. He is very aware of what occurred. He has placed his full support behind me."

"And Miss Dodd?" The man's face slowly crumpled into despair. "Was she murdered too?"

"Miss Dodd fell overboard," Clara said. "She was very distressed by what had occurred. She was not thinking rationally."

Clara did not specify that Miss Dodd had attempted suicide, that was a harsh thing to say about anyone, even when it was the truth. She felt that Miss Dodd had been placed in a dreadful position and pushed to her limits. Her toppling over the rail had been impulsive, a moment of insanity. It was plain she had not truly considered death, as she made sure to float face up in the water and had reached out to hold onto the lifebelt. A person who really meant to die would have made sure to go underwater and would not have assisted the rescuers. Miss Dodd's fall had been an impulsive act of frustration and grief. She had not deserved to die for it.

"This is terrible," the man at the desk had gone ashen

and he gripped the wooden top of his desk with his fingers so tightly they went white at the knuckles. "I can hardly fathom it. Miss Dodd is something of an institution here. She never misses a day of work and she always says hello."

He rocked back in his chair, as if reeling from the news.

"Fell overboard? Murdered? How can this all be?"

"That is what I hope to find out," Clara told him. "But I need to look in Mr Kemp's office first."

"I'm not supposed to let anyone in without his direct consent," the man said, rubbing at the back of his head and realising how absurd his last statement had been. "Mr Kemp is never going to give that consent, but I should really ask the management as there could be private documents in his office."

Clara held out the card Charles Walsh had signed once more.

"You have the consent of a senior manager and I can assure you I have no interest in business secrets, unless they somehow contributed to Henry Kemp's death. Even then, my information will be going straight to the police and no one else."

The man stared at the card a long time. He seemed very torn.

"You will not take anything from the office?" he asked.

"Not unless it is evidence of the crime committed against Henry Kemp," Clara replied, careful to hedge around the possibility.

Still the man hesitated.

"Henry Kemp was murdered," Clara reminded him, though she doubted he needed it. He just needed to be nudged into action and to realise that helping her was more important than any private documents. "To find his killer, I must explore all avenues. I have to look in his office."

Palpably upset, the man slowly nodded. Then he slipped from his chair and went to a cupboard mounted on the wall. When he opened it dozens of keys on hooks were displayed. He picked one and handed it to Clara.

"I hope this helps. I hope you find who did this."

Clara thanked him as she took the key.

"I know I shall find who did this," she promised; an easy thing to say as she already did know.

Thanking the man at the desk again, Clara and O'Harris headed up the stairs and towards Henry Kemp's private domain.

Chapter Twenty

Henry Kemp had a spacious office that overlooked the street outside. It was lined with oak panels on the walls and the ceiling. There was something rather oppressive about the dark wood, it also cast an aura of complete masculinity. This was not a room a woman was supposed to enter without permission, or to feel comfortable in.

A large bay window cast grey light from the dull day outside onto a great desk. Henry Kemp kept his work space clean and uncluttered. There were no loose papers on his desk; ones that needed urgent attention were stacked in a shallow wooden tray. A fountain pen sat in a leather case, Clara opened the box and saw that it was a black pen engraved with the initials H.K. She wondered if it was an act of vanity on Kemp's part, or a present from someone who cared about him.

Pencils and a rubber sat in a rectangular wooden tray, all ready for use. A large mechanical pencil sharpener stood on the edge of the desk. That was everything, aside from a green blotter that filled the centre of the desk.

"Last time I saw a desk this obsessively tidy it belonged to an army colonel. I had a rough landing just behind the front line and I was a bit bruised. I was escorted to his office while waiting for a transport to take me back to my base," O'Harris ran a finger down the edge of the desk as if looking for dust. "This colonel had made a temporary office in the ruins of a beautiful chateau. You could tell, even though the place was a wreck, that it had once been stunning. Only a handful of rooms remained and he had found one with this antique desk. I remember walking in and there he sat behind it, surrounded by rubble, dust and plaster occasionally falling from the ceiling, broken furniture shoved to the sides of the room. And yet, his desk was pristine, not an extra object or one out of place. It was his way of taking control of a situation that had grown out of hand. He could not stop the war, or the destruction, but he could take charge of that desk and keep it perfect."

"Are you suggesting Henry Kemp did the same? That he needed some control over his life and this room was where he could exert it?" Clara asked.

"I don't know," O'Harris admitted, slightly embarrassed that he had said so much now. "It just reminded me. Feels the same."

Clara looked around the room. There was a starkness to it. No pictures on the walls, no personal belongings, not even a vase of flowers. There was nothing except what needed to be there for practical reasons. You could look upon that in a number of ways; Henry Kemp did not like clutter; Henry Kemp preferred his work space to have no distractions; Henry Kemp had never really settled here and made the space his own.

Captain O'Harris was opening the drawers of the desk.

"As I suspected, neat and precise also."

Clara looked over his shoulder. The drawers' contents were arranged by size, shape and function. This drawer contained a diary, fresh paper, a notebook and an unopened box of pencils. The next held an address book and a few invoices that needed attention. The bottom drawer held recent correspondence from various people Kemp dealt with in the course of his work. There were further drawers on the left side of the desk, these contained blank invoice sheets ready for use, reports on the prices of wine and information on competitors, along with a drawer of promotional material that Kemp could dip into whenever he needed, probably during a meeting with a client. Clara picked out a thick piece of paper from one drawer and saw that it was a composite draft for a new advertisement for Noble and Sons. Kemp had been in the process of making adjustments to it, marking it with a red pencil. She replaced it.

"Nothing to say why the man died," she reflected to O'Harris.

"He seems to have been very organised," O'Harris agreed. He took out an invoice from a drawer. "Will you look at this? Dated 1920. I hadn't realised I never paid my last bill."

O'Harris handed the invoice to Clara and she saw that it bore his address and name. A client number for the use of Noble and Sons was prominently displayed in a corner. Henry Kemp had made a note on the top – 'who is handling the estate?' The invoice had been drawn up just before O'Harris' fateful final plane flight, when he crashed into the ocean and was missing for over a year. No one knew what had happened to him and, legally, he could not be declared dead in his absence until had he been missing for seven years. Noble and Sons were stuck, the invoice unpaid because O'Harris' estate was in limbo until such a time as he was declared dead by a court.

Which had not happened, because O'Harris had returned.

"I ought to pay that," O'Harris nodded to the invoice.

"Not right now," Clara laughed at him.

"Well, no," O'Harris laughed back. "But at some point."

The office was not proving to be the treasure trove of information Clara had hoped for. If Simon Noble had a motive for killing Kemp, it seemed most likely it was related to the business; they had no real personal relationship after all. Yet there was no evidence, as far as

Clara could see, of any problems with Kemp's work. He seemed efficient and organised, though it would take a thorough examine of every file and invoice to truly rule out financial mismanagement or neglect. Henry Kemp would have been smart enough to mask any such behaviour from a casual observer.

There was a knock on the door of the office. Clara had left it open when they entered. An older man now poked his head around and looked in.

"Hello," Clara said politely.

The man stepped through the doorway. He was short with a nearly bald head, just wisps of white, cotton-like hair above his ears. He wore round spectacles with gold frames and a grey suit. He approached Clara and held out a hand.

"Mr Manfold," he said.

Clara shook his hand and then O'Harris came around the desk and shook it too.

"I am assistant manager here," Mr Manfold explained. "I have just been informed of the dreadful incidents of last night. I can barely believe it."

Mr Manfold clutched his hands together in an effort to mask that they were trembling.

"How long have you worked at the firm?" Clara asked him.

"Nearly thirty years," Manfold said. "I started in the warehouses and worked my way up. I became first a clerk in the office and then an assistant manager just as the war began."

"You've known Henry Kemp a long time, then?"

"All the time he has been here," Manfold agreed. "Assistant manager is really the limit of my progress. I can't go higher. The Nobles like people with a good foundation in maths. They have to have been to university for that."

Mr Manfold said all this with complete honesty and not even a hint of hurt or sarcasm. He was one of life's unassuming souls, who was grateful for every advantage attained, but not expecting of anything more. Clara was not sure whether to feel sorry for him or to admire his calm acceptance of a situation he could not change. Perhaps she might feel both?

"Have you noticed any problems with Henry Kemp recently?" Clara asked Manfold.

He ducked his head and a slight flush came to his cheeks as he lied.

"I don't know what you mean."

"Henry Kemp drank too much, and while he was working," Clara pointed out. A thought then struck her and she looked around the room again. "Actually, I am surprised I have not come across any bottles of alcohol in his office."

"Mr Kemp never drank in the office," Manfold replied, clearly deciding it wasn't worth continuing to lie. "He had his principals, even in his dissolution."

"Why did he drink?" O'Harris asked. "Most alcoholics have some sort of reason for regularly reducing themselves to oblivion. Was he depressed?"

"Mr Kemp was difficult to read," Manfold admitted. "I found him very private and wary of letting anyone know his thoughts. I worked with him nearly every day, yet I really can't say I knew him. I know more about Mr Brown who mans the front desk than I ever did about Mr Kemp."

"What about his relationship with the Nobles?" Clara asked.

Manfold looked worried, rather as if he had been asked to steal something from Arthur Noble's pocket. Clara guessed he was a man whose loyalty to his employer was largely based on his fear of losing his position.

"I shall not let them know you spoke to me," she promised him.

Manfold's face still bore the expression of a man who has just been told he has been condemned to hang in the morning.

"Arthur Noble has always been very supportive of me,"

he said, the words somewhat forced.

Clara doubted that statement.

"Did Arthur Noble come to this office often?"

"No. Maybe twice a week," Manfold admitted. "I rarely met with him. He always came to see Mr Kemp or to take part in a board meeting."

"What about Simon Noble?"

"He comes with his father," Manfold nodded.

"Have you ever noticed him arguing with Henry Kemp?"

Manfold's mouth dropped open. Clara might as well have asked him if the king liked to pop in for tea. He seemed more astonished by the question than anything.

"I have never heard a raised voice between Mr Kemp and the Nobles," he insisted.

Clara was disappointed. No one seemed to know of any reason that Simon Noble should wish Henry Kemp harm. It was proving very frustrating.

"When did you last see Mr Kemp?"

"Yesterday afternoon," Mr Manfold replied. "I was supposed to have the day off, but he asked me in as he had some issues with a couple of invoices."

"What sort of issues?" Clara asked.

"Oh, it was just a misunderstanding, really," Mr Manfold said quickly.

Clara felt his excuse was too hastily declared.

"Tell me about this misunderstanding," Clara persisted.

Mr Manfold hesitated and he clutched his hands together harder. He glanced briefly at the open door, acting as if he was regretting coming into the office. Finally, with Clara staring at him hard, he found he had to speak.

"A couple of clients had been accidentally invoiced twice," Mr Manfold explained. "One complained, the other unwittingly paid the surplus invoice before they realised. Clients can get very angry about such mishaps."

Clara could well imagine. The sort of people who used

Noble and Sons were cut very much in the cloth of the company's owners. They had money and they had power, they liked to hold onto the former and exert the latter.

"Mr Kemp had received a very unpleasant phone call from the gentleman who had paid twice for the same order. I do not know the details, but I believe it was rather upsetting and rude," Mr Manfold blushed even deeper as he confessed this about one of the company's customers. "Mr Kemp was upset and wanted to know how the error had happened. He summoned me and was almost in a fury when I arrived."

Mr Manfold seemed to tremble again at the memory.

"Mr Kemp very rarely loses his temper, but when he does…" Manfold licked his lips nervously. "We resolved it all, of course. It was just a mistake. Mr Kemp had asked me to complete the invoices and send them out during our busy season over Christmas. Normally he tracks all the invoices and checks each one before it is sent, but during the festivities time gets very tight. I did the invoices as asked, but Mr Kemp forgot he had told me to send them off immediately and wrote out his own. It was just a clerical error."

Clara felt that Mr Manfold was holding a lot back. A clerical error, maybe, but had it been made while Kemp was deep in drink? If that was the case, was it the first sign that Kemp's drinking was starting to interfere with his work?

"Mr Kemp was rather concerned that one of the clients might be at the same New Year's party yesterday as him," Manfold continued. "I noticed he had a glass of whisky on his desk, which was most unusual."

"Henry Kemp did not handle customer complaints well?" Clara surmised.

Manfold looked wary of the question, like it might be a trick. Slowly he responded.

"Mr Kemp hated people criticising him or feeling that he had done something wrong. He was upset yesterday. When he realised the situation was his own fault, I think it made him feel worse. He apologised to me and then said I could go," Manfold's gaze moved to the desk in the middle of the room. "An accidental extra invoice is no reason to kill a man, is it?"

"No," Clara agreed.

"I am so sorry for Mr Kemp," Manfold was rubbing his hands together now in his distress. "I thought a lot of him. He was a very good manager."

"Except for the drinking," O'Harris prodded him. "People keep telling us how wonderful Kemp was, which is all very well, but it does not tell us why anyone would want to kill him. I rather feel people are being altogether too nice."

Mr Manfold took a shaky breath.

"Mr Kemp was very good at this job," Manfold insisted. "He had his demons. What they were I cannot say, he never discussed them, but they were there nonetheless. They were what made him drink. They were destroying him slowly."

Manfold deliberately took a pace back from Clara.

"I have to returned to my work," he said. "I am sorry I could be of no real help."

He scuttled away. Captain O'Harris gave a snort after he was gone.

"No one has a bad word to say about Kemp!"

"There has to be something," Clara replied. "Only, it is not in this office. I think we need to pay a call on his parents. The man downstairs should be able to tell us where to find them. They deserve to know what happened to their son."

O'Harris had no quarrel with that. They left Kemp's immaculate office, feeling no further forward. Kemp kept his secrets close. Even so, something had happened between him and Simon Noble. Something that had resulted in a very deadly series of events.

Chapter Twenty-one

Henry Kemp's parents lived in Hove. It therefore made logical sense to visit them first, before Clara headed for home and the opportunity to deposit her luggage and change her clothes. She did, however, ask the young man at the desk downstairs if she might use the company telephone first. There was a telephone exchange in a small room behind his desk. Clara had noticed the door as they came downstairs. Many of the lines were internal and, during a normal working day, a girl would be stationed in the room to connect calls. Currently she was not around, the offices operating with so few people that day that it was unlikely anyone would need to use the telephone.

There was an outside line for the telephones as well as an internal one. Customers and suppliers could all communicate with Noble and Sons via the telephone wires and from the comfort of their own offices. A number of Clara's neighbours would have found this astonishing, even though the telephone was not precisely new. But to have one in your own home was still a novelty for many. Clara was one of the few exceptions; her work meant a phone line directly to her house was essential.

"It will only be a quick call, to let my housekeeper

know why I have not returned home yet," Clara patiently explained to the man, who was looking deeply reluctant to comply.

She didn't add that Annie, her friend and housekeeper, would become very anxious about her wellbeing if she did not arrive home when expected. Especially if she learned police had been called to the Mary Jane. Gossip like that spread swiftly through a town and Annie always seemed to be well-connected to the gossip grapevine.

"It is not for the use of the public," the young man said at last, his face illustrating his uncertainty.

"Then, perhaps you can make the call? All I need you to do is pass on a message about why I have been delayed," Clara then began to dictate to him an unnecessarily long and complicated message that he should relay word perfect to Annie.

As she had hoped, panic came over the young man's face as he was confronted with this epic dialogue which he could not possibly hope to pass on correctly. He hastily interrupted Clara.

"Maybe you best relay it yourself," he conceded. "No one will know."

Clara, triumphant but masking her satisfaction, smiled politely.

"How kind."

She was allowed into the telephone room and the young man made sure the wires were connected to enable outside calls. Then he left her in peace. The phone barely rang before a breathless Annie picked it up.

"Hello!"

"Hello Annie," Clara said pleasantly.

"Clara! Where are you? Maud Mumford came by and said there were policemen swarming all over the Mary Jane! She saw them when she went to the docks to see if she could get any haddock for supper. No one is being allowed off the ship!"

"Inspector Park-Coombs made an exception for me," Clara replied. "I am currently in Hove pursuing a matter for him."

"Oh Clara! Can't you even go for a night out without stumbling onto a crime?"

"Apparently not," Clara replied, a little hurt by the suggestion, as if she could not enjoy herself unless someone was being murdered. "Anyway, I thought I best let you know where I am."

"How did you get to Hove?" Annie asked in amazement.

"Captain O'Harris called for a car," Clara explained. "His driver brought it over."

There was a short pause on the line and Clara could almost feel Annie's grin. She realised suddenly that the knowledge was making her blush. She was relieved Captain O'Harris could not see.

"The captain is still with you?" Annie asked.

"He is assisting me," Clara agreed, trying to make it sound very bland and practical.

"Assisting?" Annie said with a chuckle. "He really is smitten, isn't he?"

"Oh Annie!"

"Well? Is he not? A dinner of dancing and celebrating was interrupted by a crime you have somehow got yourself involved in solving, and he is still sticking with you," Annie sighed happily. "I was wrong about him before. I thought he was reckless and irresponsible. I've had time to change my mind. When you are all done, make sure you bring him home for dinner."

"I will," Clara smiled. "And Happy New Year to you and Tommy. Did you have a good evening?"

"Tommy insisted we stay up until midnight," Annie gave a small huff. She deemed eleven o'clock a little late for bed, midnight was unthinkable. Her parents had been farmers and she was raised to early nights and early mornings. "Then he fell asleep in the armchair at ten. I had to wake him before the clock chimed."

Clara laughed.

"As long as you got to wish in the New Year

170

together!"

The embarrassed silence that followed told Clara that it was now Annie's turn to blush.

"We saw it in just like any other day really," Annie said, somewhat brusquely. "I'm going to cook a steak and kidney pie for dinner. I'll make extra for the captain."

Annie always made far too much, even when they did not have guests, but Clara said nothing.

"That will be lovely," she responded. "I shall see you later."

"Yes, and get this thing solved before you do. I always prefer my dinner when you are not mulling over a case. You and Tommy will insist on discussing the details. Nothing worse than having a murder debated over the salt and pepper pots."

"Sorry Annie," Clara apologised. "I promise we won't discuss it, even if I haven't solved it before tea."

"Hmph," Annie huffed down the line. "I'll believe that when I see it!"

Clara returned to O'Harris in the front hall of Noble and Sons.

"You are invited to dinner," she told him. "I am informed it will be steak and kidney pie."

"Lovely," O'Harris grinned. "And, let me guess, Annie wants this case solved before then so we aren't late for dinner?"

Clara raised an eyebrow at him, wondering if he had been listening into her conversation.

"Isn't that what Annie always wants?" O'Harris added, as they walked to the front door.

"True," Clara said. Annie's one rule in life, that Clara was horrific for breaking, was that everyone should be home in time for dinner. "We best not let her down."

"We'll never hear the end of it if we do!"

Clara hid the smile of delight that nearly crept onto her face. O'Harris was beginning to think of himself as part of the Fitzgerald household and therefore under the stern auspices of Annie. That made Clara not just happy, it gave her a strange little thrill inside. She was not yet prepared to admit to herself that her feelings for O'Harris went beyond friendship. She was still feeling stung by the terrible grief that had engulfed her when he disappeared. It was not his fault, but it still left her a touch wary.

Captain O'Harris' driver was waiting by the car. The rain had eased a little, but the grey clouds overhead threatened a great deal more before the day was done. He opened the rear door for Clara and O'Harris.

"Where to now, Sir?" he asked as he climbed in the front.

"It's a place called Primrose Cottage at the bottom of Trumpery Lane. I think I'll need to find a map," O'Harris mused.

"Not to worry, Sir," Jones opened the glove compartment and produced a recently purchased map of Brighton and Hove. "I came prepared."

Jones glanced back at them with a sheepish grin.

"Good man," O'Harris laughed.

"I'm learning," Jones answered. "Thought the map was a good idea, however."

He unfolded the paper map and pinpointed their location. Then he started scanning the names of the roads around it for Trumpery Lane.

"I don't imagine it will be terribly far from here," Clara sat forward and leaned on the back of the front passenger seat. "Henry Kemp bought the place when he moved down here. He would not have picked somewhere miles away."

Jones was running a finger over the map. A horse and cart rattled past outside, the horse sploshing through the puddles forming on the road.

"Here's Trumpery Lane," Jones indicated the spot. "There aren't any cottages listed."

"Private homes do not always appear," O'Harris said. "At least we have a place to start."

They drove to the location on the map. The rain began again as they headed from the urban areas of Hove into the surrounding countryside. Clara judged that it would take perhaps half-an-hour on a bicycle for Henry Kemp to reach Noble and Sons. Longer if he was walking, of course. There might be a bus he could catch, but the services outside of the main roads of town were usually infrequent and not always conveniently timed.

Trumpery Lane contained no more than five old cottages spread out along the twisting road. They appeared to all have names rather than numbers. Jones drove slowly so they could see each clearly. Primrose Cottage proved to be on the right-hand side, situated between a place that called itself Half-Acre Farm and a house called The Hawthorns. Each property had large tracts of land around it. Primrose Cottage also stood on a sizeable plot; though not a big cottage, it was surrounded by a large garden, the front of which was currently looking bedded down for the winter, but in the summer was probably a riot of colour. Clara could only guess at the names of half of the plants and shrubs planted there, but she could see enough to know that when they were blooming it would look like a true cottage garden, the sort magazines like to reprint photographs of.

The cottage itself looked to be sixteenth century or thereabouts. It was whitewashed, but the old timbers were visible and had been painted black. The contrast was stark on the dull, grey day, especially with the grey thatch roof cresting the entire building. A pea green door was set in the middle of the house with a deep window on the right and a slightly smaller one on the left. A brick chimney popped up from the thatch and blossomed with coal smoke. There was a peacefulness about the entire place. As Clara stepped through the garden gate she felt awful that she was about to disturb that peace with some truly terrible news.

With Captain O'Harris just a step behind her she approached the pea green door and stood on the small step before it. She knocked on the wood and held her breath a little as she waited.

"I don't like being the bearer of bad news," Clara whispered to O'Harris as he stood just behind her.

"This is not your fault," he pointed out.

"That is not how people always see things," Clara said. "Blame tends to fall on the nearest person handy, even when they don't deserve it."

She was silenced by the handle of the door turning and a woman appearing before them. She was tall and very thin, perhaps unhealthily so. She wore a green dress a few shades darker than the front door and extremely thick stockings. The ensemble ended in a pair of red tartan slippers lined with lamb's wool. She had a narrow, pinched face. The mouth seemingly screwed up in a perpetual expression of rebuke and her eyes small behind a pair or wire-frame glasses. Even when wearing the glasses she appeared to be constantly squinting at Clara. Her hair was in the process of going completely white, though it retained a hint of golden brown in places. She did not look welcoming.

"Who are you?" she demanded.

"I apologise for the interruption," Clara began as politely as she could. "I am Miss Clara Fitzgerald, this is Captain O'Harris. We have some unfortunate news concerning your son, Mr Henry Kemp. You are Mrs Kemp?"

"I am," Mrs Kemp answered. "What has happened to Henry?"

She looked a little confused and the colour was draining from her face.

"Is it very bad news?"

"It is, I am afraid," Clara saw no reason to beat about the bush, drawing things out was only more torturous for the person involved. Better to have it out in the open and face the consequences then to hum and ha over the matter. "Henry was stabbed last night while aboard the liner Mary Jane."

"Stabbed?" The woman started to shake. "He was with his firm, on a night out. They always celebrate New

174

Year's together."

"Yes. That is true. There was a moment when Henry found himself alone and someone attacked him. I am so very sorry."

Mrs Kemp pressed a hand to the middle of her chest and seemed to sway backwards.

"I think you ought to sit down," Clara said hastily, reaching out an arm to steady the woman.

"What's going on out there, Ethel?" A man's voice called from the room on their right.

Ethel Kemp blinked fast.

"You need to come through and explain this to Henry's father," she said to Clara.

Then she turned and marched into the front room. Clara hesitated for a second, then she shrugged her shoulders at Captain O'Harris and followed.

The front room was furnished in further shades of green. The large sofa and two armchairs were upholstered in green leather, the shade reminding Clara of pond weed. The floor was wooden, but a large rug covered most of it. Lamps were dotted about the room, there was no electricity in the cottage, no overhead lights, so the lamps contained oil, though there were also candles in brackets on the walls. The space in-between them was taken up with pale, insipid watercolour landscapes. A coal fire burned in a large brick fireplace at the far side of the room. It was billowing smoke into the room as well and Clara guessed the chimney needed a sweep.

Lying on the sofa, his legs covered by a blanket, was an old man who Clara guessed was Henry's father. There was a similarity between the man and his late son. Mr Kemp looked his age, which had to be somewhere in his sixties. He was incredibly thin, like his wife, and with the same pinched, almost anxious expression. They looked like people who always expected the worst. Mr Kemp examined Clara and O'Harris with wary eyes. He rumpled the blanket in his hands, clutching onto its edge like it would save him from impending disaster.

"What is it Ethel? Who are these people? What has happened?"

Ethel Kemp took a long, deep breath, then, in a tone of doom – like a judge pronouncing a death sentence – she spoke to her husband;

"Henry is dead, Bill. Our son has been murdered."

Chapter Twenty-two

"Murdered?" Bill Kemp's eyes stared at Clara, the shock of what he had just heard making his gaze glassy and fixed. "I don't understand."

Ethel Kemp collapsed suddenly into the armchair near him and dropped her head into her hands.

"Who would want to harm my boy?" She wept to herself, the tears hard to fall, but her emotion plain.

Clara hated these moments. There was no easy way of explaining to someone that their loved one was dead. She dreaded being the bearer of bad news and yet, in the line of work she had chosen, it had become a necessary evil. She wished Simon Noble was here to see the distress he had caused Henry Kemp's parents. Then again, it was just as likely he would not have cared.

"I am so very sorry," Clara said, knowing her empathy sounded hollow under the circumstances.

"What happened to him?" Bill Kemp asked her, his gaze still fixed and odd, as if he was looking without actually seeing.

"Last night someone stabbed your son," Clara explained. There was no point peppering the statement with polite euphemisms. Nothing could change the facts and bluntness could be easier at times. "The police and I are still trying to work out precisely what occurred."

"Who are you?" Ethel Kemp abruptly demanded, raising her head and glaring at Clara.

Clara knew the hostility was more due to the news she had just heard than any real anger towards herself.

"I am a private detective," Clara explained patiently. "When your son was found, the ship we were all on was out at sea and the police could not be easily summoned. I happened to be aboard as a guest and was asked to investigate the matter discreetly, to determine what had led to Henry's unfortunate predicament."

"But the police are involved now?" Bill Kemp asked.

"Yes," Clara replied. "I have offered my assistance to them and they have accepted it. I am working with them to bring Henry's killer to justice."

"We cannot pay you," Ethel Kemp said sharply and Clara now saw a hint of why she was so aggressive towards her. She thought Clara was there to ask for money to pursue the case.

"Ethel…" Bill Kemp glanced at his wife reproachfully.

"I am not here to seek money from you," Clara explained, keeping her voice level and polite. "That is not how I work. I am here because of one thing, I want to bring a killer to justice."

"You know who did this thing?" Bill Kemp turned back to her, the light was returning to his eyes and he seemed to be growing more alert.

"I am fairly certain who did this," Clara admitted.

"Then arrest him!" Ethel Kemp nearly screamed at her. Her husband reached out his hand and patted her arm comfortingly.

"There is not enough evidence to do so," Clara continued steadily. "The person suspected has denied everything. That is why I am here. If I can find a motive for the crime, then I shall be a step closer to proving the person I suspect committed this murder."

Bill Kemp nodded, his face solemn. He, at least, understood.

"What motive could anyone have to kill Henry?" Ethel was growing more and more hysterical in her grief. In such a state, Clara doubted she would be much help.

"Mrs Kemp, I wonder if you would benefit from a strong cup of tea?" Captain O'Harris interjected, as if reading Clara's mind. "I would make you one, if you cared to direct me to the kitchen?"

The thought of a strange man rummaging about in her kitchen had the desired affect on Ethel Kemp. She rose from her seat and insisted that she would make the cup of tea herself. The distraction had calmed her a little.

"I'll help carry it through," O'Harris said, following her out of the room and leaving Clara with an opportunity to speak to Bill Kemp alone.

Bill had watched his wife leave, now he let out a long sigh and turned to Clara.

"Please sit down. I apologise for my wife. Henry is... was our only child and she was always very protective of him."

Clara sat in an armchair angled towards Bill Kemp.

"I wish I was not the bearer of this bad news," Clara said to him. "As far as I have been able to establish, Henry Kemp was not a man to attract enemies and the least likely person to imagine someone wishing harm to."

"Henry was innocuous," Bill Kemp said with a self-deprecating smile. "I say that openly. He was good at his job, but he would not say boo to a goose. Never had a strong opinion in his life, that boy. He drifted along, excelling at what he turned his hand to, without ever attracting attention to himself."

"Not the sort of person you expect to come to harm," Clara noted.

"Never that," Bill Kemp agreed. "His mother rather overshadowed him, unfortunately. I should have been firmer with Ethel, but we had lost two children already and she was exceptionally fretful over Henry. I couldn't find the courage to speak out. He thrived, anyway, he got a good job and bought us this lovely cottage."

Bill Kemp motioned to the room around him, which was indeed cosy and pleasant.

"I lost both legs in an accident before the war," Bill Kemp carried on, the words stated without emotion. "I still feel them, though. The doctors tell me it is all in my head, well, perhaps it is. But some days the pain I feel in those missing limbs is excruciating. I will admit that I am not a nice person to be around then. Ethel was struggling to look after me. We lived in a house in Brighton back then. I couldn't get upstairs, naturally, and there were several steps leading out the front and back doors too. So, I was stuck in the house, trapped mainly in the front parlour and I became very unhappy.

"Henry was working in London at the time. He was very successful. His mother wrote him often about my condition and our problems, he saw them for himself when he came down at the weekend. Then, one day, out of the blue, he said he had found a job in Hove and was going to buy a cottage where we could all live. I was stunned. I took him aside and asked him if he knew what he was doing and that he should not destroy his career for my sake. But Henry insisted the job in Hove was just as good as that in London.

"Well, as you can see he was good to his word. He found this lovely cottage for us. No stairs for me to worry about and a beautiful garden I can sit in during the summer. Ethel can even manage to get my wheelchair in and out the front door, over the little step. We go for walks when the weather is good. It really has made such a difference."

Bill Kemp became very silent. His eyes had fallen on his hands resting on the blanket. His mouth fell slightly open and his lower lip trembled. Emotion now began to get the better of him.

"If I had known moving here would lead to Henry's death, I would rather have killed myself than allowed it," his voice shook as he spoke.

"Who could know?" Clara said to him gently.

"Who do you suspect of this crime?" Bill Kemp asked her swiftly, his head tilting towards her.

"I would rather not say until I can prove my case," Clara replied, not wanting to reveal it was Henry's employer who had stabbed him.

"And you can't prove it without a motive?"

"It will be difficult," Clara agreed.

Bill Kemp considered this for a moment.

"Henry did not make enemies, not like some people. I cannot think why anyone would wish him harm."

They were going around in circles and soon Ethel would be back. Clara was not sure they would get another chance to talk so freely. Ethel Kemp struck her as the sort of person who would not allow a bad word to be said against her son, even if that meant failing to catch his killer.

"Did Henry ever mention the people he worked with?" Clara asked Bill. "Miss Jane Dodd, for instance? Or Mr Charles Walsh."

"I have heard him mention both those names," Bill Kemp answered at once, looking hopeful that he could provide useful information at last. "Mr Walsh came to the cottage once or twice when they needed to work out a tricky contract or something. Henry hated going all the way into Hove on the weekends. Mr Walsh seemed very pleasant. He did not…?"

"Mr Walsh is accounted for at the time of your son's death. I do not think he was involved. He is very upset as well."

"I don't know this Jane Dodd," Bill Kemp frowned.

"She was the secretary at Noble and Sons."

"Was?" Bill had been alert to Clara's use of the past tense.

Clara hesitated, she wasn't sure how much of the full extent of the tragedy of last night she should reveal. In the end, she could not see how it would hurt for Bill Kemp to know that someone else cared extremely deeply for his son.

"Miss Dodd lost her life last night too," Clara said.

At that moment Ethel Kemp reappeared in the room.

"What is this? Someone else died last night?" She had composed herself and looked like the woman who had greeted them on the doorstep. Her face was slightly hard and her pinched expression had returned. Clara was beginning to think that Ethel Kemp was an extremely highly-strung person who thrust down all her inner emotions deep inside. The pinched expression was caused by her constant repression of her feelings. What would happen if she unleashed them? Perhaps Ethel Kemp did not want to know.

"Among the Noble and Sons party last night was a lady called Miss Jane Dodd," Clara explained to Ethel. "She was the secretary for Arthur Noble, but was frequently in and out of your son's office as part of her duties. She had known Henry since he began with Noble and Sons and she thought a lot of him. She took his death very hard and threw herself overboard."

Bill Kemp gasped at this news. His wife glowered.

"What would she do a silly thing like that for?" She demanded.

"I believe she cared very deeply for Henry," Clara explained.

"Huh!" Ethel Kemp's scowl had deepened. "Well, my Henry knew better than to get involved with a woman. He was loyal to his mother."

Captain O'Harris was stood behind Mrs Kemp and he cast a wide-eyed look of amazement at Clara. She was concentrating on Ethel.

"You did not want your son to marry?" She asked.

"Certainly, certainly," Ethel Kemp quickly backtracked. "But he would never find anyone who knew how to take care of him like I do. I know all his quirks and dislikes. There was no woman out there good enough for him. So, I don't know what this Miss Dodd was doing getting herself all emotional over him."

Bill Kemp cast an apologetic look in Clara's direction.

He lifted his hands up, the palms out in a gesture of – see what I mean? Clara was beginning to feel sorry for Henry.

Ethel Kemp was laying out the tea things on a small table she had brought before the sofa.

"Henry had a good life with us. We are comfortable," she carried on. "How could anyone compete with that? What did he need with someone else? Some stranger? Henry was never good at making friends, he was a family person."

The cups rattled rather fiercely in their saucers as she plonked them down.

"Henry did not need company. He was content by himself."

Clara wanted to interrupt this rant and point out that Ethel Kemp had made that decision for her son, and that he had been too 'innocuous', as his father had put it, to fight her. However, there was little sense in offending the woman. Henry was dead and whatever he had needed or did not need was now a moot point.

"Henry Kemp knew a lot about wine," Clara changed the subject.

"He knew what he needed to know," Ethel Kemp maintained. "He was extremely professional."

"What did he drink when he was at home?" Clara was trying to ease into the topic of Henry's heavy drinking. There was no way Ethel would allow her son to be called an alcoholic in her presence, but she might let something useful slip.

"Drink at home?" Ethel Kemp looked at Clara in amazement. "There is not a drop of drink in this house! We are a teetotal family. Something that always made me uncomfortable with Henry's work. None of us ever touched a drop."

Clara was so stunned by this response that for a second she could not think what to say. Bill Kemp was staring at her, something about his face suggesting he wanted to speak, but didn't dare before his wife. He suddenly turned to Ethel.

"My dear, I feel the need for one of my pain tablets," he said.

"Oh Bill," Ethel sighed. "Can't it wait until after we have drunk tea?"

"No, my dear," Bill said, pulling a face. "I am starting to feel so uncomfortable."

Ethel Kemp looked at Clara with an expression of apology.

"I shall go and fetch it."

She rose and left. Bill Kemp turned to Clara sharply.

"The pill has to be dissolved in water, it will take her a while. I was aware that Henry was drinking. Up until recently he never had a drop in the house, but, the last few weeks I had a hunch he was drinking in his bedroom. He keeps it locked, so his mother cannot get in."

Clara found this intriguing. If there was any clue as to a motive for Henry's murder, she hoped it might be among his private belongings.

"Might I take a look in his room?" She asked Bill Kemp.

"You may," Bill said. "But you will need to find the key. Henry always kept it with him."

Clara was puzzled; they had not found a key on Henry.

"Henry began drinking more heavily in recent months," Captain O'Harris said. "Do you have any ideas why?"

Bill Kemp pursed his lips.

"Henry was very private, but I am certain something was upsetting him. He was not himself," Bill rubbed at his lower lip. "It was as if he knew a secret that was gnawing at him. I was worried for him."

"A secret?" Clara became excited. "A secret that, perhaps, cost him his life?"

Chapter Twenty-three

Ethel Kemp did not like the idea of anyone entering her son's bedroom.

"It was his private space."

"Ethel, my dear, Henry is gone and these people are trying their hardest to discover who killed him. If they can find a clue to his murderer in his bedroom, surely that is a good thing?" Bill Kemp spoke patiently.

His wife's mouth twisted and turned like she was sucking on an extremely sour sweet.

"Henry never let me in there," she declared, and Clara felt that here was the nub of the problem.

Ethel Kemp was an extremely jealous and insecure woman. She wanted to pry into every detail of her son's life and control him so completely that he never did anything outside of her direction. Henry Kemp had countered that in one small way, by preventing her from accessing his bedroom. It was the one place where he could be in complete privacy.

Clara speculated that some of Henry's drinking issues stemmed from his unhealthy relationship with his mother and her ability to overpower him and make him feel as if his life was not his own. It still amazed Clara at how selfish some people could be, and how they muddled up that selfishness with caring for someone. Henry had been surrounded by people who used him for their own ends while never giving a thought for how he was affected. Not just his mother, but the Noble family who had treated his murder as an awkward inconvenience. And then there was Simon Noble who, no doubt, killed Henry for his own selfish ends. Only Miss Dodd had truly cared about him.

"Henry kept nothing personal in his office," Clara explained to Ethel Kemp as patiently as Bill Kemp had spoken to his wife, though she was really rather fed-up with the delay. "There might be something in his bedroom that could tell me why he was killed. A diary, perhaps, or a letter. Some clue that I can present to the police as evidence."

"It's locked," Ethel grumbled, clutching to a final straw. "Henry said there had to be some place I could not go. He said it to my face."

Ethel looked affronted.

"He wouldn't even let me clean in there!"

"The lock might be breakable," Captain O'Harris said to Clara.

"Breakable!" Ethel Kemp gasped in horror.

"Ethel!" Bill Kemp was doing his best to sit up on the sofa, his face was flushed with anger. "Let them in the damn room! Our son is dead! Do you not hear yourself? Dead and you argue about such stupidity as a locked room!"

"Do not call me stupid, Bill," Ethel rebuked him, but her voice wavered with tears. "I can't see how entering Henry's bedroom will bring him back."

"It won't!" Bill replied to her in exasperation. "But it might mean they can find the proof that will put a killer behind bars! I want to see justice done for our son, even if you don't!"

"I never said I didn't!" Tears fell down Ethel's face. "You are too harsh to me Bill Kemp. Henry was my blessing, my precious boy. I shall never be the same without him."

"Let them in the damn room!"

"Do not swear at me!" Ethel screamed. "None of you know how I am feeling, none of you! I have lost my boy, my only boy! Nothing will ever be the same, nothing! You can all do as you please, but leave me alone!"

With that, Ethel Kemp fled from the room and a moment later they heard the slamming of a door. She had retreated to her bedroom.

"I apologise for that," Bill said softly. "Ethel has been blind for so long to what others need. I should have stood up to her while Henry was alive. I should have made him move out, but he felt duty-bound to look after us. We have no income other than what Henry brings in."

Bill Kemp paused.

"It was just easier to say nothing. I am a cripple and I need Ethel's help. I suppose I felt fighting her too strongly would be to my detriment, so I allowed her to overwhelm Henry and keep him from having a real life away from us. I am not proud of the fact. It took his death to realise how much I had simply taken him for granted."

Bill pulled the blanket up a little, using it as a sort of protection from the world, like hiding beneath the bedsheets at night when a noise scares you. He was a very frightened man, one whose own life had been taken out of his control. He was completely dependent on Ethel for the most mundane of tasks, and the flipside of that dependency was that she was able to take charge of every aspect of his existence. The distress and despair this caused him was palpable.

"Go open Henry's room any way you have to," Bill said quietly. "I'll deal with Ethel. And, find the person who did this to my son."

"I will," Clara promised him. Then she left the room and stood in the hall for a moment, glancing about to see which room might have been Henry's.

The cottage was almost square and the hallways formed a cross in its centre, dividing it into quarters. At the front was the parlour where Bill Kemp sat and opposite was the kitchen. The hall was then intersected by another corridor that ran behind the two front rooms. Three doors faced onto this corridor. At least two were bedrooms and Clara guessed the third would be for some sort of bathroom. Bill Kemp would need a bespoke space for his personal needs, preferably indoors. These three rooms were split unevenly by the main hallway, which ran from the front door to a backdoor that was almost perfectly opposite the former. The unevenness of the divide meant that the room on the right of the hallway stood alone and was slighter bigger than the bedroom on the left, which had some of its space taken up by the bathroom. Clara's instinct was that the room on the right was Henry's. His father would need easy access to the bathroom and it made better sense for his parents to have the left bedroom.

Clara walked over to the door and depressed the metal handle, it was old and curved, made of iron and then painted black. The handle dropped but the door did not budge.

"Can I have a look?" O'Harris asked from behind her.

Clara stepped out of his way and he jiggled the handle up and down thoughtfully a few times, before crouching down and staring through the keyhole.

"It's a pretty old lock," he said. "We have some similar in my house. I learned how to pick them. We had one on a cupboard that was rather prone to locking itself. The key had been lost to it years ago, so we learned how to crudely pick it. Saves on calling out the locksmith."

"You could have changed the lock," Clara pointed out.

"You don't stay rich in this day and age by spending money frivolously," O'Harris grinned at her.

He depressed the handle again.

"What I need is a screwdriver, or something similar."

Clara walked to the kitchen and started to search through the drawers. She half expected Ethel Kemp to appear and berate her for going through her kitchen, but the woman did not emerge from the bedroom. Clara was feeling ashamed that things had reached such a point that the woman had snapped. She surely could have handled the situation better?

Clara was mulling over all this when she opened a drawer and came upon a selection of work tools, including a screwdriver with a wooden handle. Carved into the handle were the initials W.K. Bill Kemp. Bill was usually a nickname for a man called William. Clara had not asked what work Bill Kemp had done before his accident. Now she noted that all the tools in the drawer had the same initials on them. She picked out the screwdriver and headed back to O'Harris.

"Will this do?"

O'Harris took the screwdriver and nodded. He worked it in the lock and depressed the handle carefully, before pressing on the door to take the weight off the lock. He squinted into the keyhole and raised and lowered the head of the screwdriver.

"I can see the latch," he said. "These old locks, the keyhole is positively enormous. There is a little spring, if I can just…"

There was a click and O'Harris fell forward as the door unlocked and opened. He went to his knees and gave a laugh of surprise.

"Easier than the old cupboard!" He declared.

Clara pushed the door back further and looked into Henry Kemp's private world. She had not really given thought as to what to expect, but she had never imagined the room would be such a mess. Henry Kemp's office had been pristine, almost obsessively neat. His bedroom was the opposite.

Dirty clothes had been discarded on the floor. The bed was unmade and the blankets were slipping off the edge while one pillow appeared to have been hurled across the room. Shoes lay where they had been kicked off and books from the spacious book shelf were scattered everywhere. Some were lying open, spine upwards, as if Henry had been in the process of reading them and had become distracted. Loose papers were also everywhere, but mainly in piles on the bed, on a desk in the room, on a chest of drawers, and in several stacks here and there. Perched on top of one, and looking about ready to fall off, was a typewriter, a page still sitting in it with the last lines Henry had typed displayed.

As Clara stepped into the room she noted that everything was thick with dust, except where Henry routinely placed and removed things. The top of the chest of drawers was grey, but there were finger marks in the dust where Henry had apparently grabbed the edge. The rug had not been beaten in ages and was flecked with specks of dirt and crumbs of food. The floor needed a sweep too. Clara could see little balls of fluff and hair that had crept into the corners and gave away that a broom had not entered this room in some time. Cobwebs hung from the ceiling edges and the windows. Clara guessed there were more under the bed and behind the furniture.

Captain O'Harris picked up what was the most obvious feature of the room; he held in his hand a bottle of whisky, empty. There were dozens of bottles all about the room. In one corner they had been precariously stacked into a tower, others were discarded on the floor or were perched on whatever surface was handy. If there had been any doubts about Henry's drinking habits the bottles swept them away. There was a smell in the room, stale and alcoholic, rather like an ill-kept pub. Henry Kemp's personal space revealed a man who was rapidly unravelling, who was struggling to keep up the façade of being all right. He was a man in chaos, whose life was faltering out-of-control and the only place he could express his real anguish was in the bedroom he kept locked up.

"Makes you want to open a window," O'Harris said as he stepped inside. "Here is the real Henry Kemp."

Clara picked up a shaving kit from the chest of drawers. There were elements of the room where the neat, fastidious Henry emerged. The shaving kit was one of them. Kept in a wooden box, each item had been washed and dried after use and replaced with care. The same could be said about Henry's clean clothes which were hung up in the wardrobe with precision and military-style order. But, then again, these were the parts of Henry's world that enabled him to keep up his façade outside his room. He had to keep them tidy.

"Poetry," O'Harris had picked up one of the books from the floor and was reading the title. "He liked poetry, but the dark, morose stuff."

He flicked through a few pages.

"Utterly depressing if you ask me," he closed the book and placed it on the bedside cabinet.

"Cycling magazines," Clara picked up a magazine with an illustration of a man riding a bicycle speedily down a country lane on the front. "That was his passion."

"Not his only one," O'Harris had removed the partially typed sheet of paper from the typewriter. "It seems he was something of an amateur poet himself."

O'Harris frowned as he read the lines.

"It must be rather New Age stuff, I don't understand it."

Clara had picked up a piece of paper from a stack nearest her and discovered the same thing. A series of lines were typed on it, presumably they were meant to be poetry, but they almost struck her as gibberish. She imagined Henry became inspired when he was drinking and the results were these strange contortions of words.

"This one is about the war," O'Harris said, having started to go through a pile of papers. "At least I think it is. There is stuff about mud and people being blown to pieces."

"Henry served in the war," Clara nodded. "Perhaps another reason he drank?"

"Certainly that whole bloody affair left its taint on everyone who went through it," O'Harris said grimly. "Was this Henry Kemp's way of coping?"

"I don't think any stretch of the imagination can call

this 'coping'," Clara glanced about the room at its dust and cobwebs and its many, many empty whisky bottles.

"Oh heavens!"

They both glanced to the door and saw that Ethel Kemp had appeared on the threshold of the room. On seeing the state of the bedroom she had put her hands to her mouth to stifle her shock. Her eyes drifted about the room, taking in each new horror as she came across it. The whisky bottles made her eyes go wide.

"I never imagined…" she looked a little pale and put out a hand to lean on the chest of drawers, at once taking it off again as she felt the soft dust beneath her fingers. "Oh Henry."

"It is going to take us a while to go through this all," Clara explained to her.

Ethel was not listening. She had lifted up a whisky bottle and was staring at it like it was some exotic article she had never seen in her life before.

"Henry didn't drink," she said to herself.

Clara glanced at O'Harris. He shrugged his shoulders. Ethel Kemp could not be prevented from seeing the revelations of Henry's true existence now.

"I'll start with the papers this side of the room, while you do those over there?" He offered.

Clara agreed. With a last glance at Mrs Kemp, who was still examining the whisky bottle in some horror, she set to work, hoping to find something among the poems and scraps of paper that would tell her why Henry Kemp had to die.

Chapter Twenty-four

The utter disarray of her son's room had at least given Ethel Kemp something to think about other than his death. She fetched her dusting rags and a broom, along with a mop and bucket, and began the process of giving everything a good clean. It was quite obviously a job she had wanted to do for some time, though she could not have envisaged the state he had allowed the room to get into. She said nothing about the whisky bottles, but collected them up with an expression of distaste, loading them into a large cardboard box she had found.

Clara and O'Harris had to work around her, sorting through the piles of papers as swiftly as they could, before Ethel Kemp came past with her broom and insisted she needed to sweep where they were standing. Clara felt the need to go through the drawers of the furniture before Mrs Kemp could get to them and potentially remove something. She did not think the woman malicious, as such, but she might spot something she thought Clara should not see and, out of prudence, take up what could be a valuable clue.

Henry Kemp's chest of drawers revealed nothing more than might be expected; socks and underwear, ties and neatly rolled leather belts. One drawer contained boxes of expensive cufflinks and tie pins.

"He received them every year at Christmas from Mr Noble," Ethel Kemp said, looking over Clara's shoulder as she went past with her bucket of soapy water. "I dread to think how much they cost."

Clara moved on to the bedside table, which O'Harris had managed to unearth from a pile of loose papers, books and discarded pyjamas. His own searches had yet to turn up anything beyond poem after poem, and the odd piece of prose. There were often several versions of the same poem, each typed on its own sheet of paper and numbered at the top in pencil to show which variant they were.

"He had enough material for several volumes," O'Harris remarked, looking slightly fed-up at sorting through the reams of rhyming couplets.

"I can't offer any insight into poetry," Clara shook her head. "It largely all goes beyond me. I don't mind a little rhyme, but some of the more high-brow stuff leaves me cold."

"You are too practical for poetry," O'Harris grinned at her. "This stuff is for people who live in the clouds all day and end up residing in rooms like this."

O'Harris glanced about the room, his eyes pausing on the cobwebs and dusty surfaces.

"Henry Kemp was hardly impractical," Clara pointed out.

"No, but he had to work hard at it. This was the real him, the man he wanted to be. Well, sort of."

"Maybe I'll stick with being practical then," Clara observed.

She opened the top drawer of the bedside cabinet and the first thing that came to light was a leather bound book. Clara was excited as she thought it was a diary and she waited for a moment when Ethel Kemp had gone to empty her bucket of water, before removing it. The cover was black and soft, the leather was slightly worn at one edge where the book had been opened regularly. She turned to the first page and her excitement faded. It was not a diary, but an address book. Clara was about to put it back, when she remembered that Henry Kemp's official address book had been in his office. If that one had been for his business contacts, then who were the people in this book?

The addresses were either local or for people in London, old contacts and friends from Henry's time there, she guessed. Henry's obsession with privacy was also apparent; the book contained no names, each addressee was merely indicated by a set of initials. Clara flipped through the pages, trying to see if any of the initials made sense, but she could not fit a name to any of them. Considering that everyone she had so far spoken to implied that Henry had no personal friends and kept himself to himself, the book was a curiosity. Clara decided it was best to keep hold of it and hid it in her handbag.

There was nothing further in the drawer of the cabinet that seemed important. She found a packet of cigarettes and matches, and an incomplete collection of cigarette cards showing famous cricketeers. There was a blue velvet box tucked at the back and when Clara pulled it out and opened it, she found Henry's war medals.

Ethel had returned to the room with her bucket and she spotted the box in Clara's hand. She placed down the bucket and walked over.

"I wondered where he had put them," she said softly. "I hated every day that he was away fighting. I tried to find a way to prevent him going, but that was the one thing he would not back away from. He insisted he had to go."

"When was he called up?" Clara asked.

"The summer of 1917. I had been able to stop him from volunteering. He was almost elated when he was conscripted. The one time he defied me," Ethel ran her finger over the face of a medal. "I thought I would lose him in that war. I never thought I would lose him at home."

"What unit did he serve with?" O'Harris asked.

"The Royal Artillery," Ethel explained. "He never

195

really talked about what he did, I know he was in charge of a lot of big guns. He was never injured, fortunately. He came through without a scratch. When he returned home everything went right back to exactly as it always was."

Clara doubted that. No man could fight in a war of the scale of the last conflict and come home perfectly the same as they had left. The scars were not always physical, but she had seen them plain enough in her brother and in O'Harris.

"I'm going to take these to Bill," Ethel said, a tear forming in her eye as she took the box off Clara. "He was very proud of his boy for earning these."

She departed the room hastily. Clara let out a little sigh of sadness, her shoulders sagged. O'Harris glanced at her.

"All right?"

"I always feel a little odd when I come across someone who survived that war only to be murdered at home in peace time. It seems almost as if fate was trying to catch up with them."

"I hope not," O'Harris frowned. "I've cheated death more than once, in war and peace, I'm hoping for a very long and boring life."

"And I am sure you will get it," Clara reassured him, touching his arm. "Though not the boring part, at least not while I am around."

"You are most certainly not boring Clara!"

Clara laughed as she went to Henry's desk. So far, her search had turned up very little and she was beginning to feel she was on a wild goose chase. Supposing there really was no hard evidence of the motive for Henry's murder? Supposing it was something only he and Simon Noble knew about? Then there would be simply no hope, none at all. Because, unless Simon Noble confessed, they would never have the reason for the killing and without that how could they hope to make a court convict him?

Her laughter had faded as she began to open the drawers of the desk. She felt deflated. Not yet defeated, but coming close. She could almost feel Simon Noble laughing at her, his nasty smirk on his face as she confronted the possibility of never having the proof to convict him. It was far from a happy thought.

The desk contained more bundles of paper, some were fresh and yet to be used. There were also piles of poems, older ones. Henry Kemp had started off by keeping his work in his desk but, as the poems mounted up, the desk drawers had proved too small and then the paper had to be stacked in piles. Henry had been a prolific writer, perhaps it might almost be said he was obsessive. Clara took out each stack of poems from the drawers and went through them, just in case. Strange phrases caught her eye as she thumbed through.

Blood blossoms blue.

Dirt upon the soul of man.

Skulls crack like robin's eggs.

There was nothing peaceful or pretty about these poems. Even those written before 1917 had a dark aura to them. The words were bitter, empty and full of misery. Was this an insight into Henry's soul? A poet wrote from the heart, about things that mattered to them. Henry wrote a great deal about death and suffering, there was also a lot of imagery of 'trapped things'. Birds in cages, dogs lunging at the ends of chains, prisoners in irons. Remorseless depictions of creatures and people who had lost their freedom and had no hope of regaining it. Impotent beings, brought to the brink of despair by their mental prisons, as much as physical ones. The more Clara read, the more she felt sorry for Henry. He was a man suffering, that was plain enough.

Clara rubbed at her eyes. She was not sure she could take anymore talk of blood and bones. She was beginning to think she ought to give up, that there would be nothing but more unhappy poems in among the papers when she glanced at something that was not a poem. It was a letter, muddled in the middle of a pile, though perhaps muddled was not the right word, because a paperclip had been fastened at the top, the one and only piece of paper with a clip. It almost seemed as if Henry had marked this page as subtly as he could and then hidden it among others, just in case his mother gained access to his bedroom. She would have even less reason to go through the papers than Clara and would probably only glance at the first few before deciding they were not something she wanted to read. The letter would be safe among them, but the paperclip meant Henry could lay his hand on it easily when he wanted to.

Clara pulled the letter out. It had been sent to Henry and the address in the top right corner was back in Brighton. The writer had addressed him as H.K. and had signed themselves P.Y. Another aspect of the secrecy Henry Kemp veiled himself in. The letter's contents were equally cryptic.

Dear H.K.

You sounded unhappy in your last letter and I am sad for you. If you cannot see a way forward, I can only offer council and suggest you go with your heart or perhaps do nothing. After all, must you act? Surely you can ignore what has happened and continue on as normal? I wonder that you feel so strongly on this matter, as it cannot affect you greatly, rather it affects those who are perhaps not worthy of your deep consideration? I say this all as a friend who thinks dearly of you, and who does not wish to see you suffering. Life must go on, and there are things out of your control, which must be accepted. If you come round on Sunday we can discuss this further, but I hope you will put all thought of it out of your mind for the time being. Better for you to forget about it, then perhaps a solution will offer itself spontaneously? I have always found a problem mulled over is a problem worsened, while one that is allowed to fall to the back of the mind, will be suddenly solved.

Your dearest friend, P.Y.

The letter was remarkable for several reasons, not least that here was evidence that Henry Kemp did have a friend, one that no one else appeared to know about. What was this problem that was upsetting him? The letter was undated, which made it difficult to know if this was a new issue or something that had happened years ago. Yet, the ink looked vivid and fresh, not like the ink of letters written years past.

"I have something," O'Harris called out.

In his hand was a similar letter. There was the paperclip at the top and the names were replaced with initials.

"What does it say?" Clara asked urgently.

Dear H.K.

I would be delighted if you would come over on Sunday for tea. I have missed your company, though I fully understand that you are extremely busy. I have been remiss with my letter writing, as I have been unwell and found composing words difficult. Please bring me some of your latest work, as I feel the need to see fresh words and your poems always excite such discussion. I hope you are well and that you are finding your work satisfying, as you have mentioned to me before.

Your dearest friend P.Y.

O'Harris looked up at Clara.

"Who is P.Y.?" He asked in amazement.

"I don't know, but they seem to have been someone Henry confided in. Look for more letters from them. He seems to have marked them with a paperclip and hidden them among his poems."

They started to go through the piles of paper with renewed optimism. O'Harris was the first to find another letter.

"The same writer," he declared. "Dear H.K., I am worried about you. Your recent complaints seem to have worsened and this burden that sits upon you weighs you down too greatly. I understand, though you suggest I do not. You are a man of great principles and I fear these make you vulnerable to the harshest slings and arrows this world has to offer. Please come over one Sunday so we may discuss things in a logical fashion. I shall support whatever you decide. I never intended to sound dismissive of your worries, only to imply that you must sometimes put these things to bed to preserve your own wellbeing. What, after all, can you really do? But please, call over soon so we might talk. Your dearest friend P.Y."

O'Harris showed her the letter.

"This one is dated. It was written last August."

"There was something troubling Henry," Clara surmised. "Something that was crushing him and he was drinking to try to escape it."

She rummaged through the pile of papers nearest her.

"Here's another!"

"And another here!" Called O'Harris.

Within the span of ten minutes they had found ten letters all from the mysterious P.Y. Some were innocuous, but several of the later ones continued to discuss the big burden fallen on Henry's shoulders.

"We have to find P.Y." Clara said.

Just at that moment she heard Ethel Kemp returning and hastily shoved the letters into her handbag. As Ethel entered the room, she glanced up at her.

"I think we are done Mrs Kemp."

"Oh," Ethel Kemp looked around at the room. "I hope you found something useful."

"Maybe," Clara replied. "I shall keep you informed of what happens. Once again, I am so very sorry."

Ethel escorted Clara and O'Harris to the front door, as she let them out she seemed to pause, as if suddenly she did not want them to leave. She almost put out a hand to catch Clara's arm, but then she stopped herself.

"Henry did not deserve to die," she said solemnly, then she shut the door on them.

"Rude to the last," O'Harris shrugged his shoulders. "Well, Brighton next?"

"Definitely," Clara agreed. "Time to meet P.Y."

Chapter Twenty-five

Locating the address of P.Y. involved getting the map out again. Jones located the street name and plotted a route.

"About twenty minutes," he conjectured, before starting the engine and slipping away from the hedge outside the Kemp cottage.

Clara glanced back at the property and thought of the sadness that had now filled it. Despite the rudeness of Mrs Kemp, she felt sorry for her.

O'Harris had gathered up all the letters from P.Y. – six in total – and was trying to glean something from them.

"It's all so cryptic, but most certainly Henry has been worried about something for months," O'Harris thumbed through the letters. "This one talks about P.Y.'s concerns for Henry's health, and this one refers to him making a difficult decision."

"That could mean a lot of things," Clara replied. "He might have been considering moving out from under his mother's gaze, for a start. Maybe going back to London?"

"Hmm, that would be a tricky decision," O'Harris rearranged the letters back into chronological order. "Next question, is this P.Y. a male or female acquaintance?"

"The latter could raise all manner of new possibilities," Clara said slyly.

"Was Henry Kemp contemplating marriage, you mean?"

"If P.Y. is a woman," Clara answered. "Which means poor Miss Dodd was barking up the wrong tree altogether."

"Miss Jane Dodd," O'Harris sighed. "She's the victim in this case who is always going to get forgotten, isn't she?"

"Her tragedy is no less great for the fact she jumped herself," Clara became solemn. "I won't let her be forgotten."

Jones glanced in the rear view mirror.

"This is the road," he spoke.

Clara and O'Harris both looked out of their respective windows. The number of the house given on the letter was ten. Clara quickly saw that the houses on her side of the road were odd numbered. Ten would be on O'Harris' side.

"We are in the higher numbers, so far," he said to Clara as she turned to him. "Twenty-four, twenty-two."

He paused as Jones took them further down the road.

"Ah, fourteen, twelve, ten!"

Jones pulled the car to the side of the pavement and Clara and O'Harris stepped out. The rain had eased and the sun was peeking through the clouds and making the puddles glisten. Number ten stood back from the road. It was a villa-style property with a formal front garden. There was an immaculate lawn, split by a brick path. In the centre of each section of lawn was an ornamental palm tree, planted in a circular bed lined with smaller, white bricks. The beds had been recently tilled and looked as fresh as the day they were planted. The whole garden was lined by a red and grey brick wall, with hydrangeas sitting in beds before them. The hydrangeas looked glum in their barren winter sleep, but in the summer they would be glorious.

Clara opened a grey-blue gate and walked up the path to the house. The villa was two-storeyed and painted white, with the windows and door a pale green. Two grand picture windows looked onto the front lawn. The door was sandwiched between them. A Christmas wreath of holly and ivy was still hanging on the door itself. Clara was careful not to disturb it as she knocked.

There was a long moment before movement could be heard inside and the door was carefully opened. A woman stood before them. She was in her seventies, with perfectly white hair that had been swept up into a high bun. She had a soft face, barely marked by time, though her eyes had taken on the watery blue hue of old age. She was dressed in a plain grey dress and the reason for her difficulty in opening the door was explained by the fact she was propped up on two walking sticks. She leaned forward because of the sticks and so seemed to be peering at them.

"I do apologise for disturbing you," Clara said immediately, feeling guilty she had summoned the woman to her door. "We have a rather odd question to ask. Does anyone reside in this house with the initials P.Y.?"

The woman was startled for a moment. Then she smiled.

"That would be me. I am Patricia Youngman."

Clara felt relieved, she had feared the address would somehow prove a red herring too.

"Why do you ask?" Patricia started to frown.

"I believe you wrote these letters to Mr Henry Kemp?" Clara motioned to the letters O'Harris was holding and he showed them to the woman.

She glanced at them for a moment, then nodded.

"Yes, I wrote those," a look of concern came upon her face. "Has something happened?"

"I am afraid so," Clara said sadly. "Might we come inside and explain?"

"I think you best," Patricia agreed. "You will have to bear with me."

She moved unsteadily back from the door, allowing Clara and O'Harris to enter.

"My maid has the day off," she continued, turning around awkwardly and heading into a room on her right. "I won't be able to offer you tea, I'm afraid."

"No matter," Clara reassured her. They followed Patricia into a sitting room handsomely furnished with large sofas and several tall bookcases. There was a fire crackling in a large hearth with a tiled surround. Abstract lilies and irises curled across the shiny tiles in deep greens and purples.

"I broke my hip back in November," Patricia continued as she gingerly lowered herself onto a sofa. "It is taking forever to heal. Please sit."

O'Harris and Clara sat on the sofa opposite.

"I am not used to inactivity," Patricia said with a disagreeable sigh. "Fortunately, I am fond of reading, though even that is trying my patience."

Clara could not help but look at the many bookshelves in the room and estimated there had to be a thousand books, at least, upon them.

"What do you read?" She asked.

"Everything," Patricia shrugged her shoulders. "Science, history, gardening. There is a little bit of everything. Not much fiction though. I like to read something I can learn from."

Patricia Youngman picked up the book that had been left on the sofa when she rose to answer the door.

"This one is about the Ancient Greeks and the first democracy. Are you a keen reader?"

"Yes, but I rarely get the time," Clara smiled. It felt to her as if they were dodging around the real issue, pushing it out of the way with pleasantries. She decided it was time to be blunt. "We have some news concerning Henry Kemp."

"Is he all right?" Patricia asked anxiously.

Clara's face spoke for her. Patricia groaned.

"Was it the drink?"

"Mr Kemp was attacked last night," Clara explained. "He was stabbed and sadly did not survive. We are trying to find out the motive for this attack and thought you might be able to assist us."

Patricia accepted this information almost calmly, but she fell silent for a long while. Eventually she looked up.

"You found my letters to Henry," Patricia pointed to them, still in O'Harris' hand. "Henry was concerned about his mother discovering them and he made me only sign with my initials. I was not supposed to write my address on them either, but I forgot once or twice. Habit, you see."

"Fortunate for us," Clara admitted. "You seem to have been the one person Henry confided in, at least that is what I am hoping."

Patricia gave a sad smile.

"Henry's life had not turned out as he had intended. I dare say that is the case for most of us," Patricia looked around her living room. "I have this beautiful home and enough money to keep me comfortable until the day I die, but even I have regrets. I had plans to marry and have children. I was convinced that that was the path I would follow in my life when I was a girl. But the man I loved died and I never found another."

Patricia shrugged her shoulders.

"I understood what it was to have your plans for the future snatched from you and for you to be unable to do anything about it. I connected with Henry in that sense."

"How did you meet?" Clara asked. "Henry, from what I have been told, did not have much of a social life?"

"He had a social life," Patricia grinned mischievously. "He kept it secret from his mother, and I suppose from those who he felt did not need to know. Henry was a member of the Brighton and Hove Cycling Club. We meet every Sunday when the weather is reasonable and go on cycling tours about the county. Henry did not always participate in those, but he did attend our evening meetings and was very good at writing articles for the club magazine. I met him through the club.

"I have been a cyclist for much of my later adult life. It is a fabulous way to keep fit, unless, of course, you go for a ride on your bicycle in November and slip on some ice. I hit the ground rather hard and, well…"

Patricia rubbed at her hip.

"My doctor was furious. But I have cycled through every winter since 1891. Henry was understanding, thankfully."

"I grasped, from your letters, that you and Henry had been friends for a while and he would visit for Sunday tea?" Clara asked.

"That is true," Patricia was still rubbing her hip as if talking about it reminded her that it hurt. "Henry would come around after the club cycle. He preferred talking to people one-to-one, he found groups slightly intimidating. I can't even recall now how it all began, but it became quite a habit. I enjoyed his company. I will miss him dreadfully."

Patricia's face became ashen.

"Murdered," she whispered to herself, then louder. "I am finding it hard to contemplate such an idea. I have never known someone to be murdered before. Not anyone I knew, anyway. I have known a lot of people who have passed on. The older you get the more it seems to happen, but to have his life snatched away…"

She tailed off and seemed to lose herself in her own thoughts.

"When we first arrived, it almost seemed as if you had been concerned for a while something might happen," O'Harris interjected.

"Oh," Patricia came back to herself. "I suppose that had been on my mind. Henry was struggling. I can think of no better way to describe it. Life had taken a turn he had not expected and he was not coping with the idea that he had plateaued and could expect little more from the future. He felt trapped and also finished. I tried to talk him around, but I saw he was sinking. And, of course, there was the alcohol."

"You knew he was drinking heavily?" Clara asked.

"I could hardly miss it," Patricia shook her head as if the idea was absurd. "Anyone who knew him would have spotted that he was in a desperate state. He drank heavily these last few months. I was growing more and more worried about him. I feared he might do something reckless."

"Was that what you meant in the letters by a burden being upon him and he needing to make a difficult decision?" Clara asked, fearing that Patricia would no more hold the key to this situation than anyone else.

"In part," Patricia agreed. "But there was another situation that was causing Henry a great deal of trouble. It was the reason he was drinking heavily and I felt he needed to resolve that situation first before he could manage his own problems. While that burden was still upon him, he would have a reason to drink and drown his sorrows."

"What was the problem?" Clara asked, hope returning.

Patricia hesitated.

"I was sworn to secrecy," she said. "Henry would only tell me after I promised I would never speak of the matter to anyone. I know he is dead, but…"

"If this decision had an impact on his death, we must know of it," Clara explained to her. "And, we can only know if it had an impact on his death if you tell us about it. If it is of no relevance, we shall not breathe a word of it."

Patricia pressed her lips together, uncertain what to do for the best. She was still looking at the letters in Captain O'Harris' hand.

"Do you have any suspects for his murder?" She asked.

Clara sensed that her answer would make up Patricia's mind as to whether to speak or not. She could, however, only answer truthfully.

"I do. I believe he was stabbed by Simon Noble, the son of his employer."

Patricia let out a long breath through her teeth.

"Now, that is unexpected!" She gasped. "But it makes my decision easier. If you want to know Simon Noble's motive for wishing Henry Kemp ill, you can find it in the drawer of that bureau over there."

Patricia pointed to a bureau by the door. O'Harris rose and opened it. Under Patricia's directions he opened a small drawer and removed several papers.

"Correspondence," he said as he flicked through them. "Between Simon Noble and another company."

"Another importation company," Patricia specified. "Henry brought those papers to me just a couple of weeks ago. He asked me to keep them safe while he made his mind up on what he was going to do."

"What do the letters say?" Clara asked. O'Harris was bringing the papers back to the sofa and handed them to her.

"In essence they are communication between Simon Noble and this other firm, Ignatius Importation, concerning the possibility of the latter buying the former," Patricia stated.

Clara could hardly believe her ears.

"Simon Noble was thinking of selling the company!" She gasped.

"And Henry knew about it," Patricia nodded. "I would say that goes a long way to giving Simon Noble a motive."

Chapter Twenty-six

"Here is an interesting little piece of information for you. I happen to be of the same generation as Arthur Noble's father, Joshua Noble. He was just a few years my senior," Patricia continued conversationally. "Joshua's father was another Elias and he used to golf with my father. Hove is really more of a large village than a town, we might be connected to Brighton but we see ourselves as separate. You tend to know everyone who happens to be in the same social circle as you."

"How well do you know the Nobles?" Clara asked.

"I knew the late Elias and Joshua the best. As I say, Elias and my father often golfed together. My father was involved in the Great Western Railway. He was a senior director. Both he and Elias were working men who understood what it was to have to strive hard for a fortune. They were sometimes looked down upon by those at the golf club who had merely inherited their wealth," Patricia shrugged her shoulders, deeming this unimportant. "Joshua was five or six years my senior. I can remember attending a number of the same social functions as him as we grew older. He was always a remarkably arrogant young man."

"That seems to be a trait that runs through the family

line," O'Harris noted somewhat sarcastically.

Patricia smiled.

"I know Elias and my father talked about the possibility of my marrying Joshua, but I had my heart set elsewhere," Patricia's smile became sad. "I find myself wondering, on occasion, what might have been had I married into the Noble family."

"I don't think you would have liked it," Clara assured her.

"Probably not," Patricia's good humour returned. "In any case, Joshua married some heiress to another company and expanded the Noble firm. He died just over a year ago, you know. I remember reading his obituary in the newspaper. Over the years I had lost touch with the Nobles. After the death of my father there was no real connection between me and Elias, and Joshua moved in his own circles.

"I hadn't given much thought to them for a long time, until I met Henry Kemp. Did you get to meet him before… Well, just before?"

"Unfortunately, my acquaintance with Henry Kemp occurred at a time when he was not at his finest," Clara admitted.

"He was drunk," Patricia said flatly. "Yes, that had become a problem for him lately. It was all the turmoil surrounding the discovery that Simon intended to sell the firm."

Patricia paused.

"No, it was more than that," she gave a gentle sigh. "That was the straw that broke the camel's back, but he was struggling before then. Henry felt trapped. I was perhaps the only person who he felt truly free to talk to. I had no agenda, you see? His mother was oppressive and only wanted to keep him close for her own sake, while his father was just interested in an easy life. I am being blunt, I know."

"I have met them both," Clara replied. "I understand and I appreciate bluntness."

Patricia was pleased to hear this and she sat a little more upright.

"If he could not talk to his parents openly, he could certainly not talk to his work colleagues. He did not know how trustworthy they were, they might have reported any criticism he gave of the Nobles back to them. No, I alone was neutral and Henry talked with me," Patricia's smiled returned. "We met through the cycling club. That was another source of escapism for Henry. We happened to sit next to each other at a club meeting and we introduced ourselves. When I asked where Henry worked, he told me Noble and Sons. Naturally I explained that I used to know Joshua Noble and so we began to talk.

"That was just before Joshua passed away and Henry had met him a few times. We shared impressions of the man. Henry was reticent, but I was not! He soon discovered he could talk freely with me and we became friends. The more I grew to know Henry, the more I realised that he was in a terrible position. I forget the first time I invited him to Sunday tea, but it was after a cycle meet. He wasn't sure at first, but I persuaded him.

"I liked Henry a lot. He was honourable, but that meant he placed others too often before himself. His parents in particular. Did you know he had a high-flying job in London?"

"I had heard," Clara nodded.

"It paid him twice as much as he earned down here," Patricia declared.

"That I did not know," Clara responded, mildly surprised. "I was told Noble and Sons was the better paying job."

"That is what Henry told everyone. Especially his parents. He didn't want anyone to know the truth. He gave up a job that paid a lot of money, and which had huge prospects to come home and look after his mother and father. It was a sacrifice he made willingly, but not without regret. There was another thing he gave up when he came, something much more personal. His freedom,"

Patricia became solemn. "Henry had only broken free from his mother's grasp the first time with great difficulty. She detested him living in London and not being under her constant watch and full control. I have little time for that woman, I suppose you can tell.

"Anyway, his father was in an accident and lost both his legs. The impact was hard on his parents both emotionally and financially. Henry could have stayed in London and sent money to them. But, as I said, he was honourable and terribly loyal. He knew his mother was not coping and he felt guilty staying away. In the end he resigned his London position and moved to Noble and Sons. I know he missed London dreadfully, and his independence, but there was nothing he could do."

"He could move away again," O'Harris pointed out.

"You don't understand the emotional burden his mother placed upon him. She would have made him feel so guilty if he had even proposed the idea. Leaving to serve in the war was hard enough. His mother made herself sick with worry, or so it appeared. I don't think that woman has enough soul to make herself sick over someone. But she knew how to manipulate Henry.

"I think, also, the war knocked Henry for six. He saw things that shook him and maybe it made him feel bad about thinking of leaving his parents. There were fathers and mothers who would never see their sons again, and who would give anything for an opportunity to be together once more. He started to project those feelings onto his own mother. He always was far too generous to her."

"How well do you know her?" Clara asked.

"I never met her," Patricia replied. "But I didn't like how she treated her son. Perhaps I would have found her company pleasant in person, you tell me, seeing as how you have met her?"

"I don't think I could go so far as to call her company pleasurable," Clara said carefully. "But then, I don't think she is a person to encourage friendship."

"She certainly did not encourage Henry to have friends. I was a secret, I know that. Poor Henry was in such a terrible position. He felt he had no future, only the endless trial of caring for his mother and father. He was just about coping, because he actually enjoyed working at Noble and Sons, not that the Nobles were the nicest of souls either. But the work was interesting and he was doing well. Then he learned about the plan to sell the company and he was thrown into a new turmoil."

"Why was that?" Clara asked. "Surely, if the company was sold, Henry would move with it as senior manager. Simon Noble was not selling because the company was in trouble, was he?"

"Noble and sons is doing better than ever," Patricia agreed. "Selling it had nothing to do with the business itself, rather, it is to do with Simon Noble's desire for instant money and not having to work for it. He has no interest in the firm and doesn't want to run it. Selling it would not only provide him with a huge fortune, which he could comfortably live off for the rest of his days, but it would take away the chore of working for the company. Even if most of the working is done by people like Henry. I guess Simon Noble was too lazy to even be bothered about attending the twice weekly meetings, if he could help it.

"No, the reason Henry was so concerned stems back to that strong streak of honour he always had running through him," Patricia gave a sad chuckle. "He was a man of another age. When Henry discovered Simon Noble's plans he was torn because, on the one hand, he felt he should be loyal to Simon Noble, and yet, on the other, he knew how devastating the sale would be to Arthur Noble, and Arthur was the one who hired him."

Patricia shifted a little in her seat.

"I ache after a while," she explained apologetically.

"Can I get you something?" O'Harris offered. "A drink, perhaps? I feel rude sitting here without offering."

Patricia waved the suggestion away.

"I would have been here alone had you not come knocking, and I would have coped just fine," Patricia adjusted a cushion behind her and settled again. "That's better. Now, I need to explain to you how strong a tie some members of the Noble family have with the company. Noble and Sons was founded in 1764 as a coffee importer. However, the rising duty on alcohol introduced an interesting side-line and they became involved, at arm's length, with smuggling. Then the taxes on alcohol were reduced, coffee was not quite the grand thing it had once been and the second Mr Noble hastily moved into wine importation.

"The family never looked back. They became inherently linked with the company and the prestige it granted them. Each generation was schooled to take it over and continue the Noble name. It was a legacy, a means of immortality. Elias believed in that, as did Joshua and his son Arthur. The name was important, it gave the family meaning as well as a small fortune. To throw that all away seemed like sacrilege to Henry. It would feel even worse to Arthur Noble. Simon was planning the move after he inherited the company and his father had handed over full control. There would be nothing Arthur could do. Equally, younger brother Elias would be cast off without an income. The firm has always been passed into the sole control of the eldest son. Younger siblings receive an income from the firm, but nothing more.

"When Simon sold the company, he would take all the profit for himself. He had no qualms about leaving Elias penniless. He had even been to a solicitor to discover if there was any legal requirement for him to split the money with Elias. He discovered there was none."

"How utterly despicable!" Clara said. She had found Simon Noble obnoxious and selfish, but she had never thought he would be so cruel as to leave his own brother without a penny to his name.

"Henry thought so. He discovered the plans by accident," Patricia explained. "It was August last year and

Simon Noble had not attended one of the weekly meetings, stating he was unwell. During the course of the meeting some papers were required urgently and Henry recalled that Simon had requested them and taken them to his office. He was sent to fetch them by Arthur Noble. He had to search through the drawers in Simon's desk to locate them and, while doing so, he stumbled over the letters you have in your hand."

Patricia motioned to Captain O'Harris.

"He skimmed them, thinking they were the papers he wanted, but when he realised their content he felt sick to his stomach. After the weekly meeting, he made copies of the letters to return to Simon's drawer and he kept the originals. He hoped Simon would not look at the copies closely enough to realise they were fake. Eventually he brought the letters to me and asked me to keep them safe."

Clara took the letters from O'Harris and glanced through them. One was from a solicitor in respond to a letter asking where Simon stood in regards of Elias and the firm. Another was a valuation of the firm's holdings, and yet another was from a company who were responding to an enquiry Simon had made to them, saying they would be willing to buy the firm for a set amount. The figure they stated in the letter had so many zeroes that it made the mind boggle. Clara whistled through her teeth as she saw the extent of Simon Noble's duplicity.

"Exactly," Patricia spoke. "Henry knew he could not sit on this information but he was afraid to act. What if he was not believed or Simon explained away the evidence? Arthur Noble might choose to believe his son, however improbable the explanation, over his employee. Yet, Henry would feel awful if he did not tell Arthur and something could have been done to prevent the firm leaving the family. He did not know what to do for the best, and that was when his drinking became extremely serious."

"Maybe everything got to him at last," Clara pulled the papers into a pile. "Maybe tonight he could not take the burden any longer and it slipped out when he was alone with Simon Noble."

"And, to preserve his plans, Simon killed him," Patricia mumbled glumly. "I do not know Simon Noble, but it strikes me that he is a man who puts the greatest value on money and would act violently to protect his wealth."

"Henry perhaps confronted him below decks in the ship's kitchen," Clara theorised. "He was drunk and perhaps let slip what he knew by accident more than design. A spurt of anger got the better of his tongue. He blurted out what he knew, told Simon he was going to reveal the truth to his father and Simon could not allow that to happen. Well, there is my motive."

"You are welcome to the letters," Patricia said. "They are of no value to me anymore."

Her face fell. The reality of everything was sinking in.

"Henry Kemp was a good man but, more importantly, he was my friend. He was his own worst enemy in many regards, but he always tried to do what was right," a tear suddenly crept down Patricia's cheek. "He did not deserve to die. Of all the men in this world, he surely did not deserve this."

Chapter Twenty-seven

The car drive back to the Mary Jane seemed to take a torturously long time. All the way Clara was burning with questions for Simon Noble and also feeling an eagerness to confront him. She had won, hadn't she? Now she would knock that smug look off his face. Only, nothing was ever certain until a suspect had been arrested. And even then, there was always the court proceedings to endure.

Clara glanced through the letters again. They provided clear motive, but the elements were still disjointed. No one had seen Simon Noble stab Henry Kemp, there was always that reservation hanging over everything. There were plenty of other people on the ship who could have committed the crime, though what motive they might have was debatable. The letters only indicated that Simon had a reason to be angry with Henry. Did a person really kill someone because they planned to sell the family business? Clara played the doubts over and over in her head, trying to think how a good solicitor would. Simon Noble would have someone who could work every angle. Clara had a nasty feeling there were still too many gaps in her case.

They pulled up at the docks. The police were still

stationed on the gangplank, but in the hours that had passed a number of guests who were of no relevance to what had happened, had been allowed to leave. Dock workers were keeping an eye on the liner, pondering what was going on. They were even more curious when the fancy car that had left earlier returned. Clara and O'Harris hastily exited it and ran for the gangplank.

The police constable recognised Clara and let her through.

"Do you know where Inspector Park-Coombs is?" She asked him as she nipped past.

"No, Miss, sorry."

Clara headed back to the captain's cabin, deciding this was the most likely place for Park-Coombs to still be. The letters were growing hot in her hand, her palms beginning to sweat with the tension of the moment. She almost felt as if they were burning her.

At the door to the captain's cabin she paused, collected herself and knocked.

"Just a minute," Park-Coombs' deep voice boomed from inside.

Clara relaxed a fraction, knowing she had found him. She glanced at O'Harris, who smiled. It did not still the anxiety inside her.

Park-Coombs opened the door and allowed a pair of passengers to exit, before he motioned for Clara to join him inside.

"Any luck?" He asked as soon as the door was shut.

Clara handed him the papers.

"Simon Noble was secretly planning to sell the family company and Henry Kemp learned of this. He was torn between telling Arthur Noble or not. I surmise that last night he became so drunk that he blurted out to Simon Noble what he knew. Or perhaps they had spoken about it before and last night merely presented an opportunity."

Inspector Park-Coombs took his time to examine each letter and document.

"Arthur Noble will be very unhappy about this," he

218

mused. "I know a little about the family, the business has always been very important to them. At least, to the older generation."

"I think it would be safe to say that if Arthur knew his son was going to sell the company as soon as he inherited, he would not get the chance. That would be a lot of money Simon would lose, not to mention his father might have cut him off without a penny for even considering it," Clara said.

"Let's get them all in here and have a chat," Park-Coombs agreed. "I would like to see the look on Simon Noble's face when we reveal to his father what he was planning."

Park-Coombs went to the door and called out to a police constable stationed nearby to fetch the Nobles. Then he returned to the room and waited with Clara and O'Harris.

"We are a step closer," he told them. "Simon Noble had a very good reason for wanting Henry Kemp silenced."

Clara hoped a jury would see things that way.

Around half an hour later, the three Nobles appeared in the room. Arthur entered first, looking fed-up. Clara half expected him to demand to be allowed to go home. Simon came second, an arrogant smile on his face. He was convinced Clara could not touch him and his nonchalance was beginning to unsettle her. She wanted to wipe that smile from his lips, she was just not sure she had quite enough to do that just yet. Elias brought up the rear, keeping behind everyone and with his head down. Aiming to keep out of trouble.

The three men were offered chairs by Park-Coombs at the table. They sat in a semi-circle; Simon, Arthur and then Elias, facing Park-Coombs, Clara and O'Harris. Clara sat opposite Simon Noble, determined to watch every twitch of his face as she revealed what she now knew.

"Thank you for joining us," Park-Coombs began politely.

"I am tired of this ridiculous performance," Arthur Noble snapped. "I should have been home hours ago. I am supposed to be welcoming guests this evening."

"You may wish to cancel them," Park-Coombs said calmly.

"Whatever for?" Arthur snapped.

"Because I believe your son murdered Henry Kemp last night," Park-Coombs continued in the same placid tone. Park-Coombs never became excited during an interview and he rarely allowed anger to slip through. His calmness was usually unsettling to his suspects.

Arthur Noble went very still as the inspector spoke. The implications of what he had said had stunned the normally bombastic man into temporary silence. His cheeks reddened and Clara was not sure he had taken a breath in a while. She awaited an anticipated explosion.

"How dare you call my son a murderer!" Arthur Noble reacted somewhat predictably. "We are leaving this ship at once! I will not have my family accused of being criminals."

Arthur Noble rose from his chair and Simon was quick to follow. Inspector Park-Coombs spoke in an even tone.

"I have some information here you will wish to see, Mr Noble. Information that will make you hesitate at defending your son so belligerently."

Clara was watching Simon Noble's face, but he did not blanch or even startle. She started to feel her doubts returning. He seemed too calm and confident. However, Arthur Noble had hesitated.

"You have no proof my son is a murderer!" He yelled, but he hadn't move closer to the door.

Maybe he had had his own doubts about Simon?

"Would you like me to show you your son's bloody shirt?" Inspector Park-Coombs asked him politely, rather like he was offering him a cup of tea. "The blood on it is most certainly that of Henry Kemp."

Arthur no longer moved. He glanced at his son, then back at the inspector.

"Please sit down, so we can explain properly," Park-Coombs persisted. "You will want to hear this."

Arthur Noble did not look convinced, but he did slowly sit down again. Simon was now the only one left standing and the first signs of discomfort were creeping onto his face. He gripped the back of his chair with a hand and his knuckles went white, then he sat down and glowered at Clara. His expression said it all, he was challenging her – do your worst.

"Explain to me what makes you think my son did this thing," Arthur Noble asked, his voice threatening, though also uneasy.

"Henry Kemp remained on board when everyone else was evacuated," the inspector began. "He was seen going down below. One of the first lifeboats to return to the Mary Jane was the one that contained Simon Noble. Simon was witnessed leaving the lifeboat and going off on his own to look for Henry Kemp. Miss Dodd had been upset about Henry remaining aboard and she had insisted that someone should look for him when the lifeboats returned. They assumed this was what Simon was doing when he went off alone, however, we may also conjecture he had other motives."

"Conjecture is not proof," Arthur Noble declared fiercely.

"I shall present you with proof," the inspector was not intimidated. "At some point Simon Noble found Henry Kemp in the ship's kitchen. He was witnessed standing over Henry's body."

"Witnessed by whom?" Arthur Noble demanded.

Simon Noble was grinding his teeth, but kept his mouth shut.

"The witness did not see Simon commit the crime," Inspector Park-Coombs continued without answering Arthur's question. "Simon has already told us that he merely came across Henry already dead."

"Completely logical!" Arthur Noble interrupted swiftly.

"Except," Park-Coombs continued patiently. "Simon informed no one of the discovery. Instead, having somehow stained his shirt with Henry's blood – I shall allow you to conjecture on how he did that – he went to his cabin and changed his shirt. He then returned to the party as if nothing had happened. A very peculiar thing for an innocent man to do who has just come across the body of someone he knew."

Arthur Noble was going that dangerous red colour again, but even he was struggling to find an innocent reason for Simon's actions.

"When we interviewed you all after Henry Kemp had been 'discovered', Simon made no indication that he knew of what had occurred. I find that very suspicious, but, as you have pointed out, that is not proof of anything," Park-Coombs paused to await a response from Arthur, but it did not come. He carried on. "The problem we had, despite our doubts, was that there appeared to be no reason for Simon to have murdered Henry. I therefore sent Miss Fitzgerald out to speak to people onshore. She has returned with some very interesting information. Perhaps, Miss Fitzgerald, you will explain what you discovered?"

Clara was only too glad to do so. Her eyes shifting between Simon and Arthur, she pointed at the papers before the inspector.

"Henry Kemp was devoted to the company of Noble and Sons and felt a deep loyalty for you, Mr Noble."

Arthur Noble seemed unaffected by the comment. Perhaps he assumed all his employees should be intrinsically loyal to him.

"By pure chance, Henry discovered that your son, Simon, was intending to sell the company as soon as he inherited it."

"Lies!" Simon Noble finally could be silent no more. "I would not do such a thing!"

Arthur Noble did not look at his son. He appeared shaken, as if he too was struggling to rationalise Simon's actions.

"These papers were found by Henry Kemp in Simon Noble's desk. They reveal Simon's plans. Henry was deeply torn as to what to do with this information. However, I believe he was planning on telling you everything, Mr Noble."

"This is nonsense!" Simon Noble flapped.

Clara pushed the papers over to Arthur Noble. At first he would not look at them, then he lifted up the top one and frowned as he read the words.

"It's true," he said bleakly. "You were going to sell the company Simon."

"No, it's not how it looks!" Simon bleated to his father. "I was trying to discover the company's worth, that's all."

"This letter implies you had already settled an agreement with our chief rival to sell once you took over Noble and Sons," Arthur's tone was flat, he could hardly believe what he was reading. "How could you? The company is the family. Selling would be a betrayal of me and your grandfather, and all those Nobles who have gone before us."

"Who cares?" Simon barked, no longer pretending. "I don't want to run the damn thing and sit in on damn awful twice weekly meetings for the rest of my life. I could have made a fortune!"

Arthur looked at him bleakly, something had been ripped out from him and he suddenly looked his age. He didn't seem to recognise his son anymore.

"Does this all come down to money?" Arthur said. "Was that worth more than our family pride? Is that why you killed Henry?"

"I didn't kill Henry," Simon snapped. "I didn't even know that he had these papers. I had no motive because I did not know that Henry was aware of my plans and no one can prove otherwise!"

Simon glowered at Clara, challenging her again.

"I think I can prove that you and Henry had spoken about this before," Clara said carefully. "Henry Kemp kept his bedroom locked and no one was allowed to enter it because he kept his private papers there. He carried the key on him at all times, but the key was not with him when he was found. Someone had searched his pockets and taken the key. I think you wanted the papers back that Henry had copied. You knew he would have secured them somewhere and you searched his pockets for a clue to where they might be. You found the key, but did not know what it unlocked. As it was on Henry's person you knew it was important and now you would have time to search his office and find what it fitted.

"That key proves you were searching Henry's pockets and that you knew about the papers he had taken."

"You are saying that whoever has that key on them must have searched Henry and is probably his killer?" Simon Noble clarified, then he grinned. "Well, that person will still have that key on them, I would imagine. Not the sort of thing they are going to risk losing. So, search us all for it and that will reveal your killer."

Simon Noble rose from his chair and held out his arms, inviting them to search him. Clara did not like how this was going. He seemed too confident. Park-Coombs rose nonetheless and searched Simon. He went through every pocket in the man's suit, but there was no key.

"Now search Elias," Simon said darkly.

Elias Noble rose from his chair and waited patiently to be searched. Park-Coombs flashed a brief look of uncertainty at Clara as he strode over to the younger brother and repeated the process of going through all his pockets. When he reached an inner pocket of Elias' jacket he paused, then he pulled out a key. It might have been a key to a safe, but Clara knew it was the key to Henry's bedroom door. And it was in the pocket of the wrong man. Park-Coombs frowned as he held the key before him. Clara's heart sank a little. She didn't look at him, but she knew that Simon Noble had that Cheshire cat grin on his face once again. He had fooled them once more.

Elias Noble had not raised his head, he was staring at

a knot in the wood of the table. But he coughed politely and spoke clearly.

"I shall confess," he said without hesitation. "I murdered Henry Kemp. You ought to arrest me now."

Chapter Twenty-eight

Clara could feel Simon Noble grinning at her. She refused to look at him. She kept her face stony calm and tried to think of a good way to counter Elias' confession.

"Charles Walsh saw you on the sun deck during the time of the murder," she said.

Elias didn't even blink.

"He is mistaken."

"If you killed Henry Kemp, why did Simon's shirt have blood on it?" Inspector Park-Coombs was frowning at Elias.

"He saw what I had done and looked to see if Henry was alright, but he wasn't," Elias said placidly.

"But you didn't get covered in blood?" Park-Coombs plucked at his jacket cuff.

"No, I didn't," Elias said, still what that infuriating dullness to his tone.

Clara wanted to wring his neck. She knew he was doing this to protect his brother. The confession was worthless as all the evidence pointed to Simon, but it would muddy the waters bringing up that nasty spectre of 'reasonable doubt' once again.

"This is…. This is…." Arthur Noble blustered and puffed out his cheeks. Suddenly he grabbed a hand to his chest.

"Are you all right?" O'Harris asked him sharply.

Arthur seemed to sway on his feet. Park-Coombs turned around quickly.

"Someone get him a glass of water," he ordered.

Since neither Elias or Simon moved, Clara headed to the nearby drinks cabinet and produced a glass of water. Arthur was offered it and he sipped the contents between gasping breaths.

"I want... my... solicitor," he said.

"I have not charged your sons," Park-Coombs told him, trying to reassure him. "And, at this moment in time I won't be."

"I don't want it for them!" Arthur spat out, followed by having to take several breaths before he could speak again. "Want to... change my will... so these two... traitors... don't get the firm."

"Father!" Simon Noble's grin was now lost. "You don't mean that! The papers were meaningless. Henry got the wrong idea. I was trying to assess the company's worth, that's all."

"I read them!" Arthur Noble hissed at him. "Do not lie!"

"But who will you leave the company to?" Simon's wheedling tone had turned hard. "You will be putting it out of the family if you do this!"

"Your sister... Gertrude..."

"Gertrude!" Simon Noble almost stumbled back in amazement and Clara wondered if he too was about to suffer a heart attack. "She's a girl!"

Arthur Noble did not reply, he was concentrating on breathing.

"I think we need the ship's doctor," Clara said.

"And... my... solicitor..." Arthur gasped angrily.

O'Harris said he would run for the doctor. Park-Coombs kept a hand on Arthur Noble's shoulder and tried to calm him. Simon Noble paced, occasionally throwing out rough comments to his father who was pointedly ignoring him. Elias stood in silence. Clara tried to catch his eye, but he resolutely stared at the floor. Whether it was loyalty to his brother, or whether Simon had offered him a share in the fortune he intended to gain when the company was sold, Elias was not now going to break his promise. The confession would stand, as ridiculous and as pointless as it was.

"Clara, maybe a cup of tea would help?" Park-Coombs looked at her a little desperately. "And, some cold cloths for Mr Noble's brow, he seems boiling hot."

"I'll see what I can do," Clara replied, glad enough to get out of the room.

She hurried down to the deck containing the kitchens, feeling a twinge of unease as she found herself walking once again to the room where Henry Kemp had met his end. She was feeling awful. It looked as though Simon would get away with murder, and if his father was to now die he would inherit the company anyway and get everything he wanted. Clara had never felt so terrible about a case. She had never faced such failure before.

Clara was running to reach the kitchen and in her haste she nearly stumbled over a small black object that was sitting in the middle of the corridor. She stopped herself in time and looked down at what first appeared to be a discarded fur muff. The muff lifted up a little head and meowed at her.

"You must be Jack, and what an awful place you have sat yourself," Clara declared, reaching down to move the cat out of harm's way. "Ah, I see, a warm pipe runs under this piece of floor."

She picked up the cat, which was lovely and toasty. He purred at her.

"I really think you will get trod on down there, however…"

Clara froze. Ahead of her, down the bottom of the corridor, she could see the shadow of a person. Her mind was flicking back to the testimony of the young sailor. Someone else had been in the corridors near the kitchen other than Henry Kemp. What if that person had returned?

Clara knew it was a long shot, but she was at a stage when she would take anything she could get. She put down the cat and ran to the bottom of the corridor. The shadow had vanished before she reached the turning. She feared it was an illusion and that no one would be around the corner at all. She almost fell over her heels as she spun to the right.

There was a man walking down the corridor with empty trays.

"Hello!" Clara called out.

The man did not react. She started to follow him.

"Hello! You there!"

The man was reaching another turning. She was waving at him now, calling out. He made no response to her shouts.

"He won't hear you."

Clara was startled by a voice behind her. She spun and saw that one of the kitchen lads had appeared at the turning of the corridor to see what was going on.

"He is stone deaf," he explained.

Clara turned back to her escaping shadow man. He had turned down another corridor. She ran after him and finally grabbed his arm. He turned around in surprise and almost dropped the trays.

"I must speak with you," Clara said, hoping the man lip-read.

He frowned. He was wearing the uniform of one of the waiters who had served them yesterday evening. After a moment he nodded. Clara almost sagged with relief that he understood. She motioned with her arm for him to follow her and she took him back to the kitchen.

Food was still being prepared for the guests who had been detained. Clara glanced around the staff and saw the kitchen lad who had briefly spoken to her.

"Who is this gentleman?" She asked him.

"Mr Greene," the lad answered. "He used to be part of

the crew, until he retired. Sometimes the captain hires him for a little job, so he gets some extra money."

Clara turned back to the deaf gentleman.

"Mr Greene?" She asked.

Greene nodded with a smile. He was in his seventies, his face lined from many long years at sea. He wore a beard about his chin, it was white as snow and frizzy. He looked a little puzzled at being accosted.

"Mr Greene, where were you last night during the mine emergency?"

Greene's forehead furrowed.

"What mine emergency?" He asked her, his voice extremely loud.

The kitchen staff could not help but overhear. They now wandered over.

"You did not evacuate the ship with the others?" Clara asked again.

Greene shook his head.

"I've not left the ship since I boarded yesterday."

The cook dipped his head in shame.

"We forgot him," he mumbled. "I can't believe we did that. If something had happened…"

Greene was staring at him, unable to read his lips because he had his head down, but noting his expression.

"Mr Greene," Clara persisted, tapping Greene's arm to draw his attention back to her. "You walk back and forth along that far corridor a lot during your job?"

"I take the full trays from the kitchen along that corridor to top deck, and I bring them back the same way."

"Last night, did you notice a gentleman wandering about this deck? He was very drunk."

Mr Greene nodded.

"He bumped into me," he said. "He knocked all my trays out of my hands. Luckily they were empty."

"Did you only see him once?" Clara asked, feeling somewhat desperate now.

Mr Greene shook his head.

"I took the empty trays to the kitchen, then I took the rubbish bins to empty into the big container below. It took me longer than I expected because I dropped one of the bins on the stairs and I had to clean the mess up. Eventually I returned to the kitchen," Mr Greene scratched his head. "No one was around, which I thought off. The man was in the kitchen mumbling to himself. I went to look for everyone. I did a circuit of this deck and I was just getting back to the kitchen when I saw another man walk in. He was dressed like a guest."

"What happened?" Clara was almost trembling with excitement.

"I thought I should tell them that guests are not meant to be in the kitchen," Greene said. "I should have told the other fellow, but he didn't seem to be doing any harm. As I stepped to the doorway of the kitchen I saw that the new man had picked up a knife and was waving it at the other man. I was about to say something when he struck out at the first man and stabbed him. I quickly made myself scarce."

Mr Greene looked abashed.

"I should have said something, but everyone started to return and, the next time I checked, the hurt fellow was gone and everyone was acting normal. I figured he had been taken to his cabin. Is he feeling better this morning?"

"Oh my," the cook put a hand to his face.

Clara let out a soft sigh.

"The gentleman died," she told Greene.

Greene blinked his eyes furiously.

"He died?" He said. "I… I panicked when it happened. I thought I would just step away for a bit and then come back to check everything was fine. No one said anything to me about someone being murdered, otherwise I would have said something."

Greene looked about him at the kitchen staff.

"I'm not a coward!" He declared. "But I am old, and… and you don't talk about the guests' private business. I only retreated to the linen cupboards for a short time, just to recover myself. My nerves are not what they used to be."

No one was listening to Greene's feeble excuses. He had witnessed a murder and run away. His ignorance of the latter investigation could be excused by his deafness. He had not heard the captain's announcements that his crew should assist Clara's enquiries, he had not been able to. He had spent longer in the linen cupboard than he realised and when he returned to the kitchen everything had been cleaned up and Henry Kemp's body removed. It would have been easy to imagine that nothing serious had happened at all.

"Would you recognise the man who held the knife?" Clara asked Greene, ignoring the fact he had runaway from a crime scene. She had other things on her mind now.

"I would," Greene said. "My ears are broken, but my eyes still see good."

"I need you to come with me, please," Clara took his arm and led him back along the corridor.

"What is happening?" Greene asked.

"I need you to look at some people and tell me if one of them was the man with the knife," Clara told him.

Greene pulled a face and hesitated. Clara almost lost her grip on his arm.

"We shouldn't gossip about guests," Greene started to back off.

Clara reached out for him again, catching hold of his sleeve.

"Mr Greene, a man died last night. You are the only person who saw what happened. I need you to point out the killer, otherwise this man will walk free and never be brought to justice for his crimes, do you understand?"

Mr Greene stood as still as a statue, his face was contorted into an anxious grimace.

"I can't, Miss."

"Why not?" Clara demanded. "It is your duty!"

Greene suddenly flopped against the wall of the corridor and started to give tense, tiny sobs.

"I want to, Miss, I want to help," he said, his voice broken by his emotion. "But I can't."

"Please, explain to me," Clara begged him, touching his arm in sympathy now. "Help me to understand."

Greene's weathered face was wet with tears. He had once been a powerful man, but those days were gone and he felt every year of his age. He took a handkerchief from his pocket and wiped his face.

"I'm as poor as a church mouse, Miss," he said. "Since I had to give up the sea, me and my wife live on a pittance. She is very sick, probably dying, but we can't afford a doctor. These last five years we have lived in an alms-house, else we would be on the streets homeless."

Greene sniffed and the tears threatened again.

"I don't like what I did, Miss. It was an awful thing. I stood by and watched a man be attacked. I hoped he was all right, but I had to run. I had to. I had to think of my wife. Our alms-house is part of a charity scheme supported by the Noble and Sons company."

"And you recognised Simon Noble," Clara understood.

"I met him when we applied for our house. The Nobles take part in approving those who reside in their alms-houses. He was there. Do you know how hard it was for us to get that house? How close we were to destitution? I couldn't put my wife through that again," Greene could not hold back the tears any longer, they ran down his face. "I know I was cowardly. I know. But I did it for her. I had to. I love her and she is my responsibility."

Clara squeezed his arm.

"I truly understand what you are saying," she said. "And I can see why you acted the way you did. However, things are different now. There is a lot of evidence that proves Simon Noble was at the scene of the crime, all that we need is for a witness to testify to seeing him strike the fatal blow. You are that witness, Mr Greene."

"I'll lose my home," Greene sobbed.

"I promise, on my honour, you will not," Clara was begging him now. "Please, come forward so that a murderer does not walk free. I will not allow harm to befall you or your wife. I swear to it."

"What can you do, Miss, honestly?" Greene looked at her sadly.

"You would be amazed at what I can do, Mr Greene," Clara took his hand and held it tightly. "Just trust me. Now is the time to step up and do your duty. Will you help me, Mr Greene?"

Greene hung his head. He said nothing.

Chapter Twenty-nine

The occupants of the room had fallen into silence. Arthur Noble was being tended by the ship's doctor. The immediate emergency seemed to have passed, though he was still insisting on having his solicitor summoned to the Mary Jane, just in case something was to occur that would prevent him changing his will later. Captain Pevsner had sent out a messenger after he heard what was happening.

Simon Noble was sullenly standing by the porthole window, gazing out at the ocean. He clenched his fists and his face was set in a grimace of rage. Even if he was going to get away with murder, he had lost.

Clara entered the cabin and closed the door behind her. She looked around at the people assembled. Inspector Park-Coombs nodded to her.

"I've asked for a large pot of tea to be brought up," Clara said. "How are you feeling Mr Noble."

"Bloody awful," Arthur Noble gasped. He still had a hand on his chest, though his breathing was fine now.

"It was a scare, but nothing major," the ship's doctor said, standing up from his patient. "Nothing a little exercise and weight-loss wouldn't resolve. Your heart would be a lot happier if you were a few stone lighter, sir."

Arthur snorted derisively at such a comment. A light tap came at the cabin door. Clara answered it and a crewman entered carrying a tray of tea things. He kept his head down as he moved towards the table and started arranging everything. Simon Noble looked over. At that moment the crewman happened to raise his head and their eyes met.

"You recognise the man over there, Mr Greene?" Clara asked.

Mr Greene pursed his lips together, then he nodded uneasily. Simon Noble's face drained of colour, even if his expression did not change. Clara might have been the only one who noticed it.

Inspector Park-Coombs now started to pay attention. He glanced at Simon Noble, observed his pallor and then turned back to the old man placing tea things on the table. Clara placed a hand on Greene's arm to attract his attention.

"Mr Greene, might you tell Inspector Park-Coombs where you last happened to see Simon Noble?"

"What is this?" Simon Noble barked before that could happen. "Who is this old fool you have brought in? Some sort of trick? Who would believe a word he says?"

"He hasn't spoke as of yet, Mr Noble," Park-Coombs pointed out to Simon coldly. "From your reaction, I would guess that what he is about to say is quite incriminating."

Greene had not been able to hear Simon Noble's words, but he had eyes in his head and had been able to see the man's rage. He started to tremble. Clara kept her hand on his arm. It had taken a great deal of persuasion to get Greene up here. She had promised him that she would judge Simon Noble's reaction before asking him to speak. For that reason, she had placed him in charge of the tea tray, so that he had a valid reason for coming into the room.

Clara was afraid Mr Greene might lose his nerve now

that he had seen Simon Noble's face.

"Mr Greene has been anxious about speaking up before," Clara directed her attention to Park-Coombs and Captain O'Harris. "He fears it will be to his detriment if he speaks out, that there will be repercussions for him and his wife."

"I'll say there will be repercussions!" Simon Noble snapped.

Inspector Park-Coombs moved in front of him and faced Mr Greene.

"You have my word, Sir, that no harm will befall you for speaking the truth."

Mr Greene did not look convinced. His face betrayed every bit of his nerves and Clara was certain he was about to back down and refuse to talk. What happened next took everyone by surprise.

Arthur Noble rose from his chair and the movement attracted Greene's attention. He looked even more frightened as his benefactor stood before him. Arthur Noble was still red in the face from his heart attack, he was breathing deeply just from standing up, but he spoke firmly to Mr Greene.

"You have my protection, Mr Greene. I want to hear the truth of this matter. I want to know what my son did. You need fear nothing, Mr Greene. Upon my honour, you will suffer no repercussions, do you understand?"

Mr Greene seemed dazed, as if the sight of Mr Noble, a man he owed everything to, had stunned him. Then he nodded slowly.

"I understand," he croaked.

"Father!" Simon Noble protested.

Arthur Noble turned sharply, the colour in his face shading to an unpleasant purple hue.

"Do not call me father, after what you have planned!" He yelled at Simon. "I did not raise you as my successor, for you to sell my company – the family company – the second you could, to get your greasy paws on my money. Your grandfather must be turning in his grave! He was so glad the day you were born, thinking that Noble and Sons' future within the family had been secured for another generation. Instead you have betrayed us all!

"And as for your attack on Mr Kemp – do you know how hard it is to find managers of his calibre? He was worth a dozen of you, my boy!"

Simon Noble took a pace backwards. Up until that moment there had been a glimmer of hope that all might be resolved, that his father might come around. Now he understood that everything was to be taken from him. He kept backing up, until his legs hit the sofa beneath the porthole and he collapsed unceremoniously onto it.

Arthur Noble had turned back to Mr Greene.

"What did you see?" He asked him.

Mr Greene had watched Simon stumble away in astonishment. He looked Arthur Noble in the face, his trembling had stopped. Resolved, he spoke;

"I happened to walk past the kitchen doorway and I saw Simon Noble arguing with another man. Mr Noble picked up a knife and he thrust it at the other man. The other man gasped and then fell to the floor. I… I was afraid to stay any longer."

No one spoke after Mr Greene had finished. Arthur Noble slowly returned to his seat. He seemed satisfied, in a strange way. Elias Noble had been hovering in a corner. He stepped forward, closer to the table.

"I would like to retract my confession," he said quietly. "Simon told me what he had done and gave me the key. He said, if anyone asked, I was to say I had killed Mr Kemp, as no one could prove it and it would never go to court."

"What did he promise you in return?" Clara asked him.

Elias hung his head.

"Simon told me he was going to sell the company when he inherited it. If I helped him, I would get a share of the profits."

"Why did you not come to me?" Arthur Noble asked his son, his tone had lost its fire, it sounded more disappointed than anything else now.

"I didn't think you would believe me," Elias said simply.

Arthur Noble looked bleak. Clara surmised that he realised that was true enough. Without hard evidence, Arthur would not have wanted to believe his eldest son and heir was about to betray him.

"Well," Inspector Park-Coombs broke the silence, "I think that about wraps things up. Simon Noble, I am arresting you for the murder of Henry Kemp."

Simon Noble laughed miserably.

"Stupid fool! He would have kept his job, you know? He was one of the company's main assets. Why did he have to be so bloody loyal?"

~~~*~~~

They were once more leaving the Mary Jane. Captain Pevsner was stood at the bottom of the gangplank looking up at his old liner. He looked forlorn and lost. A man who had glimpsed into his future and disliked what he saw. Clara and O'Harris met him as they walked from the ship.

"Thank you for all your assistance, Miss Fitzgerald," Captain Pevsner held out his hand for her to shake.

Clara appreciated the gesture; a lot of men would not have offered.

"What happens now, Pevsner?" Captain O'Harris asked. "Are you really going to scrap her?"

Captain Pevsner stared up at his ship. The sun had broken through the rain and gave the old vessel a gentle golden glow.

"She is passed her time," Pevsner said sadly. "Better she go to her rest with grace and under her own power, than to be towed in because her engines have failed and her hull is as leaky as a sieve. She deserves dignity."

Captain Pevsner smiled wistfully.

"I suppose the same goes for me. Time to become a

landlubber."

"I wish you all the best Captain," Clara told him. "I am glad I was able to join you for the last voyage of Mary Jane."

Captain Pevsner looked surprised.

"Really? Considering all that happened?"

"Really," Clara assured him. "I am only sorry I could not have resolved the situation more discreetly, but hopefully it has not soured things too much for you."

"I have come to think of it as a fitting final drama in the saga of Mary Jane. She has seen some times, you know. I hope to God we never see the like again," Captain Pevsner gave them a naval seaman's salute. "Safe sailing, you two."

O'Harris and Clara returned the farewell and then began walking back towards O'Harris' car.

"Miss Fitzgerald?"

Clara turned and saw that Charles Walsh was running up to them.

"Mr Walsh."

"I wanted to say thank you, for solving this mystery," Charles Walsh came to a halt before her and looked suddenly nervous. "It's a weird thing to say, isn't it? Thanking you for discovering my employer killed my colleague."

Walsh gave an anxious cough.

"I think Miss Dodd would very much have appreciated it. I regret not being able to stop her from doing... what she did."

"You did not expect her to toss herself overboard," Clara reminded him gently. "That was her decision."

"I suppose," Walsh tapped his feet and was clearly keen to be moving on. "Mr Noble approached me a short while ago. He wants to promote me into Henry's position. I feel slightly odd about it. Dead man's shoes, and all that."

"Don't," O'Harris said. "Henry would not have minded. And the company needs a steady hand in the difficult times ahead."

"Yes," Walsh shook his head, as if he didn't really believe what had happened. "Neither Simon or Elias Noble will inherit the company now, or so I have been told. It is going to Mr Noble's daughter who I have never met. Hard to think of the company in a woman's hands."

"Don't knock it," Clara winked at him. "Women are fully capable of doing a man's job."

"Oh, yes, it is not that," Walsh quickly corrected himself. "It's just… will they have to rename it Noble and Sons and Daughter?"

Charles Walsh grinned at them. He gave them a jolly farewell then hurried off, heading for his own home before the evening closed in. Clara would be glad to get to her house too. She followed O'Harris to the car and slipped inside when he opened the door. The captain climbed in the other side and gave a sigh.

"To Miss Fitzgerald's house, Jones."

The car slowly rolled off.

"Quite a remarkable New Year's," O'Harris mused, relaxing back into the leather seat. "I'll not forget this one in a hurry."

"Sorry about that," Clara said.

"Nonsense! Best New Year's I have ever had!" O'Harris remarked. "But I do have to ask one thing."

"What is that?" Clara smiled at him.

"Did I do all right?"

Clara laughed.

"You were absolutely fine!"

"A worthy side-kick?"

"Positively!"

O'Harris beamed, his smile stretching from ear-to-ear.

"Good. Glad to be of assistance. And, if you ever need someone to back you up in the future, I'll happily take up the task. I'll be the Watson to your Holmes."

Clara was grinning now.

"Next time I might even get paid for solving the case," she chuckled. "I rather did this one out of a sense of duty."

"Well, personally, I am expecting a complimentary crate of champagne and wine from my import company, if they have any sense in the matter," O'Harris raised an eyebrow.

"I think Charles Walsh will arrange something," Clara agreed. "Still, how about we end our first day of 1922 in a rather quiet and boring fashion?"

"Sounds delightful," O'Harris said in amusement.

"Dinner at mine then?"

"Perfect."

"Jones, you'll join us too?"

Jones, who had not really been listening to the conversation, heard the invitation and was almost startled enough to run the car into a lamppost. O'Harris reached forward and patted his shoulder.

"Don't worry, old boy, you'll get used to her," he said mischievously. "She is rather unconventional."

"I shall gladly take that as a compliment," Clara smiled.

Printed in Great Britain
by Amazon

79507745R00144